When two knowlec
head in the courtroc
justice. John Merrin.... .... g~ ~~ any means for victory
and Malcolm Prescott is blinded by pride. The careers of
these two men grate on each other until a 30-year cover-
up is disclosed by a disgruntled detective and brings about
justice for an innocent man. Merriman becomes the one
fighting to right a wrong. Great courtroom drama.

—Pat Guerry Hodnett, author, *Dragon Smoke*

Wilmot Irvin tells a good story about the big tent that is the
Practice of Law, a tent large enough to house the ethically
challenged John Merriman, Esquire, who, like the Prodigal
Son, finally manages to get it right.

—Bert Goolsby, author, *Harpers' Joy*

Merriman's Second Chance is a well-written novel that
explores such timely subjects as morality, power, and ethics.
The plot involves professional rise and fall, racial issues,
women who stand by their fallible husbands, men who
strive for career success, and courtroom drama so popular in
today's fiction and television. It's a hard book to put down,
a thought-provoking read, and another quality addition to
the diverse collection of writing published by Red Letter
Press.

—Carmella Broome, author, *Carmella's Quest*

In *Merriman's Second Chance*, Irvin, himself a lawyer, has
given us a legal drama in which long-standing wrongs get
righted, justice does prevail, and redemption, however
tardy, is ultimately realized. This novel should be required
reading in all law schools.

—Robert Lamb, author, *Atlanta Blues*

Merriman's Second Chance

Wilmot B. Irvin

Red Letter Press
Columbia, South Carolina

Published by Red Letter Press
6148 Rutledge Hill
Columbia, SC 29209
RedLetterPress@gmail.com
http://redletterpress.googlepages.com

First Edition
[Reprint March 2015]
Printed in the United States of America
Library of Congress Control Number: 2009937555

ISBN-13: 978-0-9661199-5-4

For all the lawyers I have ever known

PART ONE

CHAPTER ONE

"I desire to practice the law again."

John Merriman delivered the declamation in his distinct stentorian timbre, this time flavored with a hint of humility. There was a quaver in his rich, strong baritone, but it delivered the message Merriman meant to impart. He was sixty-three and penniless.

The meeting of the Commission on Character and Fitness was a solemn occasion. Six of its seven members were seated at the burnished mahogany bench inside the windowless chamber of that body's offices. Each was frowning. Each knew John Merriman. None wished to reinstate the scoundrel, yet they knew they would.

The Commission's lawyer stood.

"Mr. Merriman has completed the requirements for reinstatement. His six-month suspension has run its course." He paused and sighed, as if tired to the bone. Then, grudgingly, he came to the point. "Our investigation has unearthed no valid reason to oppose his request."

A smile, barely perceptible, took form in the corners of Merriman's mouth and eyes.

The commissioners retired to an outer sanctum. After a perfunctory recess they returned to the inner chamber. Merriman stood. The chairman announced the inevitable result.

"Your request for reinstatement is granted, Mr. Merriman. May God have mercy on our courts and their litigants."

CHAPTER TWO

With a brisk step and the assistance of a cane, Merriman walked the two blocks from the court building that housed the Commission's well-appointed chambers to his shabby office on the ground floor of a dilapidated building on the corner of Northampton and Champagne Streets.

It was misting rain. Withdrawing a single key from the pocket of his tattered vest, Merriman unlocked the door and entered. To his left was a straight-backed chair. On its seat lay a cracked cedar shingle with two eye hooks screwed into its top. He turned the board over to its painted side and read with pride: "John Merriman, Attorney at the Law." He exited the dismal chambers long enough to hang the advertisement on a pair of rusty nails sunk into the brick mortar just to the right of his office door.

He was back in business.

He had always practiced alone. The solitude masked the depravity of his practice to nosy outsiders. He was in his thirty-seventh year at the Bar. He had been reprimanded three times. And there was the one suspension. He was guilty of many more offenses than those. But there was no secretary, no office manager, no law partner, not even a clerk. And file cabinets could not talk. So the Office of Disciplinary Counsel was none the wiser.

His stock in trade was petty criminal defense and automobile accident cases. There was little paperwork involved. He always got his dirty money for the criminal work up front. And his standard fee for the wreck cases was an unabashed forty percent. His overhead was next to nothing. He had runners who worked for the police department that sent him clients. He nearly always settled the wreck cases, and his criminal clients routinely entered into plea bargains. They were as guilty as sin, and so was Merriman.

He walked to his desk and sat down. It was pine with a

walnut veneer. The top was littered with old newspapers and letters. The receiver of his telephone was off the hook. That way, if anyone called during the period of his suspension, they didn't hear the mandatory recording that notified callers he was suspended from the practice. It just rang busy instead. There was an ashtray next to the phone, full of moldy old butts. It had been six months.

Merriman kept a thick foam rubber cushion on the seat of his desk chair. Years ago he fractured his spine in an altercation with a witness in one of his criminal cases. It occurred in a dive bar by the name of O'Leary's. He fought his way in, conducted his business, and fought his way out. The doctor prescribed narcotics and bed rest. Merriman rejected the advice to lie supine but filled the prescription for morphine, to which he promptly became addicted. For a while it allayed the sharp pain in his back. But by the time he swore off the drug, the fracture had clumsily fused, and the intense throb turned to a dull constant nagging ache. Thus the foam rubber cushion.

He replaced the receiver long enough to get a dial tone and then punched the buttons. The number was emblazoned in his memory. After a few rings a voice came on the line.

"Hallo?"

"Dabney, it's Merriman. You do good work."

"Well, then, I suppose congratulations are in order, counselor. By the by, when do I get paid?"

Merriman knew the answer. For a moment he considered a contrivance. Then he decided the truth was best. After all, the seventh member had not been present. And that was worth his livelihood.

"As soon as I get my first fee. You'll get half, if it takes it. And the rest will come, just as night follows day." Merriman spoke the latter clause with a lilt, taking pride in his certain literary flair.

The seventh member of the Commission on Character and Fitness was one Malcolm T. Prescott. He harbored an abiding hatred of Merriman. He knew Merriman for what he was. And Prescott wasn't about to let him regain his license to practice without a fight.

By turn of ill fortune, Prescott awoke that morning to find all four tires of his vehicle slashed and flat. When he tried to telephone the Commission to seek a delay in the proceedings he discovered his phone line was dead. He set out on foot. It was misting rain. He arrived just moments after Merriman had left the building. Prescott was damp to the bone and irate.

Dab hung up the phone. A warm sense of self satisfaction spread like a virus through his belly. He liked Merriman. The unsavory lawyer was one of his own. Merriman defended the downtrodden and sued the fortunate. Dab himself had needed the services of Merriman on more than one occasion. And on the first of those occasions, Prescott, who was then a young, inexperienced solicitor, prosecuted poor old Dab with a vengeance. It was one of the rare occasions when Merriman actually took a case to trial.

There was a ringer on the jury—one of Merriman's former clients. He persuaded the other eleven to disregard the prosecution testimony of two eyewitnesses in favor of a shifty-eyed character Merriman called to the stand at the last minute of Dab's defense. Even Dab himself blushed at the palpable lies the witness told.

But it was over, Dab's first case in this system of justice Merriman succeeded in perverting. And Dab was forever grateful.

Chapter Three

Out of necessity Merriman took a wife. Her name was May. She had money. Not much, but enough to ensure a modicum of comfort for the marriage. May knew Merriman married her for the money. It was all right with her. She was homely and there were no other prospects. Like Merriman, May was in her midthirties, and matrimonial aspirations waned daily. But again like Merriman, May was a tough bird with a keen instinct for self-preservation and little regard for the benefits of a moral life.

She asked Merriman, "What will you do when the money runs out?"

"Steal and cheat if I must," Merriman replied.

"Well," May peremptorily declared, "you already do that. What about me?"

Merriman gave honest thought to the question before answering. There was, after all, a certain code of honor, even among thieves. He felt a sudden tug at his otherwise dormant conscience.

"I can't promise, May. But I'll do my best to keep you fed and clothed."

It was good enough for May. They were married in the probate court the following Thursday, the day before Good Friday in the year of our Lord 1967.

Mercifully, no child issued from the union, but because they kept their respective distances the marriage succeeded. One would never regard the couple as an example of connubial bliss. But a certain fidelity was born to their marriage which neither Merriman nor May could trace to their heritage, and it was this quality that kept them together.

Like cancerous cells, May's money took on the innate capacity to multiply and divide. Merriman was scrupulous when it came to May's money. He advised her to invest the little corpus she had inherited, and by sheer luck, her investments turned into prudent ones. The income generated from the stocks and bonds supplemented the rather meager rewards Merriman enjoyed from the early years of his law practice.

"Don't touch the principal."

It was a credo he instilled in May by repetitive reminder, and she in turn saw to it that Merriman couldn't touch it either. Strict instructions were given to her broker—under no circumstances was Merriman to have any right to invade the accounts. Thus through mutual restraint their little enterprise succeeded. By fits and starts Merriman's practice grew and May's small fortune steadily increased.

Then came Merriman's first serious brush with Prescott. The Champagne Street office was a veritable hive of activity as Merriman prepared for trial. He was then thirty-nine years of age. His client,—a morose and obese bookie by the name of Harritt—whose defense was impeded by a lengthy criminal record, had been charged with accessory to murder. He was guilty as charged, but he had an alibi. And a corroborating witness.

Vain attempts were made to reach a plea agreement. Plea bargaining was Merriman's strong suit, and when young Solicitor Prescott turned down his best offer, Merriman felt a knot slowly tightening in his acid-filled stomach. His client steadfastly refused to take a lengthy prison term, which was a *sine qua non* for any deal as far as Prescott was concerned, and so there was nothing to do but prepare for trial.

The corroborating witness, a Mr. Dunleavy, was a shady purveyor of cheap, Japanese knockoffs of fine European wristwatches and handbags. He had a dingy storefront below Main Street where he hawked these wares alongside luggage and musical instruments of questionable origin.

Merriman scheduled an appointment to interview this key witness at two o'clock in the afternoon before trial began. Being exceedingly short on support staff, Merriman persuaded May, who was nearly illiterate, to sit in as his legal assistant. His client, who had made bail and planned to attend, was expecting a grand showing from Merriman in exchange for the hefty up-front fee he paid for the defense.

Harritt and Dunleavy crossed the threshold of the Champagne Street office at the stroke of two. May was perched at the little desk-table in the front room charading as secretary. Merriman was ensconced in his chambers, fidgeting, with the door closed. From the bottle of eighty-proof elixir he kept stashed in the bottom left-hand drawer of his desk he snuck a nip.

"May I help you, gentlemen?" May cooed.

"We're here to see Merriman," Harritt demanded. "Is he sober?"

Taken slightly aback by the question from the fat and ill-tempered Harritt, May replied, "I'll check."

Then, regaining some composure, she added, "Who shall I say is calling?"

With a dart of his black sunken eyes in the direction of Dunleavy, Harritt said dully, "He'll know."

May swished into Merriman's office and closed the door.

"They're here!" she whispered.

Bracing himself, Merriman took another pull on the flask and rose from his chair. "Get a pad and pretend to take notes." He pointed May to a rickety cane-backed chair in the corner next to his desk. With that, he threw open the door and greeted the scoundrels as if they were dear old friends.

Following a brief exchange of insincere cordialities the three shuffled into Merriman's office and took their seats. May cringed as Harritt thrust the full weight of his corpulence onto the sagging seat of Merriman's dilapidated but cushiony guest chair. By some twist of fate it held. May expelled an audible sigh of relief. Dunleavy took a seat in the stained, slip-covered wing chair next to Harritt. Merriman settled onto his foam rubber cushion.

Merriman began by lighting a cigarette. "Mr. Dunleavy, where were you on the night of August twenty-first?" He sucked a long, loud pull off the unfiltered Old Gold.

Harritt shifted uncomfortably in his chair.

"Wherever you want me to be, Mr. Merriman." The surly Dunleavy turned toward Harritt and smiled.

Merriman expelled a tubular cloud of gray smoke in the direction of May.

"Well, Mr. Dunleavy, in that case I want you to be in Harritt's apartment for drinks and dinner. You came at six-fifteen after closing your emporium, and stayed until after nine-thirty." Merriman paused and took a reading of Dunleavy's demeanor. There was not even a whimper of remorse.

Merriman continued. "It was a jolly evening with Harritt. You remember it well. Roast pork and potatoes. A nice Cabernet. Something sweet for dessert. The two of you listened to the last few innings of the Cubs game. Chicago lost. You went home." The calculating Merriman turned toward Harritt and smiled.

May nearly swooned. She had never seen Merriman at work.

"Yes," Dunleavy agreed with a smirk. "You are precisely correct, Mr. Merriman. I remember it well. Even the pineapple cake for dessert."

With no small amount of effort Harritt stood.

"Is that sufficient, counselor?"

Merriman leaned back in his desk chair and placed both hands on his splotchy cheeks. He could feel the red flush rising from his neck. "Quite sufficient, Mr. Harritt." Then he thought of Prescott and what the young solicitor might make of this perfidy.

"I'll see you both tomorrow. Courtroom two. At a quarter to nine."

After the scoundrels departed the Champagne Street office, May turned to her husband. "So this is what you do?"

"No, May. Worse than this is what I do. Do you have the stomach for it?"

There was only a momentary pause for reflection. Then she responded. "Neither the stomach nor the bowels. That's why I'll stay home from now on. You'll have to find some professional help instead."

Merriman didn't protest. May's last quarter earnings were superb.

Chapter Four

Malcolm T. Prescott derived a great deal of satisfaction from placing behind bars miscreants such as Merriman and his clients. He had served a long and able tenure as Solicitor for Cumberland County. Along the way he was often tempted to jump ship and open a private practice in criminal defense. No doubt with some effort he could have earned sizably more income than he received from the county's payroll. But his lofty conscience protected him from succumbing.

And there was another reason. He had yet to uncover a solid basis upon which to prosecute Merriman. Obstruction of justice, misprision of a felony, any old charge would do. But Prescott needed proof, not rumors. And so far, those with personal knowledge of Merriman's high crimes and misdemeanors—consisting primarily of the old scoundrel's former clients and their corroborating witnesses—steadfastly refused to rat on him.

This is precisely why Prescott was furious that he had not been in attendance at the meeting of the Commission on Character and Fitness. Oh, he knew well enough that he would not have succeeded in blocking Merriman's reinstatement. There were no grounds. But here was his golden opportunity to cross-examine the great Merriman himself, not just one of his clients or witnesses.

What a field day Prescott would have had. The Commission permitted broad discretion to its members in examining applicants for reinstatement. Every unsavory act or omission committed by Merriman throughout his notorious career, of which Prescott had even third-hand knowledge, was fair game. In his keen but narrow mind, Prescott imagined his cross-examination of Merriman to be a no-holds-barred brawl between the bright forces of good and the tenebrous powers of evil.

Prescott's favorite trial uniform was an expertly tailored white linen suit. It contrasted nicely with the usual gray or black wool-worsted ones worn by his adversaries in the court. And the white linen complimented Prescott's thick wavy head of silver hair. Prescott dreamed of prosecuting Merriman in his white linen suit, his gleaming coiffure neatly trimmed just above the ears. Merriman would be wearing his standard wrinkled gray three-piece wool blend, his disheveled dark locks dangling nearly to his shoulders. But the dream must wait. The solicitor had work to do.

Prescott was still fuming when he arrived at the offices of the Solicitor for Cumberland County. He called to his secretary. "Myrt, get Detective Barrow over here now! Tell him it's about our friend John."

He unlocked the door and entered his private office. Everything was as he had left it the night before. Neat as a pin. Not a thing out of place. Very orderly. Very good. He glanced at the telephone message slips Myrt had set in a stack next to his phone. The one on top registered a call from Merriman, just moments ago.

He lifted the receiver and dialed Merriman's office. A familiar stentorian baritone came on the line. The voice grated on the nerves of Malcolm T. Prescott. "John Merriman, Attorney at the Law," it announced with pride.

"Well, John, I see you're back into the practice," Prescott snapped.

On the other end of the line Merriman smirked. "So sorry you weren't able to be present for the hearing. Something delay you?"

Prescott controlled his rising emotion. "Yes. And you can bet I'll get to the bottom of it."

"Well, best of luck to you. By the way, I need a favor." Merriman hesitated only slightly, and purely for effect. "A continuance. Dabney Peters' trial is scheduled to begin on Monday. I can't possibly be ready by then. You know, the suspension and all." Today was Thursday.

Prescott felt the blood rush to his neck. The temerity of the man astounded him.

"As I recall, the charge against that oaf Peters is receiving stolen goods. I could get ready to try that case in a day.

So could any defense lawyer worth his salt. Sorry. No continuance."

Merriman hung up the phone and laughed out loud. He was already prepared.

CHAPTER FIVE

May puttered about her kitchen and thanked God that Merriman was back at work. It had been an insufferable six months. In his boredom he bet on everything from horses to dogs. Of course he lost every wager. What meager savings he had managed to accumulate were gone. In his own right he was nearly bankrupt.

May knew he lived and breathed the practice of law. Without it he was a spiritual destitute. The suspension had almost killed him. Perhaps now, May prayed, Merriman will reform his ways and take up an honest living.

Their lives together had been tempestuous. For the most part it was feast or famine. Thankfully May's portfolio generated sufficient income to ensure that such basic marital ends as the mortgage payment and the grocer's account were met. Every now and then Merriman hit a home run, so to speak, with a settlement from some unfortunate soul's dismemberment or disfigurement, and life was good for a while. But inevitably his luck and the proceeds therefrom ran dry, and thus she was called upon to keep them afloat.

Leland, their short-legged Jack Russell, kept a low profile under the butcher's block while May washed the breakfast dishes. Occasionally Merriman took the dog to walk. This nearly always ended in calamity. Leland resolutely refused to come when called, and Merriman was accustomed to obedience. Inevitably, some hapless widow or pitiful child would amble up, and Leland straightaway went on the attack. Try as he might, Merriman could neither coax nor cajole the terrier to quit its snapping and growling at the innocent victim. The scene inexorably turned violent, with Merriman unleashing a torrent of profanity on the willful pet.

On a whim May purchased the dog from a pet store with a sign in the window that read, "Going out of business sale." She asked the clerk whether the pup had been mistreated.

It seemed to wince at any display of affection she offered.

"Not to my knowledge," the clerk responded carefully. "But I can't vouch for the fellow that handles the night shift."

May glanced at the pup, which cocked its eye at her, and decided to redeem the beast. It cost her fifty dollars.

When Merriman arrived home that evening he spied the runt in a basket under the butcher's block.

"Have you taken leave of your senses, May?" he hollered.

She was standing barefoot in the hallway, holding a bushel of laundry that consisted mainly of Merriman's socks and underwear.

"Don't complain!" she retorted. "I purchased her with my money. And I'll feed her, too. Maybe she'll bring me some joy."

Merriman reconsidered. "What shall we call the beast?"

"I named her Leland," May replied. "After my father."

CHAPTER SIX

Detective Lieutenant Michael O'Shea Barrow had been in police work for nearly thirty years. He knew his way around the block when it came to crimes and criminals. He derived his pleasure in life from solving the former and jailing the latter.

He disdained testifying in the criminal court. The judges too often sided with the Constitution and thus the criminal. Barrow didn't need the Constitution. He knew who was guilty. The trial was an enormous waste of time. Sometimes the bugger even went free on some technicality or other. And the defense lawyers who coddled these criminals were a no-good pack of liars. Particularly Merriman.

Barrow loathed Merriman.

Prescott leaned back in his tan leather desk chair and observed the fat raindrops pummeling his office window. Barrow reclined in a comfortable chair across the desk, a feculent plug of tobacco set firm and moist in his left cheek, and studied Prescott's silvery profile.

"Mikey," Prescott began with a certain fondness, "when I walked out my front door this morning I was greeted by four slashed tires. The county owns the automobile. That in itself justifies a full investigation.

"And there's just a wee little coincidence here you might want to keep in mind, Mikey. Merriman. The hearing on his reinstatement was scheduled for nine o'clock this morning. I serve on the Commission. When I went inside to call for a postponement my phone was dead. Someone had slit the line to the house. Merriman got his reinstatement in my absence."

Prescott knew Barrow loathed Merriman.

Barrow knew Merriman loathed Prescott.

Prescott continued. "Coincidence, Mikey? I don't think so. There's a cur by the name of Dabney Peters. His friends call him Dab for short. He's up for trial Monday morning on

14

a charge of receiving stolen goods. Merriman is defending the louse. He called for a continuance just a few minutes ago and I turned him down."

Prescott swiveled his chair from the window view to face Barrow across his desk.

"Merriman has represented him many times before. Always a plea to a lesser charge that gets Dab a fine or only a brief stay in the Big House. This time I intend to slam him. No plea. Eighteen months, minimum, on a guilty verdict. He's a four-time offender. Even Judge Bailey will have no mercy." Prescott's eyes brimmed with determination.

Like a gigantic ferret Barrow rubbed his meaty hands together. "I know Dab. I've had plenty of run-ins with him. He and Merriman are birds of a feather."

Barrow stood and swaggered to the window, which he raised. Rain blew through the orifice, splattering onto Barrow's cheap shoes and Prescott's polished hardwood floor.

Prescott grimaced.

Barrow spat a splotch of nasty brown fluid from the left side of his mouth out the window and into the rain.

Prescott grimaced.

Barrow turned and said nonchalantly, "No doubt Dab traded Merriman's fee on the stolen goods charge for the slashed tires and the slit phone line."

He closed the window.

Barrow's sickening oral habit nauseated the prim Prescott, who held his tongue on that subject but warmed to the idea that Dab may be the culprit. The thought fell upon good soil and took root in his narrow mind.

Prescott rose and began to speak with an unusual fervor.

"I don't care about Dab. I'll nail him next week. I only want to put Merriman away once and for all. He's a disgrace to the profession. Find the evidence that Peters did the slashing and slitting for Merriman's benefit, and we'll indict the old scoundrel for obstruction of justice and conspiracy."

Barrow reclaimed his seat, then leaned forward to address Prescott, who was standing straight as a rail with hands pressed, palms down, on his leather-topped desk. Barrow's veined, florid cheeks glowed pink with the brilliance of his idea.

"If you get the conviction, we'll get what we want. Dab will implicate Merriman in a heartbeat if he thinks he can trade it for a reduced sentence on the stolen goods charge."

Prescott smiled broadly. "Right you are, Mikey my boy. And we'll give the rascal his reduction if that's what it takes. The conviction first, Merriman second. Just as night follows day."

Prescott, too, took pride in a certain flair for punctuating his everyday conversation with elegant phrasing. He considered himself one of the literati.

Chapter Seven

Whenever she ventured abroad May took Leland to ride. She would snap the leash onto Leland's collar and hurl the beast into the front seat of her brown and cream Packard Clipper. The rusty old rattletrap had been a wedding gift from Merriman. It was a semi-automatic. Let off the gas at twenty-five miles an hour and it jumped into high gear. The Packard Motor Car Company manufactured it in 1954. It was the automotive equivalent of a battleship. Merriman acquired it in 1966 as a kind of fee from an impecunious client.

Merriman didn't drive. Each day he walked from their Station Avenue townhouse to his Champagne Street office, rain or shine. His biological father, whom Merriman hadn't seen since birth, bequeathed him the townhouse, mortgage and all, as a guilt offering upon the old man's death in 1961. Near the heart of downtown, it was one of a dozen cinder block units in a run-down project developed decades earlier. It met the needs of Merriman and, after their marriage, May.

Five years later, his impecunious client, who happened also to be his stepfather Charlie, conveyed the Packard to Merriman in exchange for a defense to a charge of second degree criminal sexual assault. Merriman pleaded him to simple assault, got old Charlie a fine and probation for a sentence, and placed the car in storage.

Leland loved to ride. She stood on her hind legs with front paws on the dashboard, peering straight ahead while May alternately depressed the accelerator and applied the brake. Leland reminded May of a statue she had once seen entitled *Winged Flight*. Together they sped happily through the streets and alleyways of the city.

May never bothered to obtain a driver's license. Neither did Merriman trouble himself to obtain current tags or insurance for the Clipper. While in flight, May and Leland violated enough state and municipal laws to put them behind bars for years. They didn't care.

Merriman's mother Brocadia was alive and well. She missed the Packard but not the second husband. Charlie Forsythe had been his name. His dalliance with the ladies was legendary. Fortunately for Brocadia, Charlie suffered an irreversible coronary embolus while engaged in an erotic act with a young tart he met in a bar. For his debauchery Charlie paid the ultimate price. The coroner pronounced him dead but, by all appearances, quite happy. His railroad pension and a modest death benefit inured to Brocadia's well being.

Merriman kept the Packard.

Occasionally Brocadia came to dine with Merriman and May. May was no chef, but neither was Brocadia a gourmet. Merriman preferred beef or lamb over pork or chicken and adamantly refused to eat seafood of any kind. And so, on the occasions of Brocadia's visits, May prepared either a beef stew or a lamb shank, depending upon availability. This pleased Merriman and satisfied Brocadia.

Whenever she paid a visit Brocadia insisted on a ride in the Packard. She sat alone in the back seat like some member of the royal family, while May and Leland occupied the front. Merriman stayed home, sipping cheap brandy and reading the Sunday newspaper. On one such occasion, Merriman received a disturbing telephone call.

"Yes, this is Merriman," he barked into the receiver.

After identifying himself and providing his address, the caller advised, "You'd better come over right away. Your wife has struck a tree in my front yard. An old water oak. The tree survived, but I'm not sure the Packard did."

"I'll be right there," Merriman assured the man. "Do me a favor, will you? I'll pay cash for any damage. Just don't call the police. They don't seem to like me, and my wife is a bit tardy in obtaining a driver's license."

"That's not a problem. By the way, your wife and mother seem to be fine. So does the little yapper."

"Oh," Merriman replied. "I hadn't thought to ask."

The collision had occurred when Leland spied a fox terrier on the side of the road chasing a fluffy-tailed squirrel. She flew into a rage and attempted to exit the vehicle through the partially lowered passenger window. This distracted May, who released her grip on the steering wheel and lurched over to grab the beast before she plunged to a certain death. The Packard careened off the paved road and came to an abrupt halt at the water oak.

The impact catapulted Brocadia into the front seat. May and Leland lay tangled in a knot on the floorboard. By the time the three regained their senses, the hood of the Packard had flown open and the radiator was spewing steam. The fox terrier and the squirrel had long since departed. A stoop-shouldered man wearing a woolen crew-neck sweater was standing outside the vehicle, peering in through the partially opened passenger window.

"Are you all right?" he inquired through the opening.

"Yes," May replied, feebly, clutching the whimpering Leland to her breast. "Call Merriman. He'll know what to do." She gave the man their number. Then, looking up, she observed a wide-eyed Brocadia breathing rapidly, but unharmed, in a lump on the front seat where Leland usually rode.

They never heard from the old gal again.

Chapter Eight

Dabney Peters earned a portion of his livelihood from the operation of a local hauling outfit of which he was the sole proprietor. The business consisted of an old flatbed truck onto which Dab erected an enclosure made of hog wire with a sheet of thick clear vinyl attached to the inside. The rear section of the contraption was fashioned to open and close like a gate. With the exception of sand and other varieties of silica, freight for the most part stayed on board as Dab and the flatbed hauled loads to and fro.

Foul weather presented a problem. Dab made it a policy not to haul if any form of precipitation were in the forecast. Nonetheless, he also made it a policy to have his customers sign a release of all claims for damage to their goods due to weather. In exchange, Dab promised to seek refuge under the nearest shelter if a thundershower unexpectedly popped up.

Many of Dab's customers paid in cash. Some of them also preferred that their goods be hauled after dark. And certain of these latter gentlemen required that Dab keep no record of the job. This presented unique challenges insofar as Dab's relationship with the Internal Revenue Service was concerned. He had only once been audited. When the agent asked for his accounts receivables records, Dab returned with an old derby hat full of handwritten receipts for cash which identified neither date, customer name, nor destination for the haul. After a brief inspection of the pitiful old truck, which was the only asset of the business, the agent concluded the audit with a brief sermonette on the importance of accurate recordkeeping and left an IRS brochure to the same effect. He never returned.

Dab always made the presumption that the customer was the lawful owner of the goods to be hauled. He required no proof of same, even in the face of serious evidence to the contrary. The penal code of Cumberland County addressed this issue in Section 16.1-108, entitled "Receiving Stolen Goods." Depending upon the value of the stolen property, anyone found in possession of goods which he knew, or in the exercise of reasonable diligence should have known, were stolen, was guilty of a felony and subject to fine and imprisonment. Dab made it his practice never to exercise reasonable diligence. This was his problem with the trial on Monday morning.

The goods in question consisted of two large reinforced cardboard boxes filled with automobile tires. It so happened that news reports of a theft of just such merchandise from Nate's Tire Service had been widely circulated in the days prior to Dab's midnight haul of the goods in question. It was not so much the tires that accounted for the publicity, but the fact that Nate had been stabbed in the belly while defending himself against the thieves. Nate survived the stabbing and estimated the wholesale value of the looted goods to be slightly in excess of one thousand dollars. That sum just happened to be the jurisdictional threshold for a felony count under Section 16.1-108.

The police noticed Dab and the flatbed parked under an overpass at forty minutes past midnight. An unexpected thunderstorm had arrested his haul just moments before. Through the clear vinyl wall of Dab's homemade enclosure, with the aid of a flashlight, the officers made out the words "Nate's Tire Service" stamped onto the outside of two large cardboard boxes. Probable cause was thus established for Dab's arrest and the ensuing impoundment of the flatbed and its freight.

Later that night, while Dab languished in a jail cell he shared with another misfortunate, a magistrate issued a warrant enabling the police to search the contents of the cardboard boxes. Nate was present and quickly identified the goods as the tires stolen from his establishment just a few days earlier.

The next morning, with the able Merriman at his side, Dab was arraigned before the magistrate on a felony charge of receiving stolen goods and released on a personal recognizance bond. The following week, Merriman was suspended from the practice of law for transferring five thousand dollars from his client trust account to an offshore account in the name of J. Merriman. Merriman steadfastly maintained it was an honest mistake. The client thought otherwise. So did the Commission. Merriman reimbursed the money and sweated out the next six months.

The suspension gave Merriman plenty of time to consider a defense for Dab. There was no doubt about Dab being in possession of stolen goods. The question was whether Dab knew—or in the exercise of reasonable diligence, should have known—the goods were stolen. Merriman came up with a scheme that was later dubbed by his fellow members of the Cumberland County Bar the "inanity defense"—Dab was simply too dumb to know. He wasn't crazy, just stupid. Not insane, only inane.

Solicitor Prescott anticipated some connivance or other from his worthy adversary. Merriman was capable of any trick in the book. But the inanity defense never occurred to Prescott.

Merriman spent the weekend before trial rehearsing his client's testimony. Normally Merriman would not let a criminal client take the stand in his own defense. Too risky. Particularly when the client was guilty. But in order for the inanity defense to succeed, Dab would have to testify.

Monday morning arrived. The court came to order. Judge Bailey intoned, "Mr. Solicitor, call your first case."

"May it please the court." Prescott rose as he addressed the bench. "The State versus Dabney Peters."

A jury was drawn and the trial began.

Merriman and Dab rested low in their seats at the defense table and listened while one police officer after another laid the groundwork for the stolen goods aspect of the case. Merriman had no basis upon which to dispute that the goods were stolen. In his turn Nate took the stand and identified the goods that were removed from Dab's flatbed as the very tires stolen from his establishment on the night he was stabbed.

Merriman decided to gently cross-examine.

"Nate, you saw the assailants, did you not?"

"Yes," he replied. "And I testified in the trial that put them behind bars, thanks to Mr. Prescott here." Nate cast a glance of appreciation in the direction of the solicitor's table.

"And Mr. Dabney Peters, the defendant, wasn't among them, was he?"

Prescott was on his feet. "Objection, Your Honor. This testimony has no relevance to a charge of receiving stolen goods."

"Overruled," growled the judge. He had always considered Prescott a pompous ass. "Answer the question."

Nate glanced at Dab and then turned to the loathsome Merriman. "No, he wasn't among them."

Merriman sat down.

Prescott rested his case after introducing into evidence copies of the numerous newspaper articles and television news accounts that had reported the crime. His point was made that any reasonably diligent citizen would have known those tires were stolen.

Detective Lieutenant Barrow, who was seated inconspicuously in the rear of the courtroom, permitted himself a smile. As usual, a moist and nasty plug of tobacco rested between gum and cheek.

CHAPTER NINE

It was Merriman's turn.

His first witness was an ancient and drably dressed little woman who identified herself as Dab's sixth grade teacher. That was as far as Dab went in school.

Feigning a limp for sympathy, Merriman approached the witness box on the support of his gold-headed cane. He had acquired the impressive walking stick from Dunleavy's emporium.

"Tell the jury your impression of young Dabney, Miss Alabaster."

"He was a pathetic student," she began, wincing. "I tried everything to engage the boy. I am afraid he was a dimwit. Out of pity I promoted him to the seventh grade. It was a social promotion."

Merriman glanced at his client, who, with glazed eyes, was staring dumbly down at his slightly trembling hands clasped together on the defense table. Dab was a superb actor.

"Now, Miss Alabaster, over the course of his sixth grade year were you able to discern young Dabney's reading level?"

She pondered the question for a moment. "I would be generous to say he left my class reading at a second grade level."

Merriman allowed the import of these words to settle upon the jury like a milky, morning dew. Then he concluded his examination.

"In your opinion, Miss Alabaster, was young Dabney capable of reading and understanding the daily newspaper?"

She hesitated not a whit. "Absolutely not."

Merriman had set the trap. He turned to Prescott. "Your witness."

The solicitor stood and approached his prey.

"Now, Miss Alabaster," he began gingerly, "you've not

seen young Peters since you taught him sixth grade, have you?"

She was carrying a large pocketbook and a telescope umbrella, both of which rested on her pleated skirt in the witness box. Miss Alabaster came prepared for anything.

"As a matter of fact, Mr. Prescott, I saw Dabney last Friday afternoon. In Mr. Merriman's office."

"And what, might I ask," rejoined Prescott with a smirk and raised eyebrows, "was the purpose of that little meeting?" His tone oozed suspicion.

Miss Alabaster regarded the curious Prescott for a moment. Then she gathered her belongings on her lap, as though preparing to take her leave.

"Why, just to confirm for myself that poor Dabney had obtained no level of reading aptitude higher than he had when he left my sixth grade class. I tested him," she explained. "And I'm confident he's nearly illiterate."

Merriman permitted himself a smile. Prescott had fallen right into his trap.

Prescott shuffled back to his table and pretended to study some notes on a yellow pad. He furrowed his brow. He was trying to decide whether to pursue the subject. He elected to sit down.

"No further questions." He shot a withering glare at Merriman.

Merriman stood. "Come down, Miss Alabaster." The little spinster alighted from the witness box, pocketbook and umbrella in tow, and exited the courtroom. The metal-tipped heels of her brown leather pumps tapped a pitter-patter on the heart pine floor as she went.

The inanity defense broke over Prescott's morning like a cold, cloudy dawn.

Next was Dab.

Merriman's questions intentionally evoked only the briefest of answers. If permitted to give narrative accounts, Dab would surely get into trouble. The examination played like some staccato piece from an opera.

"Do you own a television set?"

"No."

"Do you watch television?"

"No."

"Here is a newspaper article Mr. Prescott put in evidence earlier. Can you read it?"

"No."

Selecting another sample, Merriman continued. "Can you read this one?"

"No."

"How far did you go in school?"

"Sixth grade."

"Was Miss Alabaster your sixth grade teacher?"

"Yes."

Merriman paused for effect. He limped over to the jury box, cane tapping as he went, and placed his left hand on the rail. Then he raised the cane with his right and rapped it against the side of one of the reinforced cardboard boxes Prescott had placed in evidence.

"Did you know those boxes of tires had been stolen?"

"No."

"Did you know that Nate's Tire Service had been robbed three days before you were arrested?"

"No."

"Did you know that Nate had been stabbed?"

"No."

"Did you know the man who engaged you to haul the tires?"

"No."

Merriman limped back to the defense table, tapping as he went. He chanced one last question.

"Did you have any reason," he inquired of his client, and then expansively, "any reason at all, to suspect the tires had been stolen?"

"No," Dab murmured to the jury. "None at all."

Merriman turned to Prescott. "Your witness, Mr. Solicitor."

Judge Bailey intervened.

"Ladies and gentlemen," he addressed the jury, "we've been going without a break since nine-thirty." It was nearly noon. "We'll stop now for lunch. Be back in the jury room no later than one o'clock. And I remind you, don't discuss the case over the recess. Your time will come."

Still perched in a rear corner of the courtroom with his plug in place, Detective Lieutenant Barrow observed the new direction in which the wind was beginning to blow. He did not like it. Not one little bit.

CHAPTER TEN

Wherever May went Leland followed. This was not surprising to Merriman. They had been joined at the hip ever since May redeemed the beast. Merriman noticed this. It suited him. May and Leland passed the time together without bothering him. But sometimes Merriman was lonely. At night, mostly, when he thought of the absent Brocadia. He wished May had named the beast Brocadia, after his mother.

In time May took up knitting. One scarf after another fell from her needles like petals from a corolla. One morning a little tan sweater was born. She gave it to Leland, of course. Silently Merriman took offense, undeservedly so. Throughout the course of May's travail it was the faithful pup, not Merriman, who lay patiently beside the sofa while her mistress knit and pearled, knit and pearled, until the various creations issued forth. Sometimes May chose threads from shades of blue, other times from hues of brown. Occasionally a muted tan. But never red. May abhorred red.

Christmas came. Merriman despised Christmas. It reminded him of the twin follies Happiness and Joy. May loved Christmas. It gave her a reason to hope. She refused to let Merriman's bitterness put her in a foul humor. Leland rested contentedly under the butcher's block in her little tan sweater. May baked cookies while Merriman sulked.

On a whim May insisted they have guests over to celebrate. Merriman could think of no one to invite but Harritt and Dunleavy, and perhaps Dab. May selected her cousins Euphonia and Euphoria, then set about preparing her husband's favorite dish—a peppered lamb shank. For some odd reason this holiday Merriman preferred a Christmas goose. Scowling, he limped on his cane to the corner grocer's and purchased one with his own funds.

May cheerfully prepared the fowl, with sauce to boot. She was happy. So was Leland. Merriman continued to sulk and limp.

The table was set. Grudgingly Merriman opened his private bar. A bottle of champagne, purchased with May's dividends, was put on ice. The doorbell rang. It was the obese Harritt. He was wearing a red sweater.

Considering the prospect of a future fee, Merriman rose to the occasion.

"Harritt, old boy!" he hollered as to a school chum. "Merry Christmas!" Out of Merriman's mouth such talk sounded odd, especially to Leland, who cocked her eye.

Harritt produced a warm smile and a chilled bottle of Sauvignon blanc. The Christmas spirit had obviously pervaded him. He was fairly bursting from the seams of his red sweater.

"Felicitations, Merriman! And to you, May," he gushed.

May waved from the kitchen. She remembered the once morose Harritt. "Come in, Mr. Harritt. And a merry Christmas to you." The goose simmered in its juices.

Merriman opened the champagne and poured glasses all around, even for May. This surprised her. The doorbell rang again, and Dunleavy appeared. He seemed a bit tipsy, and uncharacteristically friendly. He was wearing a woolen vest of green plaid in some questionable tartan pattern. It must have come from his emporium.

Merriman sprang to the door and greeted him warmly. "Come in, Dunleavy! And have some Christmas cheer."

Dunleavy swaggered across the threshold and took hold of Merriman's outstretched hand. "Don't mind if I do, Mr. Merriman. And a merry Christmas to you! It's quite kind of you and the missus to include me."

From under the butcher's block the tan-sweatered Leland peered suspiciously, eye cocked, at the master of the house.

Merriman poured Dunleavy a brace from the bottle of Dom Perignon and refilled his own. Harritt downed the remainder of his first toast and graciously accepted Merriman's offer of another. Merriman took the bottle to the kitchen and poured May a second shot. To her great joy May's little party was becoming infused with Christmas cheer.

Just then the doorbell rang again. May's twin cousins Euphonia and Euphoria appeared. Striking little women, they were dressed identically in blue pleated skirts and white blouses. Over their shoulders rested matching furs, each adorned with head and paws of some animal of indeterminable specie. Euphonia wore her animal's parts on the left shoulder, while Euphoria carried hers on the right.

"Euphonia!" May called from the kitchen. "Euphoria! I'm so glad you came."

So were the men. Merriman introduced these radiant ones to his other guests and offered each a chair next to the fireplace. It was aglow with flames from kindling and hickory Merriman had laid and set just minutes before their arrival. Harritt and Dunleavy had not expected such a winsome treat as these fair ladies. Euphonia declined the chair but accepted a glass of Dom Perignon and hurried to the kitchen to greet her cousin May. Euphoria struck a seductive pose by the fireplace and swilled down her first glass of champagne.

Then, with a bright smile and an empty glass Euphoria proposed a toast. Even the obese Harritt rose when the lady offered best wishes for the new year to the undeserving Merriman. It was a sweet gesture, one the master of the house had not expected. Everyone stood with stems at the ready, anticipating an immediate cure from Merriman.

He checked the cabinet of his private bar and to his great relief located another bottle of May's Dom Perignon. "Good night!" he thought. "This stuff must have cost her a small fortune." Then, with a measure of grace only his spouse's largesse could have suffused in him, a regenerate Merriman refilled every glass in the house.

Last but not least of their merry little band of visitors came Dabney Peters, just in time for a glass of May's Dom Perignon.

"To the greatest lawyer in our town!" Dab proposed,

and Harritt and Dunleavy were constrained to agree, considering the ill-gotten verdict obtained by their host in Harritt's murder trial years ago.

"To the greatest husband in our town!" came another. When Merriman turned in the direction of the second toast he spied May, leaning out the kitchen door into the parlor, her face beaming with pride and pouring perspiration from saucing the roasted goose.

Overcome by these gestures of good will, Merriman searched in vain for the right words to offer in response. He kept his peace instead.

Chapter Eleven

Malcolm T. Prescott took pride in his family's celebration—recognition, really—of the Birth of Christ. The Prescott forebears had been communicants of First Scots Reformed Presbyterian Church since the dawn of the nineteenth century. A dingy stained glass window barely refracting light from the south lawn of the churchyard bore a plaque memorializing the family's frugal but nevertheless consistent contributions to the church coffers over the decades.

Every Christmas morn since the year of our Lord 1810, when old Julius Prescott was the patriarch, the family gathered on the third pew to the left of the pulpit, within spitting distance of their dismal window.

This year, with the hesitant consent of Solicitor Prescott, an oddity occurred. Each of his offspring was permitted to wear not only something silver, but something red as well. Silver in respect of their father, red in admiration of their mother. Her name was Angela. She was timid and reticent by nature. Angela tried her best to engender a tender mercy in the poor children's hearts. Prescott, on the other hand, inculcated a strict conscience of justice into their minds.

Prescott was certain, of course, that in the end conscience would conquer heart. Justice would triumph over mercy. And that is why on this Christmas morn he suffered his children's juvenile frolic of wearing their bright red scarves and fashionable burgundy skirts to the old kirk. Prescott loathed and despised the color red, in any of its shades or hues. Far too much emotion, far too little righteousness.

For her part, Angela chose from her wardrobe a subdued dress of pale blue and mocha creme taffeta. It reduced the possibility of a flare-up of marital friction. On occasion, and sometimes even at Christmas, she dared to wear an accessory of pink—shell earrings perhaps—as a symbol of her unspoken but conscientious objection.

On this brisk Christmas day, in their dated and somewhat

run-down cinder block apartment, Merriman and May and Leland set about their holiday chores: lighting the yuletide fire, preparing the Christmas goose, and chilling the Dom Perignon. Across town, in an ultra-modern and comfortably furnished four-bedroom townhouse, Prescott allowed himself a little extra time to bathe, dress, and style his coif.

With a sigh of regret he stuffed a one-hundred-dollar note into his weekly tithing envelope and thrust it into his coat's inner pocket. The sum was quite sufficient for this year's Christmas offering—generous, he decided. After all, his forebears had been pillars of the church who probably pissed away more of their wealth—and thus his inheritance—into the coffers of First Scots than God should have expected. Such unnecessary extravagance, he sighed. But there was the stained glass window that bore his family name. Prescott managed a smile.

Prescott had no intention of inviting guests to dine. Christmas was for family. There should be no outsiders. Certainly no unfortunate stranger from the highways and byways of life would be invited. He had heard of such foolishness committed by other members of First Scots and scoffed aloud as he combed his hair. And no alcohol would touch the family's lips. Prescott's conscience, and his understanding of true religion, demanded strict sobriety on all occasions, even weddings.

Like a peacock he groomed himself to perfection in order to strike a stunning pose upon his entry into the narthex of First Scots. He even donned his favorite white linen suit and silver tie. After all, the good solicitor was the rightful heir to nearly two centuries of cheap seats on the third pew to the left of the pulpit, within spitting distance of the family's dreary stained glass window.

Prescott had no friends. Most of the communicants of First Scots took him for what he was: an arrogant prick. And so when he strutted into the sanctuary, shining bright as a silvery moon on this Christmas morn, he was greeted with near-silent smirks from the men and overwhelming pity from the ladies. To this slight Prescott was totally oblivious.

Angela came behind him, cowed, as if her more heinous sins had just been exposed, while the dour children marched single-file behind her to the family pew.

As Prescott took his seat, the chimes in the old bell tower of the church pealed eleven descending quadruplets, each in G major, their tintinnabulations signifying the hour and aggrandizing the occasion. Prescott beamed with pride. It was his church. Christ would be pleased with his good works.

On any service other than Christmas, Easter, and the rare and expensive ornate wedding, the old bell itself had to suffice: chimes were for special occasions. The faithful bell's muted sounds marked life's routine celebrations of worship. The oaken clapper, striking the appropriate number of sequential rings against the bell's alloyed inner surface of copper and tin, trumpeted the appointed hour.

But this Christmas morning the chimes resonated brilliantly. On their cue the choir emerged from behind the curtained backdrop to the impressive array of stainless steel organ pipes and took their seats in the choir loft. Then the Rev. Dr. Ian MacArthur, a Scot himself, who had preached to the wandering sheep of First Scots for nearly forty years, carefully mounted the dusty carpeted steps leading to the raised marble pulpit, which had hosted many a distinguished preacher of the reformed faith over the centuries of the old kirk's existence.

Prescott's mind wandered through the first hymn. It was a carol. His thoughts were fixed on Dabney Peters' trial. How dare that scoundrel Merriman have the gall to present his client as a retarded misfortunate. Already word had circulated throughout the halls of justice that the scalawag Merriman was back and slyer than ever. The Silver Seal—a sobriquet bestowed upon the icy solicitor by his fellow barristers—had been outsmarted by the wily Merriman, so they said. But the verdict was not yet in. A mid-week Christmas had delayed the jury's deliberations—all that was left to be done in the case. Tomorrow their work would begin.

While the choir's voices joined with those of the congregation to the strains of "Silent Night," Prescott dreamed of finally nailing Merriman to the cross. After convicting the poor scoundrel Dab on the stolen goods charge, he would insist on the harshest of sentences. Prescott would consent if he must, as Detective Lieutenant Barrow had recommended, to a reduction in sentence in exchange for Dab's agreement to spill his guts about the solicitor's slashed tires and slit phone line.

Curiously, at the close of his hope-filled Christmas message, Dr. MacArthur made reference to the stern injunction of Christ found in the ninth chapter of the Gospel According to Mark. Prescott's attention reverted to the preaching when he heard Jesus' familiar warning about hell.

"And if thy hand offend thee, cut it off: it is better for thee to enter into life maimed, than having two hands to go into hell, into the fire that never shall be quenched: Where their worm dieth not, and the fire is not quenched."

Hell. Prescott considered the concept. An unquenchable fire. The undying worm. Merriman would end up there. After all, no stained glass window in this town could trace its posterity to the generosity of the Merriman clan. The man didn't even attend church. He swore and cursed liberally. He manipulated people, justified his indecent behavior, and lied and deceived constantly. He stole his clients' fees daily. He consorted with known criminals. Merriman was, in short, a sinner of the first rank. He deserved the wrath of God and the punishment of the unquenchable fire of hell and the undying worm.

Merriman was too blinded by his sin to ever cut off his offending hand, Prescott judged. He would enter the gates of hell without undergoing the essential amputation, all ten digits of his upper extremities intact and ready to burn. Prescott was confident he himself required no such self-mutilation in order to be received into the bosom of Abraham with great joy and celebration when the time came.

Suddenly Prescott felt a surge of relief. In the end, no matter how successful Merriman had been in this world by springing clients like Dab Peters from the trap of prosecution, he would surely burn in hell. And Prescott, on the other hand, would stand with the saints at the Pearly Gates, basking in the glory of his Maker, while observing with glee the torture of the great Merriman down below. Wasn't this the meaning of Christmas, after all?

Across town, Merriman and May and their guests were just sitting down to enjoy the goose, the casseroles May had lovingly prepared, and Harritt's bottle of Sauvignon blanc. Another bottle was placed on ice, just in case. Merriman demonstrated his talent at carving the goose. The juicy slices caused each mouth to water. Merriman enjoyed every second of it.

"Pass your plates for a serving. Guests first!" Merriman announced in an unusually generous and gregarious tone.

From under the butcher's block in the kitchen Leland cocked a suspicious eye.

Just then old Dab interrupted. "Mr. Merriman, would you mind if I read a bit of the Christmas story before we eat?" He pulled out of his tattered coat pocket a small New Testament, along with the Psalms and Proverbs, which he had received from the hands of a Gideon worker years before. The little book's cover was a faded brown, its corners bent and worn. With gnarled fingers scratching through the pages of the Holy Scripture, Dab searched for a passage from Luke's Gospel.

Merriman felt the air slowly escaping from his puffed-up chest, but he took his seat and replied, "Please, Dab, grace us with a reading." He thought about his inanity defense, built almost entirely upon Dab's illiteracy, and experienced a moment of dyspepsia.

Dab fumbled in his pants pocket for his reading glasses. His trembling hands placed the spectacles on his bulbous, weathered nose. He cleared his throat. "I love this passage. Miss Alabaster read it to my sixth grade class just before the Christmas holidays began. I suppose it was a sort of send-off." None at the table but Merriman cringed as Dab proceeded to read Luke's narrative of the angel's annunciation of Christ's birth.

"And there were in the same country shepherds abiding in the field, keeping watch over their flock by night. And, lo, the angel of the Lord came upon them, and the glory of the Lord shone round about them: and they were sore afraid. And the angel said unto them, Fear not: for, behold, I bring you good tidings of great joy, which shall be to all people. For unto you is born this day in the city of David a Saviour, which is Christ the Lord."

Feeling a bit dizzy from the Dom Pérignon and his erstwhile illiterate client's reading from the ancient text, Merriman thought of Brocadia and her pitiful attempt years ago to introduce her son to the essence of Christmas. He began to brood.

His reminiscing mind returned to Dab's reading, just as the old boy was concluding it at the fourteenth verse of chapter two: "Glory to God in the highest, and on earth peace, good will toward men."

Closing the little testament, Dab turned to Merriman and smiled. "Thank you, Mr. Merriman, for allowing me."

The obese Harritt, perspiring from the alcoholic beverages he had so liberally consumed, offered a felicitous toast to Christmas, to May, to the goose, and to Dabney. All around the table each celebrant but Merriman raised a glass.

"Merry Christmas to you all!" May exclaimed, as she held her stem high, filled with Harritt's good cheer. She refused to allow Merriman's gall to put her in a foul humor.

Leland rolled onto her back in her little spot in the kitchen under the butcher's block, her legs splayed upward in a pose of complete surrender. For a moment she listened to the human sounds of silverware clanking against May's good china and the titters of laughter emanating from Euphonia and Euphoria as Dunleavy and Harritt told off-color jokes and reminisced about good times. Content for the moment, Leland fell asleep and dreamed of the fox terrier and the fluffy tailed squirrel while the happy little party in the dining room finished off the Christmas goose and the Sauvignon blanc.

Christmas went.

CHAPTER TWELVE

The jury deliberated all day. Merriman paced the halls of the courthouse like an expectant father. Dab sat silently in the courtroom, reading his favorite passages from the little brown testament. Malcolm T. Prescott, pretending to be unfazed, returned to his office purportedly to work on other matters.

At a quarter to five the old bailiff found Merriman in the men's room and rasped, "Judge Bailey's ready. The jury's reached a verdict."

Merriman did not need the assistance of his gold-headed cane, nor did he limp, as he dashed to the courtroom. Dab was seated at the defense table, hands folded and trembling slightly, head bowed. Judge Bailey was already on the bench.

"Where's the solicitor?" growled the judge. "This jury doesn't deserve to have to wait on him."

The clerk of court whispered to Judge Bailey, "He's on his way, Judge. I called him as soon as we got word of the verdict."

An audible sigh of displeasure emanated from Judge Bailey. "We'll stand in recess. For exactly five minutes. Not a minute more."

"All rise," the bailiff intoned as the judge exited the courtroom.

Merriman turned to his client. "No matter what the verdict is, we tried our best case. You did a superb job with your testimony, Dab."

It was true. Prescott didn't lay a glove on Dabney Peters during cross-examination. The judge sustained Merriman's multiple objections to the solicitor's questions regarding whether the goods in the truck were in fact stolen.

"We stipulate the goods were stolen, Your Honor," Merriman declared with feigned impatience. "The only question is whether the defendant Mr. Peters knew they were."

Prescott's attempts to have Dab recant his earlier testimony that he hadn't read the newspaper accounts or seen the television news reports were totally unsuccessful. Dab stuck to his guns.

By the time Judge Bailey re-entered the courtroom, the gallery was filled with members of the Bar, curious as to whether that sly old fox Merriman had pulled off the inanity defense. The Silver Seal arrived, puffing from his run to the courthouse, just seconds before the judge took the bench. Word had reached him of the judge's displeasure with his absence.

"Nice of you to join us, Mr. Solicitor," Judge Bailey drawled, his tone oozing with sarcasm. "Now, bailiff, bring in the jury." Prescott's face turned beet red.

As the jury entered the courtroom Merriman rose, with the able assistance of his walking stick. Dabney stood at his side.

Merriman shot a glance at Prescott, who sat smugly at the prosecutor's table. The solicitor acknowledged the glance with an icy glare of his own. The tension between these two courtroom gladiators was palpable.

"Ladies and gentlemen of the jury, have you reached a verdict?" the judge inquired.

The foreman of the jury was a diminutive man, dressed in the same dark blue suit he had worn each day of the trial. He was a vice president of a local bank.

"We have, Your Honor."

"Pass it to the clerk, please," the judge instructed. "Publish the verdict, Madam Clerk."

A hush came over the courtroom. The only sound to be heard was the irritating tap-tap-tapping of Merriman's cane on the heart pine planks of the old courtroom's floor. The sound was a painful reminder to Prescott of Miss Alabaster's pitter-patter out of the courtroom earlier in the week. Her testimony was the heart of Merriman's inanity defense, and it had been devastating to the solicitor's case.

The clerk cleared her throat. "We, the jury, find the defendant, Dabney Peters," then, pausing for full effect, she

40

uttered, "not guilty."

The courtroom erupted. Judge Bailey rapped his gavel and brought order to his fiefdom.

Bowed but unbroken, Malcolm T. Prescott stood. "Your Honor, the State requests that the jury be polled."

"Very well," the judge responded. The loser of a courtroom brawl had the perfect right to ask that each member of the jury affirm that he or she agreed with the verdict. The law required that it be unanimous.

"Is this your verdict?" the judge inquired of each member. Only the foreman hesitated, then responded, "Yes, Your Honor." The rest gave immediate affirmative responses.

"Very well. Ladies and gentlemen, I thank you for your service in this case. You are excused."

With that, the jury gathered their belongings and delivered themselves from the courtroom posthaste through the rear door.

"Anything further, gentlemen?"

Merriman rejoined quickly. "Nothing from the defense, Your Honor."

At that moment Detective Lieutenant Barrow approached the solicitor and whispered something in his ear. The good detective had remained in the courtroom with an eye on Dabney Peters throughout the course of the jury's deliberations.

Prescott jumped to his feet. "I have a motion, Judge. For a new trial."

The judge scowled at Prescott. "On what grounds, Mr. Prescott? You know as well as I do, Mr. Solicitor, that once a verdict of acquittal is returned, the State ordinarily has no legal basis to seek a new trial."

"On the grounds that the defense in this case was an utter lie, a scam, and a fraud on the court."

The lawyers in the gallery, who had begun to file out, held their ground to see whether the Silver Seal had an ace up his sleeve.

Prescott continued. "Detective Lieutenant Barrow here, who has been present throughout most of the trial, tells me—and is prepared to swear under oath—that Peters has been reading a book while waiting on the verdict. That proves his testimony regarding his alleged illiteracy was a total fabrication."

Judge Bailey did not like this turn of events. "What do you say to this, Mr. Merriman?"

Merriman turned to Dab and whispered, "What were you doing, you idiot?"

"I swear, Mr. Merriman, it was only my little testament." He withdrew it from his pocket and laid it on the table.

Merriman thought of Dab's Christmas Day reading. He suddenly felt another twinge of dyspepsia. He rose to address the court. "Your Honor," he began, picking up the little brown testament, "he was thumbing through his Bible, that's all." Merriman hobbled to the bench and thrust the little brown testament onto the judge's bench.

"Is the esteemed solicitor assigning some ill motive or malfeasance to a man studying God's Word, or what little of it he can?" Merriman's dander was up now. So was the volume of his baritone. "If so, then this is not the America I know and love. And this court, should it accept such an argument, would be impeached within a matter of days!"

"Mr. Solicitor, do you wish to pursue this motion?" the judge growled.

There was a long pause before Prescott broke silence. "Yes, Your Honor," he declared with conviction. "I do."

"Very well." Judge Bailey removed his spectacles and glared at Prescott. "I don't like this, not one bit. Such a motion is highly irregular, but because the solicitor is asserting a fraud on this court as his ground, in the interest of justice I will hear it. This court will stand in recess until Monday morning. Further argument on the motion, and any testimony either side wishes to offer, will be considered then. Be here at 9:30 sharp. And, Mr. Solicitor, don't be late to my courtroom again."

The old jurist rose and marched out of the courtroom, exuding every indication of displeasure.

CHAPTER THIRTEEN

May stood at the door and watched Merriman turn the corner and limp his way to their Station Avenue townhouse. He had a scowl on his face. And he appeared older than his sixty-three years. May had hoped so much that Merriman and Dab would win the case. Dab's reading at the Christmas dinner had touched her spirit. But it appeared that they had sustained instead a bitter defeat.

She scurried inside and prepared a scotch and soda. As Merriman entered their abode she greeted him with a kiss on the cheek and the drink.

"Sit down, John, and have a bracer. Then tell me what happened today." In his cold heart Merriman knew he was undeserving of this woman.

Merriman slugged down the cocktail and set his glass on the coffee table. May took the empty tumbler to the bar and fixed him another. She returned it full to the coffee table and sat quietly next to her husband of many years.

"May," Merriman began between sips, "a trial is like a roller coaster. One minute you're up and the next you're down. That's what happened today."

May gave him his time. As the whiskey relaxed him, Merriman delivered a rambling but complete account of the day's events in court. May did not interrupt him. She could read the apprehension, and the exhaustion, in his face. When he was finished she spoke.

"But all Prescott can do is call the detective, what's his name—Barrow—to the stand." She tried her best to console him. "And Dab can explain what he was doing: thumbing through his Bible. Who could fault a man for that?"

Suddenly Merriman stood. "Miss Alabaster! I must get in touch with her before Prescott does, and poisons her mind."

He hurried to the kitchen and searched the telephone book for her listing. There it was: "Alabaster, Constance E. 745-0919."

He dialed the number. After several rings Miss Alabaster's prim voice came on the line. "Hello?" He could picture Miss Alabaster in her pleated skirt, carrying her pocketbook and umbrella to the telephone, just in case of emergency.

Merriman instantly turned on what little charm he had left after a lengthy and toilsome career of preparing and examining witnesses. He explained the predicament he and Dab were in.

"Has the solicitor contacted you about this yet?"

"No," she replied. "And if he does, I won't talk to him. I didn't like the solicitor one bit. Not one bit. But I suppose he was just doing his dismal job."

Merriman breathed a sigh of relief. "May I meet with you again, say tomorrow, to discuss this matter further?"

"Not now. I want to think this over and talk to Dabney—without you present, Mr. Merriman. What is his telephone number?"

Merriman dutifully complied. "Will you call me later this weekend? I may need you to testify on Monday morning."

"We'll see, Mr. Merriman. Goodbye for now."

As soon as he could get a fresh dial tone Merriman called Dabney Peters.

"Dab, it's Merriman.

"Oh, hello, Mr. Merriman. I was just crawling into bed. Long day and all, you know." Merriman thought he sounded a little tipsy. It was only seven-thirty.

"Listen. Miss Alabaster may be a key to our keeping the verdict intact. I've just spoken to her. Told her the whole thing." He stopped momentarily to catch his breath.

"Oh? What did she say?" Dab perked up a bit.

"She is going to call you. Miss Alabaster will demand an explanation for why you spent seven hours reading your little book, when you gave her every appearance of near illiteracy before the trial. What do you plan to tell her?"

Dab paused to reflect. "The truth, I suppose. Just as I told you this afternoon. Rote memorization. Sunday school. I still remember the passages. I read them over and over today. That's all there is to it."

"Well, Dab," Merriman allowed, "if I were Miss Alabaster or Solicitor Prescott, I would demand to know what Sunday school you attended, and the solicitor will no doubt seek a recess so that he can investigate your claim and subpoena church records verifying your attendance—I hope."

"It was the Good Shepherd Lutheran Church. On Saunders Street. You know the place. It's near the park. My mother took me there as a child. The records should bear it out. It's the truth, Mr. Merriman. I swear it is."

Merriman thought it over for moment. "All right. I'll go there myself tomorrow. Check the records. What was your mother's name?"

"Arianna, Mr. Merriman. Arianna Peters."

There was a long silence. Then Merriman finished up.

"You understand, Dabney, that a lie on the witness stand is perjury. If you add that to a charge of receiving stolen goods, you're looking at hard time in the Big House. Think it over carefully. I'll call you tomorrow after I've visited the church."

Even with the two stiff drinks May poured him, Merriman had a sleepless night. He was up at two in the morning, pacing and obsessing over the turn of events that had robbed him of an outright *coup de grace* against his nemesis Prescott. How close they had come, he and Dab, and yet how far away from his grasp victory seemed now. Justice was not even a consideration in his late-night delirium.

The next morning he showered and dressed early. With his gold-headed cane in hand he kissed May goodbye, an unusual gesture for Merriman, and thumped along to the corner of Station Avenue and Spaniard Boulevard, where he turned north in the direction of Saunders Street and the inner city park.

The Good Shepherd Lutheran Church occupied a dilapidated building on Saunders Street a block from the park. It was surrounded by mostly low-income, high-rise housing projects and a handful of cheap retail shops, a grocery, and a B-grade bar and grill that sold more alcoholic beverages than meals. Merriman hobbled up the steps to the church office and knocked on the door. He noticed a peep hole in the portal at eye level. After a moment he heard a bolt slide free and the door cracked open. The wrinkled face of an old woman greeted him with some suspicion.

"What do you want?" she demanded.

Merriman attempted a smile. "I'm a lawyer. Here on behalf of Mr. Dabney Peters."

"Never heard of him," the old gal snorted, starting to close the door.

"Wait!" Merriman called to her. "He attended church and Sunday school here as a boy. His mother was Arianna Peters. It is of the utmost importance that I speak with you." Merriman was beginning to smell disaster.

She cracked open the door again. "Arianna Peters, you say?" Through the doorway Merriman could see a desk piled high with papers and some rusted metal file cabinets leaning against the back wall of the office. "She's been dead for years. Buried in our churchyard."

"I know," Merriman replied softly, with a hint of false condolence in his baritone. Then, with an urgency that revealed his desperation, he insisted, "That is why I must talk to you about her son. His very liberty depends upon your cooperation."

"Who are you?"

"John Merriman, Attorney at the Law." He gave his best effort to stand tall and straight as he spoke these words.

The old mistress hesitated. It seemed like an eternity to Merriman. Then she opened the door wide, revealing herself to be a thick, squat-bodied woman, no doubt used to chasing off the riffraff from the nearby projects who trespassed on the church property, selling dope and soliciting prostitution.

"Come in, Mr. Merriman," she relented at last. "Welcome to the Good Shepherd."

Chapter Fourteen

Dabney Peters arrived at Judge Bailey's courtroom as instructed at nine-fifteen Monday morning. Merriman had telephoned him after meeting with the secretary of the Good Shepherd. "Stay off the sauce over the weekend, take a cold shower and a close shave, and wear your best suit of clothes to the hearing," Merriman directed. Dab made his appearance wearing an old camel's hair sport jacket, dark brown woolen trousers, and a subdued gray and black diagonally striped tie.

Solicitor Prescott and Detective Lieutenant Barrow, plug in place, were idling in the foyer of the courtroom when Dab arrived. Barrow gave him a smirk as he entered, much to Dab's discomfort. Seated in the gallery were two ladies, one being his old teacher Miss Alabaster and the other a wrinkle-faced, squat-bodied woman holding a file folder. In his telephone conversation with Dab Merriman had not discussed the outcome of his meeting with the latter.

At twenty-five minutes past nine Merriman made his grand entrance. With his gold-headed cane he tap-tapped his way to the defense table, just to grate on Solicitor Prescott's nerves. He set his tattered old brown leather briefcase—a wedding gift from May—on the table and removed its contents, which consisted of a yellow legal pad with a few notes scribbled on it and copies of records of some kind.

Dab took his seat next to his trusted counsel.

"All rise!" the bailiff enjoined. Prescott and Barrow scurried to their positions at the prosecutor's table as Judge Bailey sauntered out the door of his chambers and up onto the bench.

"I see we're all present and accounted for." The judge glanced at Prescott. "And on time." Flipping through some papers, the judge continued. "Your motion, Mr. Solicitor. For a new trial, I believe?"

The Silver Seal was champing at the bit. His eyes gleamed

bright with righteousness. He was wearing his white linen suit.

"Yes, Your Honor. The State calls Detective Lieutenant Barrow to the stand."

Merriman took his seat and prepared to take notes. There was nothing surprising about Barrow's testimony. Prescott established his presence in the courtroom throughout the trial and jury deliberations.

"All right, Lieutenant. And did you, during the course of the jury's deliberations, have an opportunity to observe the activities of the defendant, Dabney Peters?"

Barrow sucked the fibrous plug of moist tobacco to its resting place between his left cheek and gum. Prescott grimaced.

"I did. Throughout the approximately seven hours of the jury's deliberations, with only a few short breaks for, well, I assume personal needs, the defendant sat at the defense table and read a book."

Prescott approached the witness box and placed his smooth cadaverous hands on the rail in front.

"What was your reaction to this, Lieutenant?"

Merriman rose. "Object. Irrelevant."

"Overruled," the judge groused. "There's no jury here. I can decide what to consider or not, Mr. Merriman."

The old fox regained his seat.

"Well," Barrow began, "I was shocked, to tell you the truth. Mr. Peters here had just testified that he wasn't capable of reading a newspaper. But here he was, engrossed in a book, for nearly seven hours." With a slight smile he glanced in the direction of Miss Alabaster as he spoke.

Prescott strolled back to his table. "Your witness," he allowed to Merriman with a flourish of his hand.

With the assistance of the gold-headed walking stick he had procured years ago from Dunleavy's emporium, Merriman stood and approached the witness. He had no notes.

"Good morning, Detective Lieutenant Barrow. We have met before, I believe."

"You believe correctly," Barrow replied with obvious disdain.

"Now, why is it that you have taken such an interest in Mr. Peters' trial, Lieutenant? I don't believe you were involved in the case, were you?"

Barrow squirmed in his seat, pondering his answer. He loathed Merriman.

"Because Mr. Prescott asked me to sit in, that's why."

"For what reason?" Merriman pressed.

Barrow could feel the blood rise in his neck. His florid cheeks glowed bright pink.

"Ongoing investigation. I can't comment. It's, well, confidential. Police work." He glanced at Prescott.

Merriman tapped his cane on the heart pine planks. "Ongoing investigation. Very interesting, Lieutenant." The sly old fox turned and stared at Prescott as he asked, "Of whom, Detective Barrow?"

Prescott jumped to his feet. "Objection, Your Honor. Mr. Merriman is woefully off the point of this motion, and he is asking this witness to reveal confidential information about an ongoing investigation."

The court reporter, who was diligently attempting to stenographically record every word uttered in the proceedings, chimed in with his hand raised.

"Judge, I'm having difficulty keeping up with the speed of the dialogue." Judge Bailey nodded to his long-time court reporter, Mr. Pannebaker.

"Gentlemen, I have set aside the entire morning for this hearing. Slow down. I want this record to be complete and accurate. Now, as for the solicitor's objection. Overruled. Detective Lieutenant Barrow's motives are fair game. You may proceed, Mr. Merriman."

"Well," Merriman continued. "What poor soul is the subject of your ongoing investigation?"

Barrow slumped a bit in his chair. "Well, you asked me. It's you, Mr. Merriman. That's who."

Prescott grimaced.

Merriman returned his gaze to Prescott. "I see, Lieutenant.

Very interesting. And what, may I ask, is the subject of your ongoing investigation of me?"

"Object!" Prescott fairly screamed as he jumped to his feet.

"I'll sustain that objection—for your benefit as well, Mr. Merriman. You've gone far enough with this line of questioning. Move on."

Barrow's testimony had ruffled the old scoundrel's feathers. He walked to the counsel table and took a sip of water. Regaining his composure, Merriman moved in for the kill.

"Your Honor," Merriman began as he approached the bench, "may I have the little brown testament I handed to the court last week?"

The judge passed it down to the clerk, who delivered the book to Merriman.

"Detective Lieutenant, are you a man of God?"

Barrow glanced at Prescott, hoping for an objection. None was forthcoming.

"I like to think I am, Mr. Merriman."

"You respect the Holy Scripture, then, don't you, Lieutenant?"

Barrow squirmed a bit more. "I, I certainly do." He could feel the jaws of a trap closing around his leg.

"Here, Detective Lieutenant Barrow." Merriman handed the witness Dab's little Bible. "Can you tell the court what that book is?"

Barrow flipped through it, then glanced at the cover. *The New Testament, Psalms and Proverbs* was its title.

"It's the Bible, Mr. Merriman, or least the most important parts of it."

Merriman rapped his cane against the base of the witness box.

"It's the Holy Scripture, is it not?"

"Yes. Yes," Barrow replied with an inflection of impertinence in his voice.

"Turn to the twenty-third psalm, Detective Barrow."

The witness flipped through the pages to the familiar passage.

"I have it," Barrow declared.

"Now," Merriman rejoined, "read aloud the first two verses."

Barrow turned his attention to the text. "The Lord is my shepherd, I shall not want. He maketh me to lie down in green pastures; He leadeth me beside still waters."

"Now, Detective Lieutenant Michael O'Shea Barrow. You are a good Catholic, are you not?"

"I certainly am, Mr. Merriman. And proud of it, too. So was President Kennedy, if you will recall." Barrow appeared pleased with his surly response.

"Good," Merriman replied. "And when you were a wee little lad in Sunday school you were called upon to memorize this psalm, were you not, Lieutenant?"

Barrow could feel the hair on the back of his neck stand up.

"Of course I was. This passage and many others, I might add."

"Very good, Lieutenant. Now. Recite from memory the twenty-third psalm." Merriman smiled at the witness.

Barrow's ruddy complexion turned bright red. "Uh, all right. I don't see the point," he murmured, hoping for an objection from Prescott, "but I'll give it my best shot. It's been a while since I attended Sunday school," he offered.

Barrow stumbled through the recitation, missing or mangling a verse here and there, but finishing the task with valor. "Surely goodness and mercy will follow me all the days of my life, and I will dwell in the house of the Lord forever."

"Well done, Lieutenant. You butchered only portions of the good old twenty-third. Are there other passages you memorized as a child in Sunday school you would like to recite for us?"

"No," Barrow replied emphatically.

"I suppose it would help to glance back at the text of the memorized passages, wouldn't it, Lieutenant?"

Barrow grunted an affirmative reply.

Merriman turned his back on the witness and approached

Prescott, who was seated uncomfortably at the prosecution table. He pretended to be unaffected by the inquiry.

"Wouldn't you agree, Detective Lieutenant Barrow," Merriman asked, his baritone tremulous and booming, "being the good Catholic you are, who recognizes the rightful place of the Holy Scripture, that a man like you—a professing Christian who has memorized these ancient passages as a child—finds comfort in times of distress from reading over those passages—the ones learned by rote as a child?"

"Yes," Barrow conceded.

Then, cutting to the quick like a sharp paring knife, Merriman concluded his cross-examination.

"And even if such a professing Christian couldn't read the daily newspaper, he could—and should—still find solace in returning to these very passages of Holy Scripture he memorized as an innocent child in the bosom of the church?"

Barrow sat mute.

"I remind you, my good Catholic friend Michael O'Shea, that you are under oath. You swore to Almighty God to tell us the truth this day." Merriman tap-tapped as he limped back to the witness box, where he stood gazing intently into the bloodshot eyes of the witness.

Judge Bailey intervened. "Answer the question, Lieutenant."

"Yes, then. My answer is yes," Barrow confessed, his head bowed. He sucked back the brown juice of the feculent plug resting between his left cheek and gum. A trace of the nasty fluid oozed from the corner of his mouth.

Prescott grimaced.

"No more questions of this witness, Your Honor." As he returned to the defense table he caught sight of a woman in the rear of the gallery, slipping out the door. It was May.

CHAPTER FIFTEEN

For the first year of their marriage May never spoke to Merriman of her childhood. For good reason. The subject made her uncomfortable. Although he was curious, Merriman didn't pry.

To celebrate their first anniversary, Merriman took May to the Gloucester, a stodgy old restaurant in the bowel of the Prince Charles Hotel. Known affectionately around town as the Bonnie Prince Charlie, it was a seedy firetrap of an inn, but the hotel had survived for more than a hundred years, outlived three disreputable owners, and barely escaped foreclosure a half-dozen times. Worn carpets and threadbare curtains adorned its salons and guest rooms where salesmen and unwary tourists took lodging.

The Gloucester proudly displayed an A rating awarded by the State Department of Health, but while the kitchen was sanitary, the food was generally mediocre and inevitably tasteless. And cheap. This latter quality established the restaurant as Merriman's favorite. A table was always available. And for twenty dollars, including a two dollar and fifty-cent tip, he could wine and dine May in decrepit elegance and escape with what reputation he possessed relatively intact.

It was a warm spring night in 1968. Merriman ordered a cheap bottle of California Chablis and proposed a toast.

"To us, May," he gushed, "and to a long and happy marriage."

May was nonplused. "Cheers!" He added as they clinked their glasses. She hadn't expected such sentiment from the typically cold and calculating husband she had come to know over the past year. His usual expressions toward her were anything but romantic.

What Merriman hadn't told her was that, earlier the same day, he had settled a wreck case that netted him a twenty-five-hundred-dollar fee. That was big money for Merriman in 1968. He was flush with cash and oozing charm as a result.

In that moment his newfound benevolence reminded May of her father, Leland Andover. She had been an only child. Her mother abandoned them both when May was just a girl of six, leaving Andover with a sink full of dirty dishes, a stack of unpaid bills, and the single-handed responsibility of rearing their daughter. A note she left behind read, "My dear Leland, I can no longer live a lie. The man of my dreams is a long-distance trucker named Boris. In a few moments we will be on the road to the West Coast and a new life, I hope. You'll find supper in the fridge and May next door with Alice. Kiss her for me. Good luck." She signed the note, "Love (I think), Maureen."

They never saw or heard from her again. Leland was a kind, loving, and patient father. He did the best he could to raise the girl, then promptly died of yellow fever after returning from a business trip to Venezuela. May had just turned eighteen. Never successful in school, she dropped out of her senior class at Middlesex High and took a job at the Dairy Queen. She placed in a savings account the proceeds of a life insurance policy Leland left behind and supported herself by serving customers cheeseburgers, french fries, and root beer on roller skates.

May was determined to make her own way. The only relative she had was on her mother's side, a cousin by the name of Adolph. She faintly remembered him from childhood. He was slightly older than May with a lisp and a bad habit of picking his nose. Once she thought she saw him at a movie theater, index finger planted firmly in his left nostril. But when the lights came back up after the movie had ended he was gone. May resigned herself to a solitary life without kith or kin.

After a few years of rolling about the Dairy Queen parking lot chasing tips, she handed in her skates and took a job at a women's clinic that operated out of the rear of a butcher shop on High Street. There was no sign at the entrance, no advertising, and most of the clientele presented false identification and paid in cash.

At first May enjoyed the job. She answered the phone, greeted the patients, and helped them fill out the forms and sign the releases. Then one day she received a promotion. She was transferred to the back, where the procedures were performed. All of the nurses chain-smoked. The doctor, a balding, middle aged Bulgarian, had dark semicircles under his eyes, his white coat was nearly always mottled with bloodstains, and the patients usually left through the rear door in a puddle of tears.

Once when the nursing staff was short, Dr. Stambolski invited May to attend him during a procedure. The poor girl having the abortion was in her third trimester. She writhed in pain and remorse while Dr. Stambolski fought with the scalpel and the suction. Finally the dead fetus emerged on a flood tide of scarlet fluid. May vomited all over the floor, splattering Dr. Stambolski's soft calfskin shoes with her partially digested lunch.

When the bloody mess was finally over, May and Dr. Stambolski agreed that it was time for May to make a career move.

Her next stint was at the phone company, Ma Bell. Her work as an operator was frenetic but satisfying. May had a soothing voice and a steady hand, a combination that enabled her to nimbly alternate the plug wire from line to line while simultaneously calming impatient customers demanding a connection.

"Collect call from young Frankie," she cooed. "Will you accept the charges?" Of course they would.

After a few years at the switchboard, she was promoted to supervisor. The job paid well, but most of her time was spent disciplining pretty young operators who would rather be dating boys and explaining to irate customers why their calls could not be connected. But the steady work kept her from invading the savings account Leland's life insurance policy bestowed upon her, and life carried on. She stayed with Ma Bell until she was well into her thirties.

One day at lunch she met an energetic young stock broker employed by the Merrill Lynch company. He persuaded

May to transfer her funds to an investment account. May and the young man had a brief fling, but it wasn't meant to be and May found herself spending her evenings alone again. There were no hard feelings between her and Nick, the stock broker, and he continued to direct a wise investment policy for May's portfolio well into her Merriman years.

"May?" Merriman asked, interrupting her reverie. "Are you all right?"

"I'm sorry, John. I was thinking about the past." With a faint laugh she added, "That's a dangerous activity for me."

Still on his pink cloud from the day's settlement, Merriman set down his fork and murmured softly, "Tell me about it, May."

And she did. By the time she finished her life story their veal Marsala and Napa Valley Chablis were consumed. Merriman decided to splurge. He tipped the waiter an extra fifty cents and ordered dessert—a chocolate flambé—and two glasses of champagne. From this humble beginning May acquired her taste for that prestige *cuvée*, Dom Pérignon, she would one day serve her family and guests.

Later that night, when they retired to the bedroom, May knelt by the bed and offered up a prayer.

"Lord, if you're listening, I just want to say thanks. I've had my doubts, I'll be the first to admit. But this marriage just might work after all."

CHAPTER SIXTEEN

The wrinkle-faced, squat-bodied woman was Merriman's first witness.

"Will you tell the court your name, please?" Merriman began, standing at the defense table, gold-headed cane in hand.

The old gal squinted at Merriman, turned to the judge, and replied. "My name is Miranda Boatwright. *Miss* Miranda Boatwright."

"Now, Miss Boatwright, would you tell us how you occupy your time? Uh, that is," Merriman faltered, seeming a bit nervous, "how are you employed?"

"I am the chief cook and bottle washer for the Good Shepherd Lutheran Church on Saunders Street," she said with a chuckle. "In other words, I'm the church secretary. Been there forty-one years."

Merriman slowly tapped his way toward the witness box.

"Did you know one Arianna Peters?" he inquired.

"I most certainly did. A saint of a woman, if ever there was. Buried right there in the churchyard."

With a bit more confidence Merriman began to develop her testimony. "Was she a member of the Good Shepherd?"

"Of course she was," Miss Boatwright replied with a dash of impatience. "We wouldn't have buried her there had she not been."

"All right. When did she pass away?"

Miss Boatwright glanced toward the solicitor's table. The white linen suit seemed to her oddly out of place. "I double-checked her tombstone today. She slipped free of her mortal coil on the twenty-third day of August, nineteen sixty-four."

Merriman pursued. "Did she leave family behind?"

"Only the boy," the squat-bodied spinster replied. "He was a teenager at the time." Then, glancing at the man sitting at the defense table, his head bowed and hands slightly trembling, she added, "Dabney was his name. Dabney

Peters. I believe that's him there," she said, pointing at poor Dab.

"Thank you, Miss Boatwright. I won't be much longer." Merriman returned to his earlier post at the defense table. "Did the boy—Dabney Peters—attend services at the Good Shepherd with his mother?"

"I don't know about church services. He never officially joined the church. Didn't pass the communicants class as I recall. But I do know he attended Sunday school as a lad," she said. "I have his attendance record here." Miss Boatwright held up a manila file folder for the judge's benefit.

"I see," Merriman observed. "And please tell the court what your record reveals of young Dabney's attendance."

A pair of five-and-dime store reading glasses dangled just above her breast, attached to a cord around her neck. She placed the spectacles on the bridge of her nose and opened the file.

"He was a faithful student. I remember Arianna would bring him nearly every Sunday when he was in grade school. The attendance record bears out my memory. Would you like to see it?" she asked Merriman.

"No, no thank you, Miss Boatwright." Merriman feigned a courteous manner. "I believe you. Now, tell the court what young Dabney would have done while attending Sunday school at the Good Shepherd."

Her expression telegraphed the thought that Merriman's question was a ridiculously obvious one.

"Well, he would have studied the Bible, Mr. Merriman. And memorized scripture passages. Isn't that what we all did in Sunday school?"

"Of course, Miss Boatwright. Of course." Merriman had never set foot in Sunday school. He paused for a moment to collect his thoughts.

"I have no more questions for you, Miss Boatwright. Now you can ask the solicitor, Mr. Prescott, what he did in Sunday school. He may have some questions for you, too." Merriman took his seat, flashing a devious smile in the direction of his adversary.

Prescott approached Miss Boatwright with a glow of confidence. The old gal met his gaze, ready to take him on. She despised his white linen suit.

"Now, Miss Boatwright, you didn't teach young Dabney in Sunday school, did you?"

"No, I did not," came the rapid reply. Prescott concealed a smirk.

"And you didn't observe him in the Sunday school classroom, did you, Miss Boatwright?"

"No, I didn't," she repeated.

"Well, then," the ambitious Prescott drove on, "you can't tell us whether he was asleep or awake during Sunday school, can you, Miss Boatwright? Much less whether he actually memorized or recited scripture passages. Isn't that true?"

Miss Boatwright elevated her thick, squat torso to its full seated height and adjusted her cloth skirt.

"That's where you're wrong, Mr. Prescott." She eyed him carefully.

Merriman stopped doodling on his legal pad and looked up to take in the ongoing exchange.

Miss Boatwright opened her file. "It says right here young Dabney's teacher for the fourth through the sixth grade was Mrs. Greever. That old battleaxe didn't allow any sleeping in her classroom, Mr. Prescott. You can rest assured of that. And she was quite a disciplinarian, too," she retorted.

"If young Dabney was promoted from fourth to fifth, and then again from fifth to sixth, as this record confirms," she went on, holding out the file for Prescott to check, "then I can say with God as my witness that young Dabney would have memorized a minimum of six passages a year." Prescott retreated from the manila file as though she had offered him a snake.

"That's at least eighteen Bible passages, Mr. Prescott. And most of them would have been the words of Jesus Himself, taken straight from the gospels, or either passages from the psalms." She looked Prescott straight in the eye. "That was Mrs. Greever's rule, Mr. Prescott. She never granted an exception. Why, I would bet young Dabney remembers those passages to this day."

Prescott gathered himself, cleared his throat, and tried hurling one last flaming dart at the recalcitrant witness.

"And so he would have been perfectly capable of reading at nearly an adult level after such strict tutelage, would he not, Miss Boatwright?"

The old gal let out a cackle.

"Lord, no, Mr. Prescott. That's where you're wrong again. Old widow Greever drummed them passages into those children's heads whether they could read or not. All they had to do was remember where the books of Matthew, Mark, Luke, John and Psalms are located. They just followed along as Mrs. Greever read and read. Before long they had memorized them passages backwards and forwards.

"And that ain't so hard, is it, Mr. Prescott? Didn't you learn that in Sunday school?"

"Yes, Miss Boatwright," Prescott mumbled as he returned to his seat like a good, compliant little boy. "Of course I did. Just like Mr. Merriman."

Judge Bailey was beginning to enjoy himself.

"Any more questions of this witness, gentlemen?" the old curmudgeon smiled broadly, revealing discolored nicotine-and-tar-pummeled teeth from years of smoking two packs of unfiltered cigarettes a day.

Prescott grimaced.

"None for the defense, Your Honor," Merriman declared as he rose.

Then, feebly, Prescott added, "Nothing further of this witness."

Detective Michael O'Shea Barrow shivered as a draft of cold air from the north penetrated the cracks in the casement window next to him in the rear of the courtroom. He didn't like the direction of that blast, not one little bit.

"Call your next witness, Mr. Merriman."

"The defense recalls Dabney Peters to the stand, Your Honor."

"Let's re-swear him, bailiff," the judge directed. "After

all, he is the defendant."

Dab came around, placed his hand on the bailiff's Bible, and swore to tell the truth, the whole truth, and nothing but the truth, so help him God. Then he took his seat in the box.

Merriman stood and tapped straightaway to the witness box.

"Dabney, were you reading this little brown testament the other day while we were waiting for the jury to reach a verdict?" Merriman handed him the book.

"Only parts I know from memory, Mr. Merriman. That's all. It was a comfort to me."

"Very well. And tell us, Dabney, what parts were those?"

Judge Bailey leaned forward, turning his head so that his good ear was closest to the witness.

Dabney took a moment to thumb through the gilt-edged pages. "Why, just parts of them passages I remember from a child. The ones in red ink, mostly."

Merriman began a rapid-fire series of questions intended to elicit the briefest of answers and get his client off the stand as quickly as possible.

"Was your mother named Arianna Peters?"

"Yes, sir."

"Did she attend the Good Shepherd Lutheran Church here in town?"

"Yes, sir."

"Is she alive today?"

"No, sir. She passed in 1964."

"Where is she buried?"

"In the churchyard of the Good Shepherd."

"Did you attend Sunday school there as a boy?"

"Nearly every Sunday. Yes, sir."

"Was your teacher Mrs. Greever?"

"The one and the same. Yes, sir."

"Did she teach you to read at nearly an adult level, Dabney?"

"Well, she tried, Mr. Merriman." Dab paused and glanced at Miss Alabaster for strength. "I couldn't read so well. I tried, though. I really did. You can ask Miss Alabaster."

Merriman tapped over to the witness box, to better control Dabney, who was beginning to loosen his tongue a bit more than necessary.

"Dab, just listen to my question, now, will you? And answer that question only, all right?"

"Yes, sir, Mr. Merriman," came Dab's docile response.

"Did Mrs. Greever or Miss Alabaster ever succeed in teaching you to read at nearly an adult level?"

Dabney Peters diverted his eyes in shame. "No, sir," he whispered.

"Answer again, Dabney. Louder this time, so Mr. Pannebaker and the judge can hear you."

"No, sir!" Dabney fairly screamed, as if exorcizing that demon illiteracy that had plagued and tormented him all his adult life.

"Well, how could you spend so much time the other day thumbing through your Bible, Dabney?"

"I was just looking, Mr. Merriman. Just looking at all them passages I had memorized. And they all came back to me, just like as if I was sitting there with Mrs. Greever and the rest of the Sunday school class."

"How did you feel, Dabney, when those passages came back to you?"

Dab snuffled and reached for a pocket handkerchief. There was a pregnant pause in the examination. Then he collected himself and answered.

"I knew my momma was watching from heaven, just as proud of me then as she was before she died, Mr. Merriman. The day I recited the twenty-third psalm in front of the whole congregation she busted into tears. Then afterwards, she took me to the Gloucester restaurant where the waiters wear white gloves, in the basement of the old Bonnie Prince Charlie Hotel. You know the place."

"Yes, I know the place well, Dab." Merriman thought of May.

"And she bought me lamb chops and mashed potatoes and green beans and a piece of chocolate cake for dessert. That's how I felt last week, when the jury came back and said

I was innocent. It was like having lamb chops and mashed potatoes and green beans all over again, Mr. Merriman, with a piece of chocolate cake for dessert. I can't really read, Mr. Merriman. But I can remember things. And so I memorized them passages, that's all."

Merriman tapped back to the table and sat down. By his crafty examination the sly old fox had reduced poor Dab to the status of an imbecile.

"Your witness, Mr. Prescott."

Taking it all in from his perch in the rear of the courtroom, Detective Lieutenant Barrow sucked his plug, wondering what the Silver Seal might do now. He'd better do something, by God. Or this case was lost sure enough, Mikey decided.

"I have no questions for this witness, Your Honor."

Merriman seized the moment. "The defense recalls Miss Alabaster to the stand."

"Very well," the judge said in a jovial tone. "Come forward, Miss Alabaster. There's no need to swear her again, bailiff, but let me remind you, ma'am, that you're still under oath."

"Oh, I understand." Miss Alabaster clutched her pocketbook. The telescope umbrella was slipped under her arm. Merriman gazed out the window at the blue sky. There was not a cloud in sight. The old schoolmarm took her seat in the witness box, smoothed her pleated skirt, and leaned forward. She was ready.

"Now," Merriman began, "I'll be brief. You heard the testimony of Miss Boatwright this morning?"

"Yes, sir."

"And you heard Mr. Peters testify last week and then again just now, didn't you, Miss Alabaster?"

"Yes, sir."

"And, of course, you were here for Detective Lieutenant Michael O'Shea Barrow's testimony earlier this morning, were you not?"

"Yes, sir."

Merriman cut to the chase.

"Having had the opportunity to hear all this testimony, Miss Alabaster, does any of that testimony cause you to change your earlier opinion that Mr. Peters is only capable of reading at a second grade level?"

"No, sir," she declared. "To the contrary, it reinforces my opinion."

"Thank you, Miss Alabaster. I have no more questions." Merriman took his seat.

The Honorable Malcolm T. Prescott, Solicitor for Cumberland County, had no questions for this witness.

The testimony was over. Judge Bailey allowed each side to sum up its argument on Prescott's motion for a new trial. Then he issued his ruling from the bench.

"This Court finds no evidence of fraud or perjury sufficient to overturn the verdict of the jury. The State's motion for a new trial is denied. The clerk shall enter judgment of acquittal accordingly."

CHAPTER SEVENTEEN

Judge Bailey's courtroom slowly emptied out. The curious onlookers, a few local journalists, and a handful of court personnel returned to their normal travails. Dabney and Merriman sat quietly at counsel table while Prescott packed his briefcase and prepared to take his leave. Barrow was long gone. Like a lark at the door, as soon as the gavel rapped he flew away. Barrow was disgusted with Prescott. As much as he loathed Merriman, he had to concede that the old fox had out-lawyered the Silver Seal.

As he turned to go, Prescott hesitated, then made a decision of conscience. Bloodied but unbowed, like some prophet of antiquity he confronted Merriman and his client. Robed in the cloak of his own righteousness, there was a certain awesome radiance about him.

"I know the truth!" he declared. "Peters, you cur, you slashed my tires and slit my phone line. As for you, Merriman, your trumped-up inanity defense may have carried the day, but the result was a travesty of justice. You trampled upon the righteousness of the law. It won't withstand appellate scrutiny. And you can be sure I'll appeal—to the Highest Authority."

Merriman placed a restraining hand on Dab's arm, anticipating a physical response from his client to Prescott's stinging rebuke.

"You're a sore loser, Mr. Solicitor," Merriman replied with perfect equanimity. "Why don't you go home now, and soak your pompous head."

Merriman's dark, disheveled locks fell over his collar and onto his shoulders. Like some modern day Samson he pushed back his chair and stood, gripping his gold-headed cane for support. He was a good three inches taller than Prescott, and his demeanor was menacing.

"Go home, Prescott, and preach to your choir. I noticed your lackey, Detective Barrow, had the good sense to leave us in peace to celebrate our victory. I suggest you follow suit."

The solicitor was enraged. His pale blue eyes flashed white with anger.

"I don't need any suggestions from you, Merriman. But I'll leave you with this prediction: justice and righteousness will prevail. And Dabney Peters will get what he deserves—a long stretch in the penitentiary. As for you, Merriman, the next time you appear before the Board—and that day will come—I'll be present. And you can kiss your license to practice goodbye."

But Merriman would have the last word.

"Go home, Prescott, and cower before your God. You're no better than me—or poor old Dabney here—even though you dress in your white linen and carry your self-made banner of truth and righteousness like a cross." Then, stooping to meet Prescott eye to eye, Merriman delivered his own prophecy.

"One day you'll stand before the judgment seat, naked as the day you were born, alongside all the rest of us. That much I remember from Dabney's little brown testament. And I'll add this, too, Mr. Protector of the Law: 'Let justice roll on like a river, righteousness like a never-failing stream!' Check it yourself, Prescott. It's a passage from Amos, inscribed on your license to practice."

PART TWO

CHAPTER EIGHTEEN

In the months following his victory over Prescott and the forces of self-righteousness, Merriman experienced a dark, depressive episode. May noticed as much. She worried. Earlier in their marriage she had seen her husband morose, withdrawn, even isolated. But those bad times were usually precipitated by some devastating blow such as the suspension of his license to practice, or a humiliating defeat in the courtroom, or some severe financial downturn. Normally the clouds lifted within a few weeks and Merriman returned to his predictable irascible self.

This time there seemed to be no discernable external trigger to his depression. To the contrary, his and Dab's success at trial had made the headlines, and for once in his notorious career, he was showered with publicity of a positive variety. And he was completely sober—a state he rarely achieved even in the best of times. May decided that some intervention was necessary.

"John," she declared one morning, "get out of the bed." May was doing the laundry. It was time to wash the bed linens. "It's eight-fifteen. Are you going to sleep all day?" As she spoke, she snapped and folded clean, dry towels from the laundry basket.

Merriman groaned. "Leave me alone, May."

Leland was catnapping under the bedcovers. Lately she had taken up with the sullen Merriman. Birds of a feather, May decided. The four-legged traitor had sulked about her kitchen long enough.

"Get out of those covers, Leland!" May swatted a towel at the undercover lump that had begun inching forward from the foot of the bed toward the headboard, and her escape hatch. The little yapper sprang from beneath the bedspread and scampered straightaway to her spot in the kitchen under the butcher's block. May decided to deal with Leland later. First things first.

"John," she tried again, sweetly this time. May was the sole remaining creature on planet earth who addressed the old fox by his Christian name. And then only occasionally. When speaking of him in the third person, even to May, he was simply Merriman.

"I want you to go see Dr. Babb. Something's not right. I've made you an appointment for eleven today. I'll go to the office and answer your phone if you like." Merriman relied on an outdated answering machine to take his calls during his absence from the office. He procured the device from Dunleavy's emporium shortly after May's Christmas party.

Merriman pulled the extra pillow over his head. "I'll not go. Cancel it."

May expected the rebuff. She allowed Merriman a moment of contemplation. Then she pressed.

"No. I won't do it. You're going if I have to drag you."

The pillow came off. Merriman turned to look at his wife. She detected a strange flicker of fear in his eyes.

"Drag me, then."

Sims Babb was May's version of the perfect family physician. He was a little weasel of a man—short and bent forward with a face that projected out and down. But he was perceptive, thorough, and competent. And May liked him. She kept annual appointments with Dr. Babb for physicals. After all, she was in her sixties and prudent when it came to self-preservation. The doctor had seen Merriman only on the one occasion years ago when the old fox had fractured his spine in the altercation at O'Leary's bar.

Merriman and May arrived at Babb's office shortly before eleven. Of course Merriman had no insurance and thus little was required in terms of paperwork. After a few minutes' wait, a pretty young nurse summoned them to the examining room. She took Merriman's vital signs, most of which were abnormal, and inquired about the reason for the visit.

"I don't have a reason," Merriman growled. "Ask May."

Just then Dr. Babb entered. The nurse handed him the chart and exited with a comely swish and a roll of her eyes in Merriman's direction.

"Hello, May. And Mr. Merriman! I haven't seen you for years," he said, extending his hand in greeting. "How are you doing?"

"Apparently not well, according to my wife," Merriman snapped, taking the proffered hand. "I am sixty-three, you know, and so you're not dealing with a spring chicken to begin with, Doctor."

Merriman made a quick survey of his surroundings. Against the near wall stood a metal table laden with menacing stainless steel instruments useful for insertion into his various orifices. Sterile disposable products such as cotton swabs, surgical gloves and lubricating gel were stacked neatly in pigeonholes. A bed that was more like a gurney rested against the far wall. And color illustrations depicting the anatomies of both genders of Homo sapiens were taped above the bed.

"Now, May." Merriman declared. "You're the one who dragged me here. You have the floor."

May ignored her husband's sarcasm. She turned to her physician.

"Thanks, Dr. Babb, for seeing us on such short notice. I'm worried about him. He doesn't eat, he sleeps late, and seems depressed to me."

Merriman took notice of May's use of the third person.

Babb glanced over the chart.

"Mr. Merriman, your blood pressure is one sixty-five over one hundred. That's a bit high. Your pulse is ninety-four and irregular. That's not good. And your wife says you're depressed. That combination concerns me."

There was a moment of silence as the doctor's comments sank into the frontal lobe of his patient. Merriman could think of nothing to say in reply.

"Let's do a complete work-up," Dr. Babb suggested. "Then maybe we can give you some answers. Okay? Now, take off your jacket and shirt, Mr. Merriman, and let's go to work."

Merriman knew the voice of authority when he heard it.

He was cornered.

For the next hour Merriman was pricked, probed, thumped, manipulated, inspected, and required to assume various compromising positions as the doctor and nurse collected specimens, performed tests, and gathered the vital information necessary for arriving at a diagnosis. When he concluded the examination, Dr. Babb invited Merriman and May into his private office.

"All right. We've heard from May. You tell me how you've been feeling, Mr. Merriman," the doctor asked, leaning back in his desk chair.

"Terrible!" came Merriman's thundering reply. "But that's normal for me." He was hoping a bit of cynicism might lighten the mood.

"Are you depressed?"

"No. I simply despise the thought of getting out of bed in the morning and going to work. Isn't that normal, Doctor?" Merriman was playing lawyer.

Dr. Babb was wary of lawyers. And from what he knew of Merriman, he was beginning to develop a healthy suspicion of the man.

"I suppose it depends on your job, Mr. Merriman. From what I've read in the newspaper recently, you should be pleased with yourself as far as your work goes. And so, to answer your question more directly and personally, I would say no. It would not be normal for you to harbor such a thought."

"Well," Merriman drawled, shifting uncomfortably in his chair, "I was just making a bad joke."

"Stop making jokes, John," May ordered, "bad or otherwise. I'm not laughing, and neither is Dr. Babb."

The doctor cleared his throat. "I'm not liking what I'm seeing on your EKG, Mr. Merriman. I want you to visit a cardiologist. You'll need to undergo a treadmill exam, perhaps some other tests. It's important that we get to the bottom of this. Okay?"

Merriman was beginning to dislike the sound of Dr. Babb's "Okay?" It was more an imperative than a question.

And everyone in the room knew the answer anyway.

May wrinkled her face into a knot of confusion. "But what about the depression?"

"The symptoms of depression sometimes come with the territory, May. If you're sick physically, your body knows it and transmits that knowledge to your brain." The doctor leaned forward and addressed the rest of his explanation to the patient.

"And if there is a problem with your ticker, Mr. Merriman, then you wouldn't feel much like getting your brains beat out in the courtroom, I wouldn't think. But let's not get ahead of ourselves." He turned again to May. "I want him thoroughly checked out by Dr. Fairchild. Then we'll guide him from there."

Merriman took notice of the fact that Dr. Babb was also beginning to refer to him in the third person. Not a good vital sign, he decided.

Within a few days Merriman darkened the door of W. Stephen Fairchild, M.D., F.A.C.C. He had been instructed to wear comfortable clothing and a pair of running shoes. He didn't own any running shoes and had no intention of ever buying any. May paid a visit to the local Belk department store and purchased her husband a pair of Keds.

Dr. Fairchild's office was across town. May cranked up the Packard. Merriman sat in the back seat, reminiscent of Brocadia, and brooded over the upcoming invasion of his privacy. Leland rode in front with May, just like old times. May never laughed so hard in her life as she did watching Merriman shuffle his way up the brick walkway to Dr. Fairchild's front door in his baggy khaki pants, ultra-cotton Ralph Lauren polo shirt and blue tennis shoes, tapping his gold-headed cane. She couldn't ever remember seeing him dressed in anything but a suit, tie, and starched dress shirt. Merriman was of the old school.

Before he could offer the least resistance, Dr. Fairchild's staff, who had been forewarned of Merriman's potential for insurrection, immediately set about injecting him, plastering his chest with electrodes, and sending him on his inevitable journey down treadmill lane. His pace at first was leisurely. Soon enough it gradually quickened, and Merriman huffed and puffed in tempo.

"Hang in there as long as you can," the burly black technician encouraged him, glancing at the monitor. "Just let me know if you experience any pain in your chest."

The seven and one-half minutes Merriman lasted seemed to him like an eternity.

"I surrender!" he eventually cried. The tech hit the off key and slowly the cycling behemoth wound down to a stop.

"Are you a smoker?" the tech asked in a casual tone while Merriman mopped the sweat from his face and arms.

"Of course!" Merriman rejoined. "Isn't everybody?"

Next they placed him in a huge rotating device, which took lots of pictures of his heart. This portion of the torture chamber was far easier than the treadmill. Merriman had only to keep still while the machine revolved around him, snapping photos as it went.

At last it was over.

He sat in the waiting room and sulked. He wished May had stayed with him. He refused to read a magazine. There was another perspiring man in the waiting room, dressed in Nikes, a NASCAR t-shirt, and a pair of orange running shorts.

"How'd you do, pardner?" the amiable stranger asked.

"How does one really know?" Merriman responded philosophically. "They don't tell you what the rules are, much less how to keep score. I guess I'll find out soon enough."

Just then, the tech who had performed the tests appeared and invited Merriman back to see the doctor. He was escorted into a mahogany paneled, softly lit corner office. Both windows were curtained, with valances and shades. The wall behind the desk was covered with impressive-looking diplomas and such, framed and heavily matted for maximum effect, certifying that Dr. Fairchild was a graduate of this, a fellow of that, and licensed to practice medicine in the state of Merriman's residence.

On a wall of their own, a bank of photographs depicted first a young and blond Steve Fairchild dressed in cap and gown standing on the stone steps of some impressive colonnade alongside his medical school chums; another of a playful Dr. Fairchild cavorting with his fellow interns in the physicians lounge of some teaching hospital; a third, more formal picture of the young physician striking a solemn pose with his fellow cardiology residents; then a candid shot of Dr. Fairchild and his mentor—a tall, wiry-haired man in a long white coat with the trademark stethoscope dangling around his neck like a silver snake—shaking hands with a beaming, almost fawning, Dr. Fairchild; and finally, a photo of Dr. Fairchild standing next to President Reagan in what appeared to be the Oval Office. A signature was scrawled across the glossy print.

To lend a more personal touch, on his credenza Dr. Fairchild displayed an eight-by-ten image of his lovely wife, working in the rose garden of their ivy-covered Tudor mansion, tucked away in some gated community of suburbia. All in all, the office smelt of hard-earned wealth, overachievement and hyper success, odors Merriman's nostrils found at once abrasive and seductive. The carefully crafted decor had served its envy-evoking purpose quite well.

Just then a tall, handsome, athletic-looking man in his mid forties entered. He was obviously the master of the house.

"Mr. Merriman? I'm Dr. Fairchild." They shook hands. "I'm afraid I have some bad news."

CHAPTER NINETEEN

When Merriman was a boy, Brocadia did her best to raise him right. In those days divorce was still an anomaly, and Merriman bore the stigma reserved for children of that phenomenon daily. Brocadia was perfectly content to be rid of Merriman's father. He was a beast of a man. While he never abused her physically, he hurled threats and insults daily that would have shattered the nerves of Mae West.

When the state legislature finally passed the mental cruelty statute providing that such mistreatment constituted a legal ground for divorce, Brocadia was eight months pregnant with little John. She found a lawyer willing to take her case, and to her everlasting delight, the elder Merriman didn't bother to contest the claim. After the passage of the prerequisite six months built into the legislation to encourage reconciliation, Brocadia and little John, then nearly five months of age, declared their independence and were awarded the marital abode in the bargain.

Mr. Merriman was ordered to pay child support, which he rarely did, but Brocadia and the baby had a roof over their heads, she had a good paying job as an underwriter's assistant at a life insurance company, and her employer provided group health insurance that covered them both. For ten dollars a week Brocadia dropped little John off every morning at Miss Prioleau's house just around the corner, and picked him up every afternoon at a quarter after five. The evenings and weekends were hers to spend with the boy.

As he grew older, little John asked Brocadia the inevitable question: where's Daddy? For a while she was able to brush off the inquiry by changing the subject, but the child persisted. Finally, in a state of exasperation, she told little John the unvarnished truth.

"Your father is a no good son-of-a-bitch. The last I heard he was living in Cleveland, Ohio. He is supposed to help me support you, but he rarely sends a check. I don't care. I'm glad he's gone. Forget about him, son," she advised. "You're better off without him." And she was right.

It took little John, then a five-year-old, nearly a week to process this information. He asked Miss Prioleau what a son-of-a-bitch was, and she told him.

"John, I presume you learned that term from your mother. I knew your father well enough to say he fit the bill. Sometimes people refer to a male puppy dog as a son-of-a-bitch. Most times, though, people use the term to describe a man like your daddy, who just ain't worth killin'."

That did it. John Merriman never looked back. He was blessed with two good, nurturing women in his young life, Brocadia and Miss Prioleau. That was more than sufficient to provide him a decent childhood. The only time his father spoke to him was from beyond the grave. A letter came to Merriman one day, years after he reached manhood, from a lawyer in Peoria.

"Your natural father, Pickens Booth Merriman, has devised and bequeathed to you under his Last Will and Testament the real property, with improvements thereon, located at 127 Station Avenue." It was the cinder block townhouse Merriman and May eventually called home. "Finally!" Merriman cried as he perused the lifeless epistle. "The son-of-a-bitch made good on his child support obligation."

Because he was a bit of an odd duck, little John was teased mercilessly by his schoolmates in grade school. "Johnny's daddy's gone away, and left him for another day," was their favorite refrain. But as the years passed he grew tall and a bit hefty, and so he learned to survive by the old schoolyard credo, "Sticks and stones may break my bones, but words can never hurt me."

But they did, of course. And those stinging, embarrassing, hurtful verbal darts left their marks on his tender psyche. By junior high John was able to leverage his bulk to thrash any kid in his path who had the audacity to call him names. After a few such confrontations, none of the little losers dared muster the courage to resort to sticks or stones.

Johnny was taunted no more, but the scars remained.

Then came Shakespeare. Little John, who had now become Big Johnny to his peers at school, discovered the wonderful, awesome, liberating power of words. He took up drama as an extracurricular activity and his teachers soon discovered that he had real talent. Brocadia came to every school play. John was Hamlet one semester, Macbeth the next. He even played King Lear once, after the drama coach gained the confidence to take on the production.

When his voice changed around the time Johnny entered ninth grade, his newfound baby baritone provided him the versatility he needed to land parts in the local theater productions of some popular Broadway musicals.

Brocadia encouraged his pursuit of the dramatic arts. She also pushed her son to achieve academically in school. Brocadia was neither stupid nor impractical, and she figured the only chance her John had to make it to college was through a scholarship. One day the boy's ship came in. He was offered a full ride at Albemarle College, a better-than-mediocre, small liberal arts school in the upstate. He majored in English literature and participated in the drama club as a condition of his financial aid package.

Then, God engineered another life-changing circumstance into the rhythm of his formative years. The summer between his junior and senior years at Albemarle College, John took a job as a runner in a law firm back home. Mr. Pinckney, the senior member of the firm, noticed the young man's talent for both the spoken and written word, and encouraged John to apply to law school. Brocadia was overjoyed. Her son, the lawyer! How happily the words tripped off her tongue.

It was the late fifties and the economy was booming. Universities and law schools were awash with scholarship funds, and once again John Merriman took advantage of the situation. Throughout law school he continued to clerk for the Pinckney firm although old Mr. Pinckney was dead and gone. Occasionally one of the partners would invite him to come along to court when a motion was set for hearing, or to carry their briefcases and boxes of files when a trial demanded it. John quickly learned to love the art of persuasion. He resolved to become a trial lawyer.

Just after his graduation from law school, Brocadia married Charlie Forsythe. Intellectually, Merriman understood his mother's need for companionship. After all, he had left home seven years ago, paying her visits only on holidays and occasionally staying the summer with her. The cold winter months were tough on Brocadia. But emotionally, Merriman felt he had been abandoned all over again, and his relationship with Brocadia and her newfound companion slowly chilled.

Charlie was all right. He was sweet to Brocadia, but he had a roving eye and an unquenchable thirst for bourbon. He was close enough to retirement when they married that his boss, who should have fired Charlie long ago, let him finish out his career and retire with full benefits. Upon his untimely and embarrassing, but somewhat predictable, demise, Charlie's railroad pension and the proceeds of a life insurance policy secured Brocadia's future.

The house she owned as a result of the divorce from Merriman's father, coupled with Charlie's death benefits, provided assets and a modest income for Brocadia. These perquisites allowed her to step down after thirty-three years with the Globe Insurance Company and enjoy a modest retirement. She was, in a word, fixed.

Merriman became more and more isolated. He quit the Pinckney firm and opened his own office on the corner of Northampton and Champagne streets shortly after passing the bar exam. He soon developed an outlaw's persona which dogged him the rest of his career, at least until the end. Slowly but surely, the character traits Brocadia and Miss Prioleau tried to instill in him eroded, replaced not so much by immorality, but amorality. It wasn't that he had perverted his moral compass, he simply didn't see the need to use one. For Merriman, the ends justified the means.

Johnny's daddy went away, and left him for another day.

CHAPTER TWENTY

Detective Lieutenant Michael O'Shea Barrow was steamed. Not only did the solicitor for Cumberland County lose the case, he botched the motion for a new trial and stood idly by while Merriman made a monkey of Barrow—a veteran law enforcement officer—in the process. To top it all, Prescott had decided not to appeal.

"Forget the worldly appeal, Mikey," Prescott lectured him. "One bright and glorious day both of those scoundrels will have to appear before the Great Judge of the Universe and answer for their crimes. Then we'll be vanquished. Righteousness will finally prevail. And I'll be there to add my amen to the heavenly chorus of 'guilty as charged,' my good Detective Lieutenant."

The solicitor stood transfixed by this heavenly ideation, his steely blue eyes gazing beyond Barrow and skyward, upon the beatific scene concocted by his fertile imagination. "So will you, Mikey," he promised, returning to the earthly realm. "If you keep your nose clean."

Barrow shuddered. To begin with, he wasn't at all sure there was a great judge out there somewhere in the Great Beyond. A great prosecutor, maybe, but not a great judge. And he knew from past experience that he couldn't keep his nose clean, not in this world filled with devils like Merriman and Dab.

But even if there were such a judge, who was Prescott to say that Merriman and Peters would fare any worse than Barrow and the solicitor on Judgment Day? They might all roast in hell, Michael O'Shea conjectured, cringing as he pictured in his mind the abject misery of spending eternity with those damnable three—especially if Prescott wore his highly flammable white linen suit.

The detective lieutenant returned to the sanctuary of his own darling obsession. That deviant, Dabney Peters, was as free as a bird. And his cur of a lawyer Merriman was back in the lucrative practice of chasing ambulances and liberating lawbreakers. Barrow laid responsibility for this unfortunate turn of events squarely at the feet of Malcolm T. Prescott. Such was the plain, simple truth. Barrow liked to keep things plain and simple. Earthly justice was the detective lieutenant's job, even if that meant occasionally skirting the punctilious requirements of the judicial system to achieve it. He would leave the high-minded Prescott to his pearly gated visions, he decided, and get on with the dirty business at hand.

"Whatever you say, Mr. Solicitor," Mikey pretended to acquiesce. "You're the boss." He sucked on the nasty wad positioned between his teeth and gum, spat a puddle of brown tobacco-juiced saliva on the sidewalk in front of the solicitor's office, and walked away.

Prescott grimaced. And he thought he noticed a trace of sarcasm in Mikey's reply.

When Detective Barrow arrived home that evening, he engaged in his usual ritual. First, he spat the sickening remains of his plug of tobacco into the garbage can before entering the house. "It's one thing to ruin your own health," his wife Lizzie had said years earlier. "It's quite another to soil my house with that nasty stuff. You drool it all over the rugs and upholstery."

Next he went to the refrigerator and grabbed a bottle of beer. Lizzie didn't mind that peccadillo. Barrow's self-imposed limit was two. His father had died an alcoholic, and when they married, the young detective promised Lizzie she would never suffer the consequences of that same shameful dénouement on his part. He adhered to a disciplined, moderate approach to the sauce.

"Lizzie!" he hollered after taking a swig. "Where are you? We need to talk."

Usually Mikey was in no mood to talk until he had quaffed down his two pacifiers and devoured his supper. Lizzie, who was in the laundry room bleaching out the sweat rings that formed around the collars of Mikey's work shirts, suspected trouble.

"What is it?" she hollered back.

No response. She heard him settle into his Naugahyde La-Z-Boy and set his beer into the cork and plastic coaster on the table next to his chair. She laid aside the grimy shirts and joined him. He wore an unusually glum demeanor.

She took a seat on the horsehair couch. "What's the matter, Mikey?"

Her husband took another long pull off the cold, fermented brew and turned to her.

"I've had it with Prescott, that's what. He's decided not to appeal the Peters case. It's the last straw for me. I know that bugger Dab's just as guilty as sin. And as God is my witness, so does Judge Bailey. But Prescott got outsmarted by that old fox Merriman. And you know the rest. Merriman made a fool of me on the stand when Prescott pushed for a new trial."

Barrow took another pull. "I'm done with it, Liz. Prescott's way, that is. Thirty-four years on the force. I've locked up more criminals than any detective in the county. And my record for convictions is second to none. Now Prescott has, you might say, sullied my good name."

Lizzie knew better than to interrupt. Let him talk. His Irish temper was legendary.

"I've never broken the rules before. Always played fair and square. But now, with Prescott gone soft—and daft, I think, Lizzie—I have to take matters into my own hands."

Lizzie decided it was time to interject. "What do you mean, Mikey? You're not going to do something stupid, are you? You and the solicitor are old pals. And what about your job?"

"It's true what you say, dearie. We've been down a rough road together, Prescott and me. And along the way we've locked up many a hardened criminal. But there comes a time, Liz. A time in a man's life when even old friends must part company. And I'm afraid that time is nigh."

Mikey finished off the first bottle. "Get me my other Guinness, will you, Liz?"

She didn't mind. At least he was opening up to her.

Transparency had not been one of his more prominent traits throughout their marriage. She returned in a moment with another beer. Lizzie despised the taste, even the smell, of malt and hops. It reminded her of their Irish roots. Both her parents and Mikey's were immigrants, and they brought with them a love for the creamy, dark brown stout that had proven to be the downfall of many an otherwise good Irish Catholic.

"Tell me what you're thinking, Mikey," she persisted.

He released a long sigh. "Okay," he said. "Here we go. I can't do anything about Dabney Peters now. That's over and done with. And Merriman can rot in a shallow grave for all I care." He turned away for a moment, considering what he was about to reveal.

"But I know something about our good Solicitor Prescott. Something dark and hidden away—buried, you might say—in the distant past. Something nobody else but Prescott himself knows. At least nobody still alive."

He paused, then finished his train of thought. "If I talk, Lizzie, it'll cost him his job—maybe more."

"But why, Mikey? Why do you want to take him down?"

Mikey reached over and switched off the lamp that suffused a soft, dim glow over their conversation. For several moments they sat in silent darkness as he nursed his beer. Then, signaling a readiness to confide, he gulped down the last few ounces for courage and set the empty bottle onto the emerald green shag carpet.

"All right, Liz. You deserve to know." He took a deep breath and began slowly.

"Years ago, when Malcolm T. Prescott was wet behind the ears and I was a lowly gumshoe with the worst beat on the force—you remember those days, don't you, gal?"

"I remember, Mikey. Those were hard days, but good ones, too. We made love every morning, as soon as you came home from work. The sun would just be peeking its face through the window curtains, like a nosy neighbor."

"Aye," Mikey sighed. "I remember that part, too, my girl. With fondness, I might add," and his tired, crinkled eyes twinkled like stars popping through a cloudy night sky. "I wonder to this day why God never saw fit to give us little ones, as hard as we tried." They both laughed, then their eyes moistened a little as the bittersweet memories returned.

"Maybe it was my job—you know, the danger of it and all. It wouldn't be right to leave you, a poor widow woman, with a shoe full of children to raise all by yourself, now, would it?"

Mikey turned pensive for a moment, as he considered what might have been. "God knows the future, I think. Don't you, Lizzie?"

"Ah-h-h," Liz murmured, "never mind that now, Mikey. We've had a good life, haven't we? I've no regrets."

"Yes, we have," he said, suddenly craving another Guinness. "And neither do I, Liz. I promise you that."

His uncharacteristic tenderness toward her reminded Elizabeth Flenniken Barrow of the early days, when their life together was hard, but good.

"Tell me now, Mikey," she pressed him, returning to the theme. "What are you plotting in that devilish mind of yours?"

"Just this, Liz." Finally the words tumbled out and told the story that Detective Lieutenant Michael O'Shea Barrow had kept hidden in the attic of his mind for three decades.

Once upon a time, a young and ambitious Solicitor Malcolm T. Prescott prosecuted a white man in his thirties named Jake Purdy—married, with two children and another on the way—for the rape of a luscious teenage mulatto whom the police first identified only as Jane Doe. She couldn't have been older than fifteen, but Miss Doe had more curves than a Sally League pitcher and smooth, sensual, cocoa-colored skin. Her succulent array of pubescent forbidden fruit gave birth to an uncontrollable lust in the heart of her deviant assailant.

The girl's light skin tone also betrayed a scandalous rendezvous that had taken place fifteen years earlier between her ebony mother and a prominent white landowner. At the time, miscegenation was a crime. Although rarely prosecuted, it never failed to make back-page news even when the perpetrator was poor white trash. But when a well-to-do white landowner was involved, the story took on added weight—and color—and was sure to make the headlines sooner or later.

The landowner's boy Jake had just turned seventeen when the rumors persisted, gained a foothold in fact, and eventually spread to the front page. There was talk of a trial, but Prescott's predecessor exercised his prosecutorial discretion in favor of pursuing other matters and overlooked the evidence that his good friend, Jake's father, Willis, might have engaged in such an adulterous affair with a woman of color. That fortuitous circumstance notwithstanding, the vicious gossip circulating throughout the community crushed the heart of the boy's mother, forced his parents into a messy divorce, and foreclosed any possibility that Jake might slip gracefully into manhood.

In the late 1950s in Cumberland County, use of the pejorative "nigger" was a hand-me-down denigration from generations of ignorance and prejudice. The disparaging term found a comfortable, accepted—even welcome—place in common parlance and lexicon of the time, even in the ever-widening circles of educated, upper-middle-class white folk such as Jake's family and friends. Like the majority of his generation, the boy grew up inculcated by the obnoxious principle that people of color—those same human beings who worked and lived and raised families and worshiped the same God in his hometown—were members of a divinely ordered inferior breed. The genesis of this cruel misconception was perpetuated and fortified from a few white pulpits by unscholarly, twisted interpretations of the Holy Scripture itself.

Because this evil precept took firm root in the boy's mind, his daddy's delict delivered two devastating blows to Jake's vulnerable, maturating sense of emotional and psychological well-being. First, his father mixed his precious white chromosomes—the same ones he had earlier contributed to produce Jake—with those of a black woman of inferior breed. And second, in so doing, the prominent white landowner presented his son with the awkward surprise of an uninvited baby sister who happened to be colored. To Jake's way of thinking, the former was abhorrent; the latter, simply unfathomable.

In the years following that unspeakable episode, Jake's daddy drifted away somewhere, Jake wasn't sure where, and his mother remarried and escaped to South Carolina. He rarely saw her. She preferred it that way. Jake drifted awhile himself then spent a few years in the Marine Corps. But something inside him drew the young man back to Cumberland County. By that time, he was able to settle into a comfortable, anonymous life, at least as far as the past was concerned. He eventually married a young girl named Nellie who wasn't from Cumberland County originally and had no reason to suspect that Jake had a sister living there who was colored.

Before long Jake was a daddy himself. First came a girl, and then a few years later a boy. Nellie and motherhood got along just fine and provided Jake three good reasons to keep his job at the Westinghouse plant just outside of town. The next thing the happy young couple knew, Nellie was pregnant again. And that's about the time Jake got a letter from the soon-to-be Miss Jane Doe.

"Dear Mr. Jake Purdy," it began. "You don't know me, but I know you. My momma is Mae Ella Brown. My daddy is the same man as your daddy. Momma says that makes us blood kin. I put a picture of me inside this envelope so you can see what I looks like. Momma says I favor our daddy. I live with Momma at 652 Reed Street, just down from the A.M.E. Church. I don't have no brothers or sisters other than you, Mr. Jake Purdy. Momma says no colored man would have anything to do with her after I was born. So we lives alone."

After delivering this startling introduction, Miss Doe offered Jake a most generous out. "If you don't want to, you don't have to meet me."

She closed the crude epistle with "Yours truly," and signed her name: "Venus Brown (Purdy)."

Jake's first reaction to the letter was to vomit all over his trousers and shoes. Later that evening, after Jake cleaned himself up and Nellie put the children to bed, husband and wife had a quiet little conversation.

"Who was that letter from, honey?" Nellie inquired.

Jake attempted a pitiful obfuscation. "What letter, honey?"

She was having none of it. "You know what letter I mean, Jake. The one with the initials "VBP" on the back flap of the envelope."

"Oh. That letter."

"Uh-huh. *That* letter," Nellie replied sharply.

Jake considered his options. There were only two: prevarication or truth. After considerable reflection and a deafening silence, he elected the latter. It resulted in a long evening.

CHAPTER TWENTY-ONE

When the sheriff of Cumberland County received word that Venus Brown had been raped, he assigned his brightest and most promising young deputy to the case. Michael O'Shea Barrow had been with the force only two years, but in that space of time, he had amassed quite an enviable collection of law enforcement accolades. A few of his cases had actually gone to full-blown jury trials rather than guilty pleas, and so Mikey had enjoyed the privilege of working with the equally bright and promising young solicitor, Malcolm T. Prescott.

A couple of Barrow's petty cases, one involving criminal domestic violence and another charging the accused with second degree larceny, were defended by one John Merriman, Esquire, of the Cumberland County Bar. Both ended in pleas to lesser offenses, but the experiences gave Mikey a taste of Merriman's style, which left a certain bitter flavor on the taste buds of the young detective's tongue. Nevertheless Barrow was finding his depth among law enforcement officials and succeeding quite nicely in doing so.

The pernicious assault on Venus Brown was Barrow's first rape case. At that time, DNA evidence was unheard of, at least in Cumberland County. Good old-fashioned detective work, coupled with the standard forensic pathology techniques of the day such as fingerprint analysis, blood sampling, and hair follicle comparisons, was the method of choice employed by Barrow to solve the crime.

The girl waited four days to report the incident, by which point she had bathed numerous times and washed the little nightie she had been wearing. As a result, forensic evidence was scarce. Shame, embarrassment, humiliation, and fear were the reasons the girl gave her momma and law enforcement for the delay. Mae Ella was furious at her. There was, however, an extractable stain of bloody semen on Venus' cotton panties that did not match her blood type. It was a start for the boys in the lab.

The written statement Venus gave Prescott described a white man who entered her ground-floor bedroom in the middle of the night through an unlocked window while she was sleeping. His hair and eye color were by her account indeterminate. It was dark, there was no moon, and the attack lasted less than ten minutes. She distinctly remembered one clue: her assailant's breath carried a strong odor of Clove chewing gum. She recognized the scent because Clove was her mother's favorite chew.

Her intruder pressed the blade of a jackknife to her throat and threatened to slice it like a field-ripened watermelon if she uttered as much as a peep. With his left hand he ripped off her nightie, jerked down her panties, and did his dirty work. While engaged in the act of penetration, he elected to drop the knife and apply a choke hold around her supple neck instead. The bruises from his vise-like grip were still visible when she reported the crime, but she covered them for days with a turtleneck sweater so that Mae Ella was none the wiser.

Although Venus' delay in reporting the crime raised concerns, there was no doubt she had been raped. The physician's examination revealed beyond question that the penetration was forced and that Venus was a virgin. For Barrow and Prescott, Venus Brown was the quintessential victim of a brutal, violent crime. By the time of the incident, integration had swept through the South like a forest fire through dry timberland, and the nation's undisputed number one domestic issue was civil rights. All eyes were watching and judging, how Barrow and Prescott would handle the case—and play the race card.

Suddenly law enforcement got a huge break. A tearful, pregnant Nellie Purdy came forward with the letter. While steadfastly maintaining her husband's innocence publicly, Nellie had her private doubts. The ghost of Jake's past haunted her by night, and his erratic behavior following their receipt of the startling little epistle frightened her by day. To his credit Jake consented to Nellie turning the letter over to law enforcement, and even volunteered to be interrogated by Barrow. But not until he retained a lawyer.

Financial considerations impacted Jake's choice of an attorney. During their marriage, Jake and Nellie struggled to set aside a moderate sum into a rainy day fund. Nellie had in mind for its use any needs that may arise for the children. Jake interviewed several pricey, well-respected defense attorneys, but balked at the retainer fees they quoted. Then along came Merriman.

The young fox read about the incident one morning in the newspaper, noting that Nellie had curiously come forward with evidence that tended to incriminate her own husband. From the account in the paper, however, it appeared that, á la Tammy Wynette, Nellie Purdy was standing by her man, who vociferously denied any complicity.

Either way, guilty or not, it was obvious to Merriman that Jake Purdy needed a lawyer. Merriman was far enough along in his career to know the score when it came to the size of retainers criminal defense attorneys charged for handling high-profile cases in Cumberland County. He decided to get in on the action by taking an ethical shortcut, reasoning that he was only doing Jake Purdy a big favor from a financial standpoint.

Merriman thumbed through the telephone directory, found the number, and gave Nellie a call. He figured Jake would be at work that time of the morning.

"Hello? Mrs. Purdy? This is John Merriman, Attorney at the Law. A friend asked me to give you and your husband a call. He thought you might be interested in talking to me. I'm not sure why. I've been out of town on vacation and haven't seen a newspaper in two weeks. I specialize in high-profile criminal defense work."

In a period of less than thirty seconds Merriman committed at least four, and possibly five, egregious violations of the Rules of Professional Conduct—the code of ethics that governs the practice of law. And in the course of doing so, he told the prospective client's wife four whopping lies in his misguided attempt to solicit her husband's case. It was pure genius. And it was grounds for disbarment.

"I-I'm not sure what to say, Mr. Merriman," Nellie replied. "Can you tell me who suggested that you call us?"

Merriman had anticipated the question. "Oh, my goodness, no, Mrs. Purdy," Merriman responded with the perfect combination of friendly but righteous condescension.

"That would be unethical—and a breach of confidentiality. I hope you understand. I govern my practice scrupulously in accordance with the highest ethical principles." Merriman's smooth baritone imparted to the untrained ear an honorable sincerity. "I may be able to disclose that later, but only after I have established an attorney-client relationship with your husband—and then only if my friend consents to the disclosure."

Nellie was part confused, part mesmerized, by the legalese transmitted through the facility of Merriman's silver tongue. "I see," she mumbled. "Why don't I get your number and have my husband call you, Mr.—Merriman, did you say?"

On the other end of the line the sly young fox licked his chops. He had set the hook, and before long, with gentle but persistent reeling, he would have the fish safely into the boat.

"I can tell you this, Mrs. Purdy." Merriman paused, and lowered his voice. "Because of my friend's interest in the outcome of this matter, he has offered to pay half my fee. But of course your husband's decision to select an attorney to represent him in this matter should not be made on the basis of money."

Merriman allowed time for his false piety to sink in. Then he hit poor Nellie with the clincher. "From what I understand, Mr. Purdy's liberty—perhaps his very life—is at stake. Defending such a decent man as your husband is how I make my living, Mrs. Purdy."

Nellie was nonplused. "Well, I-I," she stammered, "I think that's quite generous of your friend, whoever he is. And I do appreciate the way you've explained all this," she added naively. "I'll have my husband call as soon as he returns from work. What is your number, Mr. Merriman?"

❧

To Jake's great surprise and relief, on the night he laid bare his soul to Nellie about his father's indiscretion with Mae Ella Brown and the shame he had endured over it, she didn't seem to care.

"Well, Jake, all I know is he didn't come to our wedding. And neither did your momma. I married you, Jake. Not your momma and daddy. And whatever your father did to participate in bringing Venus Brown into this world is over and done with now."

But on one point she was absolutely insistent. "Don't you ever—and I mean ever—make contact with Venus. I don't want our children to have anything to do with that whole sordid mess."

"Why, sure, Nellie," Jake said that night. "Whatever you want."

Nellie shot back, "I want that letter, then. Give it to me. And don't you ever go near Reed Street, either. You hear me?"

"Loud and clear!" came Jake's reply, as he compliantly handed over the letter.

A couple of weeks later, when the news reached the Purdy household that Venus had been raped, a pall settled over the house like a thick gray fog. It was as if someone had died. Nellie didn't speak to Jake for a day as she sorted through her thoughts. Then, the following morning, she announced, "Jake, I know you didn't have a thing to do with what happened to that poor colored girl. But we got that letter from her. And I think the police ought to know. What if she tells them about it first? You'll look guilty as sin then."

"I don't know, Nellie. I'm not so sure I like it. And one thing's for sure. It'll open up that whole can of worms about my daddy and Mae Ella. And the kids are getting old enough to understand."

Nellie could see the fear brimming in Jake's eyes.

She gazed at him square. "Jake, just answer me this. I'm

only gonna ask you one time. Did you, or did you not, have anything to do with that colored girl's rape?"

Jake looked down, feeling the weight of the shame and humiliation of all those bad times washing over him. Then he raised his head and returned her gaze, square in the eyes."No, Nellie. I did not." His denial was strong and clear.

"Then I'm taking in the letter," she informed him. "Justice will prevail."

Up to that point the police had not identified the victim by name. But Mae Ella had blabbed the news all over the black community, and it didn't take longer than ten minutes for the media to pick up the story. When Barrow was questioned by reporters about the investigation of the rape of Venus Brown, he would routinely reply, "The only investigation I plan to conduct is the one involving Miss Jane Doe." This game of cat and mouse with the news media persisted until the letter from Venus to Jake made its way onto the front page of the Tribune, thanks to the good, if impetuous, intentions of Nellie Purdy.

"All right," young Deputy Sheriff Barrow conceded at the next news conference, with Solicitor Prescott standing at his side. "This department is investigating allegations that Miss Venus Brown was sexually assaulted on April the twenty-first of this year. We are following all leads, but no charges have been filed against anyone at this point."

Barrow's clever use of the disclaimer "at this point" telegraphed that Jake Purdy had better get off his rear end and find himself a lawyer. Prescott and Barrow were fixing to take the case to the grand jury, and that bunch was sure to indict Jake. Most of the grand jurors were old enough to remember his daddy's ruinous rendezvous with Mae Ella. In Cumberland County, the sins of the fathers were presumptively visited upon succeeding generations, at least as far as this grand jury was concerned. And Prescott would not hesitate to remind them, "Isn't that what the Bible says?" Even naive Nellie understood that much.

When Jake came home from work on the day of Merriman's telephone call, he was exhausted, frightened, and confused. It didn't take his wife long to convince Jake he'd better talk to John Merriman, and quick.

Merriman was waiting by the phone. He allowed it a few rings before he picked up the receiver and announced, as nonchalantly as his rich baritone was capable of transmitting, "This is John Merriman, Attorney at the Law."

The two men soon got down to brass tacks.

"Look, Mr. Merriman. I've already talked to three lawyers. They're too expensive. What's your fee gonna be to get me out of this mess?"

Merriman had already made an educated guess of what the other lawyers would have required as a retainer and reduced it by forty percent.

"Because of my vast experience in these matters, and my close personal relationship with the solicitor, my fee is admittedly on the high end. But as I told your wife, an interested party who wishes to remain anonymous has offered to pay half my fee. That means I'll take your case for three thousand—that's your half," he lied.

Merriman guessed right. The pricey lawyers had demanded five thousand dollars. His ethical short-cut saved the client two thousand and put more in Merriman's pocket up front than he had ever earned in a criminal case before.

Jake hesitated. "I'm new at this, thank goodness," he offered apologetically, "so I'm not sure what to do. And all we've got saved up is twenty-eight hundred dollars."

Before Jake could propose paying the two-hundred-dollar balance over time, Merriman fairly shouted, "I'll take it. Forget the two hundred dollars. Meet me at my office tomorrow at ten. Corner of Northampton and Champagne. We'll go over the case then. And, by the way, bring along the twenty-eight-hundred-dollar retainer check, will you?"

CHAPTER TWENTY-TWO

Merriman guessed arterial blockages. This meant bypass surgery. Bypass surgery meant his sternum would be split in half. But that wouldn't be so bad, considering the breastbone's capacity for rapid healing. And surgeons perform more heart bypasses than tonsillectomies these days, he consoled himself.

But Merriman's real diagnosis wasn't so benign.

"You've got an abnormally enlarged heart, Mr. Merriman. Here," Dr. Fairchild offered, "take a look at the films." He slapped one up on the monitor and took out his Montblanc ballpoint. "See? Here's your heart," he pointed, explaining. His hands were smooth and steady. "It's about the size of a big green bell pepper. It should be more like a good-sized, ripe tomato. You know what I mean—a Better Boy, maybe."

Merriman studied the film. "What are you, Doc, a gardener?"

"As a matter of fact, I am," the cardiologist replied, laughing. Merriman appreciated a sense of humor in a man delivering bad news. "See this photo?" Dr. Fairchild asked, lifting the framed, eight-by-ten off his credenza. "This is my wife in her rose garden. Me, I grow fruits and vegetables in a greenhouse in the back yard. Bell peppers and tomatoes, my specialty."

"Back to the point, Doc," Merriman groused, studying the image of his bell pepper on the film.

"Okay. There's nothing surgically we can do for your enlarged heart. In layman's terms your ticker shows signs of an infection, but not the kind we can treat and get rid of with antibiotics, like a bad case of strep throat. Your condition is called cardiomyopathy."

"What causes it?" the lawyer asked.

"We can't say for sure," the cardiologist answered. "Sometimes there's a correlation to alcohol consumption, but there are correlations to lots of other triggers, too. I noticed on your chart you're a drinker. That's the only reason I mention the alcohol as one possible correlation."

There was a lull in the conversation as Merriman's brain absorbed and processed the mind-numbing information. Having engaged in the same conversation with dozens of patients over the years, Dr. Fairchild was accustomed to the lull. He waited patiently for Merriman to ask the next, inevitable set of questions.

"Three questions, Doc. With maybe some subparts."

"Okay," the cardiologist said. "Shoot."

Merriman leaned forward in the soft leather armchair. "First: is it gonna kill me? And second: do I have to stop drinking?"

Dr. Fairchild leaned back in his matching soft leather desk chair. His interior decorator had recommended a subdued medium blue for the leather chairs—professional, but not too imposing—knowing that bad news was regularly dispensed in this room.

The cardiologist looked Merriman in the eye. "Yes, and yes."

Merriman exploded. "Why the hell do I have to stop drinking if it's gonna kill me anyway?" He quickly regained his composure. "Just curious, Doc."

Dr. Fairchild nodded in agreement with the understandable sentiment. Then he delivered the cold, rational, medical response. "Because you want to die later rather than sooner, Mr. Merriman."

"How do you know?" Merriman shot back.

"Because I'm a man, Mr. Merriman. Just like you. And I'll bet the rose garden—and the greenhouse—that you've got a couple of other things you want to do in your life before you die."

There was a brief period of agonizing silence. Merriman stood and walked to the window. Taking pains to be certain that he understood, he turned and faced his doctor. "You're sure of this? So sure you don't even recommend a second opinion?"

"I already got a second opinion, Mr. Merriman. I asked

my partner, Dr. Reynolds, to take a look at the films with me. We're sure."

Merriman took a deep breath and expelled it. "Okay. One simple instruction: don't tell May. I am directing you," he boomed, in his most impressive stentorian baritone, "under the authority of the state and federal privacy laws and the protection of the physician-patient privilege, to tell no one, including most emphatically my wife, of my health condition without my express, written consent. Even if it means the acceleration of my demise."

Merriman paused, cogitated for a moment, then added for legal completeness, "I'll put that in writing today, and mail it to you."

Dr. Fairchild didn't even twitch.

"It's your call. I'll respect it." Then, in an off-handed tone, he said, "By the way, are you the guy that nailed Solicitor Prescott in that recent criminal trial? I read about it in the newspaper."

"That's me," Merriman replied with a smile. "I enjoyed every minute of it, too."

"Good!" the doctor said. "The guy's a real prick."

Merriman was almost out the door of Dr. Fairchild's private office when he remembered he had omitted to ask his third question.

"I forgot, Doc," he said, turning around, a little dazed from all the excitement. "How much time do I have left?"

"Hm-m-m." Dr. Fairchild waved Merriman back to his blue leather armchair. "Sure you don't want to wait on the answer to that one until your next appointment? You're coming back next week, you know. That's when we'll go over all the stuff you should do and all the stuff you shouldn't do. I'll have the results of all the lab work by then, too."

"Yeah, they told me. No, I don't want to wait. How much time?"

"Okay," Dr. Fairchild said. "Fair enough. Quality or quantity?"

"Both."

"If you behave yourself, you could have years left. If you smoke and drink and carouse and keep trying cases, you might not make it to next week's appointment. You understand?"

"Yeah. How much quality left?"

"How much do you want?"

Eerily, the back and forth of the conversation reminded Merriman of negotiating the settlement of a wreck case.

"As much as I can buy with good behavior." For the first time in his life the sly old fox found himself face to face with his own mortality.

The cardiologist glanced at Merriman's chart. "You're sixty-three. You smoke. You drink. You don't exercise. Your blood pressure's high." He flipped through the pages. "Your stress EKG shows abnormalities in left ventricular function. Hey, man. You're not giving me much to work with here."

Merriman smiled. He was beginning to like this guy. The same guy who just told him he's going to die.

"Come on, Doc. How much?" Merriman pressed.

"No kids?"

"No. Just a loathsome canine. Come on. How much?"

"Okay. If I was a betting man, with good behavior I'd bet you'll last to sixty-five—that's quality time. Then comes the hard part. You could linger for years."

Merriman sat quietly for a while. The only sound was that of Muzak's oldies format being piped through the office audio system at a low, soothing volume.

"Two years," he said in a hushed tone, almost a whisper. "You just gave me two good years to live, Doc."

"You asked for it, remember? And, hey. I don't have a crystal ball. I could be wrong. It's just my best professional guesstimate. You might outlive me."

The cardiologist readily perceived his patient's downcast expression. He hated this part of the job. "We could have done this a little more gently next week," he offered apologetically.

"Ah, like you said, I might not be alive next week. I'll take on faith that you really earned all those diplomas hanging on the wall behind you. You must know what you're talking about."

"Trust me, Mr. Merriman. I do." The tone of the doctor's confirmation was more matter-of-fact than arrogant.

"Well, I tell you what," Merriman rejoined. "I'll behave for two years. Then, when the quality time runs out, that's when I go for the gusto. Smoking, drinking, carousing, whatever I want. I shouldn't linger long at that pace, right, Doc?"

Dr. Fairchild scratched his head. "I don't think I've ever had a patient quite like you before, Mr. Merriman."

"Call me Merriman. I prefer it. No mister. And for God's sake, not John. From now on I get what I prefer."

"Okay," Fairchild said. "When are you going to tell your wife?"

"That one's easy, Doc. When the quality time runs out. By the way, how do you know my good friend Prescott?"

Fairchild laughed. He was beginning to like Merriman, too. "The prick goes to my church—First Scots Presbyterian. I serve on the stewardship committee with the pious tightwad. He makes it extremely difficult to maintain a Christian attitude."

Merriman stood and offered his hand. "See you next week, Doc."

"Okay, Merriman," Doc replied, taking his hand. "No drinking, no smoking, no carousing. Understood?"

"Sorry, Doc," Merriman said as he began to leave. "I'm a little hard of hearing. I didn't catch that last part. Maybe next week you could speak up just a little, huh?"

Steve Fairchild couldn't help smiling as he watched Merriman tap his way down the hall with his gold-headed cane, dressed in his Keds, khaki pants, and polo shirt.

"I'll bet he's hell in the courtroom," the cardiologist opined to himself. Then he entered a note in Merriman's chart. "Patient fully informed of diagnosis, all risks. Instructed me not to disclose to wife. Dr. Babb to be notified."

CHAPTER TWENTY-THREE

"Well, gal," an exhausted sounding Barrow said to his wife, "I'm going to bed. It's been a long evening."

"I won't be long behind you, sweet," Lizzie promised. "Just let me get these dishes into some soapy water."

Mikey had worn her out, mentally and physically, with his incredible tale of Malcolm T. Prescott, Venus Brown and the trial of Jake Purdy. Liz could hardly believe that the self-righteous solicitor was capable of what her husband had revealed. If he could prove what he said, she had no doubt that Prescott would either quietly resign or be publicly fired.

Barrow insisted he had no desire to ruin his old colleague. In his opinion, it simply was time for Prescott to step down. There was a gaggle of young trial lawyers in Cumberland County, any one of whom would jump at a chance for the prestige and challenge of the solicitor's high office. A younger, more aggressive man could stand up to the likes of Merriman, Mikey told her, and injustices such as the Peters case would never be wrought again. Then Mikey could look forward to an early retirement from the department, assured that justice in Cumberland County was in capable hands.

Lizzie liked the sound of that term "early retirement." There was so much she longed to do with Mikey, so many things they couldn't do as long as he was a bigamist— married to both Lizzie and his work. "Law enforcement is a jealous mistress," Mikey often told her, borrowing a metaphor from the legal profession.

But she was worried, too. What about his job? Prescott was a powerful figure in Cumberland County politics. And revenge is an awesome weapon in the hands of a desperate man. Who was to say that, even if Mikey succeeded in toppling Prescott, the Silver Seal wouldn't find a way to retaliate and bring them down together? Mikey had scoffed at the idea. "You worry too much," he scolded her.

"Ah, well," she muttered under her breath, "I can't think straight at two in the morning." She climbed the stairs and crawled into bed. The grimy shirts and sweat-ringed collars could wait until morning.

When Lizzie awoke it was after nine. Mikey had already left for work. The brilliant, rising sun penetrated the drawn sheers like a burglar's knife. She jumped out of bed, embarrassed at having slept so late. Mikey's evening revelation preyed on her mind. She must have dreamt about it because she had already formulated a plan. Lizzie resolved to pay a visit to Nellie Purdy.

When Lizzie arrived at the address she had retrieved easily enough that morning from the telephone directory, she found a cluster of modest, old-style brick town homes situated on a cul-de-sac in the heart of a once-prosperous area of downtown. It was a typical 1970s development, built cheap and sold fast. A few mom-and-pop retail shops and a couple of less-than-prosperous-looking office buildings hovered around the residential complex, which over time had inevitably morphed into low-income rental property populated mostly by elderly folk like Nellie.

Lizzie took a deep breath and rang the bell. There was a fish-eye peep hole in the door. After a moment she heard a woman's voice.

"What do you want?" it asked rudely.

"Mrs. Purdy? Is that you?"

"No more, it ain't," came the bitter reply. "Who wants to know? And why?"

Lizzie had rehearsed what she would say as she got dressed that morning.

"It's my husband, ma'am. His name's Michael Barrow. He's Detective Lieutenant Barrow now, with the Cumberland County Sheriff's Department."

For a moment there was silence. Then the voice behind the door spat out its response. "I remember your husband. He and that almighty Prescott put my man behind bars, for life. And they used me and my foolishness in the process."

There was another pregnant silence before the voice

behind the door delivered its ultimatum. "Go away. Leave me alone."

"Wait!" Lizzie pleaded. "Please let me come in, Mrs. Purdy. My husband wants to make amends. He's prepared to come forward, to tell the truth." Then, for a teaser, she added, "And maybe in the process Mr. Purdy will come home."

Lizzie cackled as she listened. "I already told the truth, at least to that scum of a lawyer, Merriman. And there ain't no more Mr. and Mrs. Purdy. He divorced me. First man in Cumberland County ever to divorce his own wife from a prison cell. But I don't blame him. I played right into the hands of your no good husband and his sidekick Prescott. It cost me my husband, our children, our future. Here I am now, all alone. Children grown and gone. They've disowned me, too. For what I done to their daddy."

"Listen to me!" Lizzie begged her. "I want to help you. At least hear me out."

"Ain't no use," Nellie replied, softer now, wistfully. "I ain't seen Jake since the divorce. He wouldn't even let me visit him in the prison afterwards."

"Hear me out first," Lizzie pleaded. "Then decide. I won't bother you again if that's what you want."

After what seemed like an interminable deliberation, the sounds of a rusty hasp jangling, a bolt sliding, and then a key turning in a lock announced Nellie's decision. The door cracked open. The woman behind it was gaunt and shabbily dressed with unkempt hair and a wizened face reflecting a life of desperate, shattered dreams. The room she occupied was sparsely furnished. Lizzie noticed only a sofa and a coffee table.

"It ain't much to offer," Nellie observed. "But come on in." She swung the door wide. "I'm surviving on the government dole—welfare, Social Security, and Medicaid. I'm ashamed. I never would've thought it, thirty years ago. But here I am."

Lizzie found herself standing in the center of the dingy room as Nellie sealed off the entranceway, slid closed the deadbolt, clasped shut and fastened the hasp, and double-locked the door.

"Take a seat," Nellie offered, pointing to the sofa. Its cushions were frayed and stained, and they sagged in the middle like an old saddle on a sway-backed nag. Lizzie opted for an end seat. Nellie retrieved a wooden rocker from her bedroom and sat down slowly, wincing a little from the painful arthritis that had settled into her back and knees.

"Make it quick," Nellie ordered, grim-faced and tired.

"Okay. Mikey was the lead investigator in the rape of Venus Brown. Of course, your husband was a prime suspect."

Nellie dropped her head into her hands. "Yeah, it was my fault he was convicted. I should've listened to Jake about turning over that letter."

"No!" Lizzie interrupted. "You did the right thing. Mikey said so. If Jake had withheld it and Venus was the first one to tell the police about it, things would've looked worse for Jake."

"How could it be any worse?" Nellie snapped at her. "He was sentenced to rot for life in prison. Death is better than pure misery, ain't it? Particularly if you're innocent. And just for the record, Jake's innocent. I know in my heart he is."

Lizzie stared hard at Nellie. "I know. That's why I'm here." It was a partial truth, what she said.

It took the better part of the day for Lizzie to tell Mikey's tale. Halfway through, Liz could see that Nellie was coming around. She offered tea. As they drank the weak potion, the tension between the women slowly melted away and a fragile bond of trust began to form in its place. By the end of the day Lizzie had what she came for: corroboration of Mikey's story and Nellie's trust. With the former Mrs. Purdy's support in hand, Lizzie was assured that her own husband's future was secure.

Early retirement was a reality after all. A long, lazy vacation in Italy, maybe! Lizzie dared to dream romantic dreams as she made her way home that evening, to the world of grimy shirts and sweat-stained collars. Or a relaxing cruise in the Caribbean! They deserved it, she and Mikey. It had been a long, tough, barren marriage.

Then Lizzie thought of Nellie, and of the shell of an existence eked out in those dismal quarters by that poor wench. The sharp and merciless wheels of the locomotive driving Prescott's train of righteousness had churned over Jake and Nellie, slicing them asunder on its narrow, clattering track, hell-bent for glory.

CHAPTER TWENTY-FOUR

May was waiting patiently in the Clipper when Merriman exited the cardiologist's office. Leland dozed beside her in the front seat.

"Well," she asked the old fox as he approached the car, "what did he say?"

"Give me a minute, will you, May?" Merriman grumbled, tossing his gold-headed cane through the open window of the back seat. He slid in behind her and slammed the car door.

Leland cocked a suspicious eye at him as she mounted the dashboard, preparing for flight.

They sped across town in silence.

"John!" May finally lost her patience. "What did Dr. Fairchild tell you?"

As May braked for the red light at Station Avenue Merriman casually replied. "Everything looks fine, May. Just as I thought. No blockages. No bypasses. No surgery. I'm to return next week when he receives the lab results. A medical gimmick to steal more of my money, if you ask me."

"I didn't," May retorted.

She considered Merriman's positive spin on the news, then decided that it was too good to be true, particularly when one considered the source.

"What is it you're not telling me, John?" She glanced at her husband's poker face in the rear view mirror.

Releasing a long sigh to feign his impatience with her, Merriman prevaricated. "All right, May. My blood pressure's a bit high, that's all. Too much salt in the diet. Not enough exercise. And he says I need to moderate my alcohol intake. Hah! What does he know? You could've told me that."

May turned the Packard into the driveway of their Station Avenue townhouse.

"I'm going back next week to have my pressure

rechecked," Merriman continued, reassuringly, with his little story. "And to hear the good doctor interpret the results of my lab work. That's all. Are you satisfied now, May?"

She was not. Her wifely intuition told her he was lying. But she would bide her time until next week. Then she would telephone Dr. Fairchild. When it came to her man, May would not be deterred.

In the days that followed, May noticed a marked change in Merriman's regimen. He took Leland for a brisk walk every morning—on a leash, of course—to avoid confrontations with widows and orphans. He insisted May put away the salt shaker he usually kept temptingly close at hand on the kitchen table, where they shared their meals. He cut back to half a pack of cigarettes a day. And he deferred taking a drink until six o'clock, limiting his intake to only two cocktails, whereas previously, time and quantity were not even considerations, much less limitations.

May was pleased—and reassured. Perhaps the old fox was telling her the unvarnished truth about his health after all. As the date for his appointment with Dr. Fairchild approached, Merriman's overall outlook seemed to steadily improve.

"Let me go with you to see this Dr. Fairchild," she suggested the morning of the appointment. "I'd like to meet him."

Merriman continued to sip his coffee and pretend to read the morning paper.

Under the butcher's block Leland cocked her eye, waiting for the old fox to respond.

"Well?" she pressed.

Merriman set down the paper and took a sip of coffee. "The answer is no, May. You'll just get in the way. And quit mollycoddling me. It's my appointment with my doctor, not yours," he said with a certain stern finality.

May knew when to back off. She would consider whether to telephone the doctor after receiving Merriman's version of the visit.

⚜

"Good morning, Merriman," Dr. Fairchild greeted him upon his arrival, sounding disgustingly chipper, Merriman thought.

"And a pleasant morning to you, Doc," he replied with noticeable sarcasm. "You'll be happy to know I've been a good little boy this week. Compliant in every respect. Penitence at work in my heart, I suppose."

"Ah," the cardiologist noted, his eyebrows raised. "So you're not totally deaf, then? I was considering a referral to an otolaryngologist friend of mine, but that doesn't seem to be necessary after all."

"Touché, Doc," Merriman retorted with a slight smile. "So what do you read in the tea leaves of the lab work? More happy news for your irascible patient?"

The cardiologist turned serious. "I'm afraid not. We'll get to that in a minute. Take off your shirt."

Merriman complied. After listening to his patient's heart sounds and taking the obligatory blood pressure reading, Dr. Fairchild cut to the chase.

"Your blood work confirms my diagnosis. Cardiomyopathy. Sustained loss of pressure in the left ventricle. Loosely translated? You're dying. Slowly but surely, your pump's wearing out. Maybe a little faster than I thought. But I stick by my prognosis of remaining life span I gave you last week."

"So why the hell should I continue to be a good little scout, Doc?" Merriman demanded. "There's no stopping this train, it would appear."

Dr. Fairchild was having none of it. "Come on, Merriman. Cut out the pity party. We all die of something. The reason—again—is quite simple. Do you want a couple of good years to spend with your wife, or not? If you do, then take my advice. If you want to be a selfish bastard—a burden to your loved one—and kill yourself prematurely, then reject it."

"It's a lot to swallow, Doc." Merriman's demeanor registered signs of fear and confusion, emotions Merriman rarely revealed. "I always figured I'd live forever."

"I know," the cardiologist said, softening his tone. "It

comes with the territory of being human. And, again, if you take reasonable precautions, you might surprise us and beat the odds. Who knows, Merriman? You and I might make medical history! We could publish an article in the journals. I say go for it. What have you got to lose?"

"Okay," Merriman conceded at last, his logical and analytical processes taking hold and giving way to a reasoned approach to his circumstances. "There are some things I can change, others I cannot. I suppose cardiomyopathy falls into the latter category. Right, Doc?"

"Right, Merriman."

"You'll get a kick out of this, Doc. When I was younger, and a much heavier drinker than I am now, I decided to give AA a try. You know, what did I have to lose?"

Merriman quickly answered his own question. "Pride, for one. Self pity, for another. But I needed—no, wanted—some help getting a handle on my drinking. One thing I picked up at those meetings—in those rooms, as they say—I'll never forget." Merriman put on his starched white shirt and began fastening the buttons.

"The Serenity Prayer. You've heard it, I'm sure. It's an old standard, but it's chocked full of profound truths. And those ancient verses have withstood the test of time. Doc, you've probably observed by now that I'm not a particularly religious person. Well, you don't have to be John Wesley to utter that little prayer."

"God," Merriman began, "grant me the serenity to accept the things I cannot change, the courage to change the things I can," and before he could finish, Dr. Fairchild joined in, "and the wisdom to know the difference."

Doc noticed that Merriman closed his eyes and bowed his head, ever so slightly, as he recited those simple, common verses that had brought such comfort to so many for so long.

"May's in the waiting room. Will you explain all this to her, Doc? I think I'd rather you do it than me. I'll take my morning walk. Good scout, and all that."

"All right," Doc agreed. "Are you sure you're ready for her to know this?"

Merriman stood and tucked in his shirt. "I'm sure."

"By the way, Merriman. Some good news."

"I don't believe it! From you, Dr. Moribund?" Merriman teased, a slight twinkle in his eyes.

"Your pressure's down. Not normal, mind you. But getting there. Keep up the good work."

Merriman sighed. "I'll send May in. Try to put on your best bedside manner for her, will you, Doc?" He hesitated for a moment, then added, "I, I love her, I guess you'd say."

It was the first time Merriman had ever revealed that secret to anyone, including May.

Chapter Twenty-Five

It was threatening rain on that steamy, overcast morning in June when a brash young Merriman escorted Jake Purdy to the Cumberland County Sheriff's office. Jake drove, of course. Before they went inside Merriman instructed Jake, "Keep it short and sweet. Everything—everything—you say will be used against you. Therefore, the less said the better. And no chit-chat. Got me?"

"Yes, sir," Jake replied nervously, thinking of Venus and the letter.

They waited in the reception area for over fifteen minutes. Barrow was on the phone with Prescott, receiving the solicitor's last-minute advice, while Jake and Merriman fidgeted.

"Come in! Come in," Barrow offered hospitably, as if Merriman and his client were old friends paying a social call.

"I remember you, Mr. Merriman," Barrow nodded. "Good to make your acquaintance, Mr. Purdy." He ushered them into a small conference room. On top of a walnut veneer table was a reel-to-reel tape recorder.

"No taping," Merriman insisted. "We're not giving a recorded statement. You can interview him. But when I say stop, it's over. Got me, Deputy?"

Barrow seethed under the surface, but kept his cool. "Whatever you say, Counselor." He turned to Jake.

"This is a serious matter, Mr. Purdy. We've got a young colored girl who's been raped. In her own bed, mind you. Doesn't matter to me if she's black, white, or somewhere in between, Mr. Purdy. I'm just doing my job. You understand?"

"I understand," Jake said.

"Now." Barrow turned to his notes. "Your daddy was Willis Purdy, wasn't he?"

"That's right." Jake glanced nervously at Merriman, who was nonchalantly filing his fingernails with an emery board he kept in his coat pocket for just such occasions.

"I'm told he's the father of this girl, Venus Brown. You know anything about that, Mr. Purdy?"

"Just what that letter says. The one my wife gave you, Deputy."

Barrow retrieved a piece of paper from a manila file folder lying on the table. "Yeah. The letter. You know, Mr. Purdy, that letter gives me some real concern."

Merriman interrupted. "Don't respond to that, Jake. It wasn't a question. If Mr. Barrow here has a question, he can ask it and you can answer it. Otherwise, ignore any gratuitous, irrelevant comments about what might concern him or not."

"Yes, sir," Jake replied.

Barrow glared at Merriman, who continued to file his nails with seeming disinterest in the proceedings. Merriman had correctly predicted that his little stunt with the emery board would fluster the young investigator.

"All right. Mr. Purdy, are you telling me that you didn't know that this mulatto was your half-sister until you got that letter?" He slid the document across the table and in front of his subject.

"By the way, Deputy," Merriman interrupted. "I'd like to get a Xerox of that so-called letter if you don't mind." He had never seen it. Nellie turned it over to the sheriff without thinking of making a copy.

Barrow ignored him. "Well, Mr. Purdy? You going to answer my question?"

"Uh, yes, sir. I'll try." He glanced again in Merriman's direction, but got no help. He thought of the twenty-eight-hundred-dollar retainer and Nellie and the children.

"I heard the rumors about my daddy and a colored woman when I was in high school, Mr. Barrow. But I never knew whether there was any truth to them or not."

"Well," Barrow shot back, "didn't you ask your daddy?"

"No, sir. I didn't. I was, well, kind of shocked, I guess is the best way to describe it. And it wasn't too long after that before my momma took me to live with my Aunt Pearline."

And then my daddy up and left town. I never saw him again."

"I see." Barrow let some time pass between that observation and his next question.

"Didn't that letter make you angry, Mr. Purdy?"

"No, sir. Not angry. Just confused."

"You mean to tell me you just found out for the first time that you had a sister who was a Negro, and you weren't a little bit angry? At your father, maybe?"

Merriman put the emery board back in his pocket and glanced over at his client.

"Maybe," Jake Purdy said. "Maybe I was."

"Maybe so," Barrow said. "And just maybe your wife Nellie was a little bit angry, too, wasn't she, Mr. Purdy?"

"No, she was not, Mr. Barrow!" Jake replied, slamming his palm down on the table to emphasize his point. "You leave Nellie out of this."

Merriman leaned over toward Jake and placed his hand on the back of his client's, which was still lying flat on the walnut veneer, palm down.

"Now let's calm down, Jake. No need to lose your temper. As Mr. Barrow said, he's just doing his job." Merriman removed his hand from Jake's. "Would you like to take a short break?"

Jake Purdy took a deep breath. "No, sir. I'm sorry. This whole thing's been a little hard on me, and even harder on Nellie. I apologize."

Barrow jumped in. "No need to apologize, Mr. Purdy. No offense taken."

The deputy sheriff was beginning to gain confidence. "Do you have a problem with losing your temper, Mr. Purdy?"

"No, sir."

"Well, that's good, Mr. Purdy," Barrow said. "You see, I've learned in the relatively short time I've been in law enforcement that a bad temper can get a man in trouble, Mr. Purdy. Deep trouble."

"Yes, sir," Jake said.

"Now." Barrow flipped through the file until he found

112

what he was looking for. "It says here on this rap sheet that you were arrested in Arkansas. Drunk and disorderly. Assault and battery of a high and aggravated nature." He pushed the official criminal record across the table. "You see that, Mr. Purdy?"

Jake examined the document. "Yes, sir, I see it. Can I explain?" He looked over at Merriman.

"Sure you can," Barrow said. "Go right ahead."

Merriman didn't like the direction in which this line of questioning might be taking them, but kept silent.

"Okay. I was a young kid. Fresh out of the military. Me and a bunch of my Marine buddies ended up in a bar in a little town called Hope. I got drunk. One of the locals in there that night was some long-haired dude named Clanton. College boy. Wild Bill, his friends called him. He kept teasing me about my crewcut and saying unpatriotic things about my uniform, and the Flag, and the Marines, and the President. You know, Vietnam, and all that. I had just come back from a tour of duty over there.

"Well, finally I had enough. I told him to shut up. He just kept on taunting me. His friends kept laughing at me. I lost my temper. I hit him once, hard. He went down. Next thing I knew the police were there. They handcuffed me and took me to jail. First and only time I've ever been there. Your rap sheet ought to prove that, Mr. Barrow.

"Well, the next morning they let me out. The judge told me he was dropping the charges, but if he ever saw me in his courtroom again, he'd throw the book at me. Far as I know, that Clanton boy was fine. No permanent damage. Just a bruised ego, that's all. And as far as I know, too, I ain't got no record of a conviction. Only the arrest."

"That's right, Mr. Purdy." Barrow placed the rap sheet back in his file and stared at Merriman. "Only the arrest."

Merriman, who was pretending to take notes, looked over at Barrow. "You almost finished, Deputy?"

"Not quite," Barrow said.

"Let's take a bathroom break. Too much coffee," Merriman feigned.

When they got into the men's room Merriman took Jake by the arm. "Why didn't you tell me about that arrest, boy?"

"You didn't ask me," Jake explained. "And anyway, there ain't no conviction, so what's the problem?"

"Okay," Merriman said. "Forget about it. We're just about done. Be careful. And remember. Short and sweet. No chit-chat."

When they returned to the conference room Barrow was fixing a fresh pot of coffee. "Want a cup?" he asked.

"No," Merriman said.

"No, thanks," Jake said.

"Okay." Barrow sat down. "Tell me, Jake. By the way, Mr. Purdy, do you mind if I call you Jake?"

"No, I don't mind," Jake said.

"All right, Jake. Did you go to visit Venus Brown after you got this letter?"

"No, sir. I have never laid eyes on that girl, except for the picture she sent with the letter."

"I see," Barrow said. "Now, Jake, in the letter Venus says her momma, Mae Ella, thinks she resembles your daddy. Do you think she does?" Barrow shuffled through the file. "Here. Let me show you her picture." He pulled it out of an envelope and offered it to Jake.

Jake took hold of it slowly, gingerly, as if Barrow were handing him a poisonous snake.

"I don't see no resemblance," he said, returning the photo to Barrow.

"Where were you on the night of April twenty-first, Jake?"

"Same place I always am. I went home after work, had supper with my family, and went to bed. I'm sure I was asleep by ten o'clock."

"You're sure?" Barrow asked him.

"Yep. I had to go to work the next day. First shift. Seven o'clock."

Barrow could have guessed Jake's answer. At this point, the deputy had nothing to refute the alibi. He assumed Nellie would back up her husband's story. After a few more questions he wound it down.

114

"Well, Jake, thanks for coming by. Mr. Merriman, it's good to see you again."

"Likewise, I am sure," Merriman replied with obvious insincerity.

"Here," Barrow said. "I'll see you out."

As they walked back to the reception area Barrow turned to Jake and said, "I don't know about you, but my mouth's dry from all that talking. How about a piece of gum, Jake?" He pulled out a pack of Juicy Fruit and offered Jake a piece.

"No, thanks," Jake replied. "Already got some."

"Oh, yeah. I should've noticed. What's your favorite chew, Jake?"

"Clove," said Jake. "I discovered it in the military. Never cared for tobacco. But I always keep a pack of Clove gum in my pocket. Here. Try a piece," he offered, reaching in his pocket.

"Thanks, Jake. Think I will." Barrow took the gum, still inside its paper wrapper. "Hey, I like the way that smells."

"Right," Jake said.

After they left he tagged the piece of gum and placed it in the safe, in the file alongside the envelope containing the letter and photo of Venus and the other evidence Barrow had collected. The girl's sworn statement was there with the rest, safely tucked away in a folder.

When Merriman and Jake drove away, Merriman turned to his client. "Boy, didn't I tell you—not once, but twice—no chit-chat with that fool deputy?"

"Yes, sir," Jake Purdy admitted, glancing down at his hands on the steering wheel and smiling sheepishly.

"Well, then. What was all that chit-chat with Barrow about chewing gum?"

"You got me, Mr. Merriman."

Fuming, Merriman made a note on his pad as they drove away.

CHAPTER TWENTY-SIX

Nellie was in the front yard watering her technicolor patch of thirsty summer impatiens when Jake pulled into the driveway. The ordeal of Venus' sudden intrusion into their lives, and her subsequent rape, had stressed their marriage to its outer limits. Confusion reigned. One moment they were upbeat and optimistic, the next found them in the throes of a dark depression. Each time the phone rang Nellie jumped, not knowing whether the call heralded good tidings or bad.

"How did the interview go?" she asked Jake as he parked the car.

"Okay, I guess." He wasn't really sure. "Where are the kids?"

"In school, of course." Nellie turned off the garden hose and gave her husband a bear hug.

"Sorry. I knew that. I just forgot." Jake wasn't used to being home this time of day.

"Let's take a ride," Nellie suggested. "Out in the country somewhere. I want to get away for a while, and just be with you."

It sounded like a great idea to Jake. Even four months pregnant, Nellie was a beautiful and sensuous woman. Jake craved an opportunity to escape the pressure of the investigation and spend some time alone with the girl of his dreams.

It was nearly noon. They had three more hours of freedom before the kids came home. Jake pressed the accelerator of his old Chevy to the floorboard and zipped down Highway 29. They soon found a quiet, secluded spot near the lake where they wouldn't be disturbed. By the time he parked the Chevy behind a curtain of blossoming honeysuckle, their bodies were incandescent from the heat of their desire for each other.

"What if somebody comes?" Nellie whispered as Jake pulled her close to him.

116

"I don't care, Nellie. Do you?"

"No," she said, overcome by the powerful sweet fragrance of wild honeysuckle and her yearning for his tender embrace. "I'm all yours, Jake. Just be careful with the baby."

The memory of that pleasure filled, intoxicating afternoon in June was the one thing that kept Nellie from throwing in the towel during all those years alone. The passion of their lovemaking stirred her even now, in her old age, as she recalled how gentle and patient he had been. How could this same sweet man possibly be guilty, as the jury concluded, of the violent, criminal sexual assault committed against Venus Brown?

Lizzie's visit had begun to soften the bitterness formed by years of suffering. For the first time in decades Nellie sensed a reason to keep going. She was smart enough to surmise that Elizabeth Barrow's motives were more selfish than pure, but their goals were consistent. Each woman, in her own way, sought to liberate her man.

After Lizzie left late that afternoon, Nellie took out some notebook paper and a pen. She sat down in the sag of the sofa, placed the paper on the coffee table and commenced to compose a letter to the man who had fathered her children, shared her bed, and dreamt her dream of growing old and wise and happy together—the same man whom, in her mind, she had both loved and betrayed so many years ago.

At first her hand trembled as she wrote his name. It was the first time in fourteen years she had initiated any form of communication with Jake Purdy. It took Nellie three drafts and seven hours before she was satisfied. When the letter was finished she folded it neatly, placed it into a stamped envelope addressed to Jake in care of the Department of Corrections, and grabbed a few hours' sleep before delivering it into the capable hands of the United States Postal Service the next morning.

When Jake entered prison decades earlier, he found himself vilified on nearly every front. The news of a white man—a Southerner, no less—receiving a life sentence without possibility of parole for raping a mulatto girl who was allegedly his half-sister, instantly made national headlines. The New York Times deified the courageous all-white jury that had convicted Jake, lionized the brave and erudite judge who imposed the sentence, and predicted the demise of the antiquated system driven by centuries of racism and bigotry that held sway over the criminal courts of the old South.

"For the Negro race, a new day of justice and equality has dawned in the southern sky, bright as the morning star," the inveterate Yankee rag declared in pithy journalistic prose.

Things were not much better for Jake in Cumberland County. Young Solicitor Malcolm T. Prescott and his worthy colleague Deputy Michael O'Shea Barrow were all but canonized in interviews by virtually every reporter and talking head in the state, which inspired the local populace to demonize Jake and take unearned credit for progress in the area of race relations.

The head of the state chapter of the NAACP went on record supporting Prescott in his upcoming bid for re-election, while stridently condemning in the strongest terms then printable, not only the crime itself but also the man adjudged guilty of it, who languished in the state prison alongside Negro men wrongfully convicted of equally heinous crimes against white women.

Mae Ella, flanked by every black minister in Cumberland County including the bishop himself of the African Methodist Episcopal Church, read a prepared statement from her lofty perch atop the courthouse steps to a hastily gathered clutch of local and syndicated reporters, in which she verified the patriarchal parentage of her progeny, Venus Brown Purdy. The misfortunate child, according to Mae Ella, was the biracial byproduct of her mother's own rape committed a generation earlier by the very father of the degenerate whose legacy was to assault and choke his own half-sister.

Nellie was beside herself. The third Purdy offspring, whom she carried in her womb throughout the entire trial, nearly died within weeks of the verdict as a result of a breach birth. The other two were just old enough to comprehend that somehow, overnight, their family had become the veritable pariahs of Cumberland County, if not the entire continental United States. These poor misfits were so emotionally and psychologically stunted by their family's degradation that Cumberland County's superintendent of education declared them unfit for enrollment in the public schools on the ground of imbecility.

For his part, Jake maintained a low profile and became a model prisoner. Merriman visited him a time or two, even offered to appeal the verdict, but Jake declined.

"My family's already been through enough, Mr. Merriman. Unless you tell me we've got more than a fifty-fifty shot at winning, there ain't going to be no appeal," the ex-marine decided.

Merriman, who himself had gained much notoriety from the trial, chose his words carefully.

"Jake, this case has become something of a flashpoint for the plight of the Negro in this country. Like it or not, the outcome has set off a blaze of protest sweeping the South, nearly proportionate to the sit-ins and riots propelled by that fellow King a few years ago. The chances that our state supreme court would overturn your verdict are roughly equivalent to those of a stray cat's surviving in a kennel full of coon dogs."

The first Sunday of every month was family visitation day at Killough Correctional Facility. For years Nellie faithfully attended, occasionally bringing the children but mostly just herself and a home-cooked meal. She and Jake pretended for a while that a future was in store, but they knew it was a lie. One Sunday morning when Nellie showed up at Killough with her wicker basket of fried chicken, home-made potato salad and sliced tomatoes, she was told Jake had elected to stay in his cell. The guard, a beer-bellied, thick-shouldered white man with borderline mental acuity and a thirty-eight revolver strapped to his waist, handed Nellie a note.

"Dear Nellie," it read, "don't come back any more. Find yourself another man and another life. You and the kids deserve it. Me? I'll take the necessary steps to see to the legal formalities. Mr. Merriman said he could handle it. Love always, Jake."

There was a P.S. that read, "Don't ever forget that honeysuckle afternoon at the lake."

Nellie asked the pot-bellied guard, "You married?"

"No," he replied. "Unless you could call beer and television a wife."

"Here." Nellie handed him the basket and said farewell to Killough and its inmates once and for all.

About a month later some legal papers arrived at her doorstep via the courier service provided by the Sheriff of Cumberland County. The large tan envelope bore the return address "John Merriman, Attorney at the Law." Nellie signed for the papers but never contested the divorce. The final decree was issued some weeks later.

A blurb in the "Legal Notices" section of the Tribune caught Nellie's eye one Sunday morning. "Inmate Divorces Wife From Prison Cell," the headline read. The brief news account was followed by the cold, hard fact: "Purdy vs. Purdy, Civil Action # 216654, Final Decree of Divorce entered July 31, 1973, in the Family Court for Cumberland County."

Nellie took the newspaper out to the garbage can and threw it in with the other trash. Then she went back inside and gathered her chicks to her skirt.

"Well," she told them, tears popping from the corners of her eyes, "we won't be visiting your daddy any more. Your last name is still Purdy, though. And you hold your heads high when people call you by name. Your daddy is a good, decent man. But he and I are divorced now."

Lester, the oldest of the three Purdy siblings, asked his momma, "What does that mean?"

Nellie sighed. "It means we just have to start over, Lester, honey. And take it one day at a time."

Lester ingested enough of an understanding to satisfy him for the time being. He was no imbecile, regardless of what the superintendent of education for Cumberland

County might say or do, and one day he would prove it.

"Now. You kids run along and play. Momma wants to be alone." They did, and she was.

Nellie lay back on that old sagging sofa and wept until the tears wouldn't come any more.

CHAPTER TWENTY-SEVEN

Dear Jake,

I hope this letter finds you well. I think about you nearly every day. Lester looks just like you. He joined the Marines, and they sent him to Kuwait. You'd be so proud of him, Jake. And Julie, well, she's a beautiful girl. She's married now, with children of her own. Can you imagine, Jake? You're a grandfather. Julie was crowned homecoming queen, seems like ten years ago now, at the high school homecoming game. Maybe you read about it in the paper. Do you get to read it? The newspaper, I mean. And little Jakey, he's a sweetheart. Just like you, Jake. We sure named him right. He got him a job in California, some place called Silicon Valley, working for one of them computer outfits. He doesn't remember you, of course, and that makes me sad. But life flows on, like a river. Ain't that so, Jake?

I know you told me to find a new life. There just wasn't one, honey. Not without you. But I'm all right. I did what you said, though, Jake. I have never forgot about that honeysuckle afternoon at the lake. Remember how big I was? I might as well have swallowed a watermelon. But making love to you that day was easy as pie, a sweet slice of heaven, even though little Jakey got in our way just a smidgen. I hope you haven't forgot that day either, Jake. It burns in my memory like the Olympic flame.

A woman came to see me today. Her name is Lizzie Barrow. Her husband is that deputy, Mike Barrow. I'm sure you remember him. He's some big shot with the sheriff's department now. Detective Lieutenant, they call him. He still works with that weasel Prescott, the silver-tongued devil who hornswoggled that jury into putting you behind bars and ruining our life together.

Well, Mrs. Barrow came with a mouth full. Hear me out, now, Jake. Just like I did her. Then decide for yourself whether she's telling the truth or not. I pray that she is. Because if her story is true, Mr. High-and-Mighty Solicitor Prescott might just be switching places with you, Jake. And you just might be coming home a free man.

It ain't much to look at, Jake. Home, I mean. I took an apartment on High Street when the money ran out. All the kids are gone now. So there's a place for you here, honey. That is, unless you've found another woman there in prison you'd rather stay with. Ha-ha, that's a joke, honey. But not a very funny one. I know we're divorced, but that doesn't stop folks nowadays from living together. And who knows? I might just consent to marry an ex-con! That's no joke, honey.

Well, here it goes.

Remember that letter Venus Brown wrote you? Like a big fool I talked you into turning it over to the police. Don't think I haven't regretted doing that, all these many years. But Mrs. Barrow said the same thing I told you, Jake. What if we hadn't done it, and Venus had been the first one to tell Deputy Barrow about it? I guess it don't matter now. You got convicted and I got divorced.

Turns out Venus also gave a statement, Jake. Under oath. Solicitor Prescott took it down, and Venus signed it. They kept it under lock and key. Mr. Merriman never saw it. Well, everything Venus said in her testimony at the trial was in that statement. Except she omitted one little detail. In her statement she said the man who raped her was old, maybe even sixty. She could tell by his voice, and the wrinkles on his face. Can you imagine that? A white man of that age wanting to rape a young colored girl? Now, you might just remember that Prescott didn't ask Venus how old a fellow her assailant was. And neither did Mr. Merriman, when he cross-examined her. You remember that, don't you, Jake?

Well, well. The plot thickens, as they say. Just when your case came to trial, one of the sheriff's investigators heard about a man sixty-two years old by the name of Willis Purdy. Name sound familiar? He was living with a woman in lower Cumberland County, down near the river. That woman came to Solicitor Prescott's office the day after the lawyers gave their opening statements to the jury. Remember how Solicitor Prescott strutted around in front of all them Yankee newspaper reporters and television people, bragging about how a stupid piece of Clove chewing gum would stick you with the crime? He thought he was real cute and clever, didn't he?

I was there, too, Jake, and I'll never forget how Prescott paraded like a fan-tailed peacock around that courtroom, hollering about justice and righteousness and equality under the law, and how white men have got to stand before the Lord and answer for their crimes, just like black men do? You'd have thought he was some kind of redneck preacher man. And all them Yankees just eating it up, looking down their noses at us like they ain't got no race problems back home where they come from. Hah!

Well, one of the solicitor's investigators took a statement from that woman, the day she came in. When court was over that day, the investigator gave that statement to Prescott and Barrow when they returned to the office to prepare for the next day's testimony. Now, you just try and guess what that statement said.

I'll tell you what it said. On the night of Venus Brown's rape, Willis Purdy came home before dawn, drunk as a goat. Now. Remember, Venus didn't say anything about smelling alcohol on the man who raped her. She said he smelled to high heaven of the scent of Clove gum, which just happened to be your favorite chew, according to the testimony of Deputy Barrow.

Now. Back to this woman's statement. She said Willis collapsed on the bed, spewing cuss words I will not repeat, but more than that, he ranted and raved about how he had tasted of the fruit of Mae Ella, and how that young plum was as sweet as Mae Ella herself when she was a girl. His britches were stained, prob'ly from you-know-what, and the button that held them up was tore off. That woman said she pulled down his britches and took three things out of his pockets before she threw them pants in the washing machine: Willis' empty wallet, his old jackknife, and a pack of Clove gum. While Willis was sleeping off the liquor, this woman looked in his truck and found an empty pint bottle of bourbon.

The woman said it made no sense to her at the time what Willis had said about that tramp named Mae Ella and her so-called fruit. That is, until a few months later, when she read in the newspaper about the opening statements given in the trial of Jake Purdy. By that time Willis had pulled up stakes and moved on, but she said the Lord put on her heart the obligation to come forward with what she knew.

At the time she didn't realize that you were Willis Purdy's boy. But when she read the newspaper account of Mae Ella Brown's mulatto daughter being raped by a man smelling of the scent of Clove gum, she put two and two together and come up with four.

Deputy Barrow decided to follow up on this woman's statement. His wife says he told Prescott, "We might have the wrong man." But Prescott was bound and determined to drive his train to the station—to a guilty verdict if you please, and nothing—not even the truth—was going to stand in his way. He ordered Barrow to destroy that statement. But Deputy Barrow did not. He put it in his desk drawer at the sheriff's office. He testified the next day just as planned, and answered truthfully the questions Solicitor Prescott put to him, including your chit-chat after the interview about Clove gum being your favorite chew. But when the verdict came back guilty, and all them self-righteous Yankee reporters and television crews went home vindicated, Deputy Barrow followed up on the statement that woman gave.

Willis bought that pint of whiskey from old man Akers, who ran the liquor store in the Three Rivers community, near where this woman and Willis shacked up together. Akers told Barrow that Willis banged on his door some time after one o'clock in the morning, and threatened to burn down his store if he didn't open up and sell him a pint. Akers noticed that Willis' pants were unbuttoned. He had a wild look in his eye, like a crazy man, Akers said.

Willis must have raped that poor girl and then gulped down that pint to ease the pain before going home. Lord only knows where he is now, or what might have happened to him, if he's still alive.

Mrs. Barrow says her husband told Prescott what he had learned, but Prescott instructed him that the case was closed. Period. No more investigating. And she says her husband has been living with that injustice for all these years. He's prepared to come forward.

Listen, Jake. They got DNA testing now. And Mrs. Barrow says that stain of blood and sperm on Venus' panties is still available. The DNA test could prove that wasn't your semen. There might have been a blood-type match just like they said at trial, but there ain't no two people, not even father and son, who have the same DNA.

Are you willing to give another sample? It ain't one hundred percent necessary. They've got the old one. But the newfangled DNA tests work better with a recently drawn blood sample.

Do it, Jake! What have you got to lose? It's been fourteen years since I talked to you. I don't know whether you're still a believer, still a praying man like you were when we were young. I admit I ain't been faithful like I should. But for some reason I don't understand, God has given us a second chance.

I'm coming to visit you next Sunday, Jake. Please pray about this. And please don't turn me away.

I still love you, Jake.

Nellie

CHAPTER TWENTY-EIGHT

Detective Lieutenant Michael O'Shea Barrow had just popped the aluminum cap off his first bottle of Guinness when Lizzie rushed in the front door.

"Well, Mikey," she said, "the old gal has agreed to do it."

"What in the name of the Blessed Virgin are you talking about, woman?" he asked her, his face a contorted mask of confusion.

Lizzie was so absorbed in her plan, she had forgotten that her husband had not the faintest idea what she had been up to all afternoon.

"Sit down, Mikey."

Lizzie led him through the short version of her afternoon as he took slow, steady pulls from the brown pint bottle. She reached her climax with the declaration that Nellie had agreed to persuade her estranged husband to submit another vial of his blood for the cause of justice.

"You've got some nerve, woman," Mikey growled at her. "What if she had run you out and called Prescott? Where would I be then?"

"I thought about that, Mikey. I promise I did," she soothed. "Call it a woman's intuition. Call it something worse than that, if you like. But the end justifies the means, Mikey. She's agreed to help us."

The detective lieutenant polished off the pint and leaned back in his Naugahyde La-Z-Boy. He could have made the case without the old gal, but having a fresh vial of Jake's blood for the boys in the lab was icing on the cake.

"All right, Liz. Now. You listen to me. I've decided that Merriman is the one to set the trap. He's a past master at setting traps anyway."

"But . . ."

Before she could come out with one of a myriad perfectly justifiable reasons to distrust the sly old fox and leave him out of it, Mikey cut her off.

"Hush, Lizzie. This is my business, not yours. Now do as I say and listen for once, will you?"

Sufficiently chastened, Lizzie took her place on the sofa and heard him out.

"Remember," Mikey started, "it was Merriman who got duped years ago. And by his nemesis, I might add. Merriman loathes and despises Prescott. And as they say in the courts, vice versa.

"My point is simply this, Liz. Once Merriman finds out that Prescott withheld—and destroyed—critical pieces of evidence that could well have exculpated his client, he'll lead the charge with a vengeance to haul Prescott before the Board of Commissioners and the judge. He'll do our work for us, Liz. Don't you see? And what can little old Mikey do but tell the truth if I'm subpoenaed to testify, aye?

"Prescott committed three serious lapses of professional judgment, my dear." In his excitement to explain, Mikey eased into his official law enforcement jargon.

"First, he didn't turn over to Merriman the partially exculpatory written statement we obtained from Venus, in which she clearly described her assailant as a man older than Jake Purdy. We've got rules, Lizzie, that require us to turn those documents over to defense counsel. It's called fairness—and justice. The bloody U.S. Constitution itself requires us to do it.

"And second, to pour just a dash of salt into an already-festering ethical wound, Solicitor Prescott disregarded credible evidence that another man—Willis Purdy—committed the rape. He ordered me to destroy the very statement incriminating Willis that was given by the woman who shacked up with the old devil down by the river.

"Well, I didn't. I hid it in my desk drawer for a while, and later brought it home. It's been sitting right here ever since," Barrow said, pointing with pride toward a squat, cast iron box standing against the wall. "In my safe, just in case the day should come, Lizzie, when I would need it."

The detective lieutenant ambled over to the safe. He spun the dial of the combination lock several times to clear the tumblers, turned the knob clockwise to its first numerical destination, then counterclockwise to another, and finally back again clockwise to the dial's final resting place. He jerked the long, cylindrical handle and, to the accompaniment of a loud clunk, pulled open the heavy door to the old Otis safe.

There it was on the middle shelf, all alone, a slightly faded legal-sized paper whose bottom corners were curled with age, stapled at the top onto an old legal blue backing, bearing the notarized signature of one Janelle Foxworthy.

"See? Here it is. Exhibit A," Mikey joked, examining the document carefully, then handing it to Lizzie. "Be careful with it, girl," he admonished her unnecessarily. Lizzie well understood the significance of preserving intact the statement.

She took hold of it and read it through quickly at first, then again slowly, painstakingly. "The young plum was as sweet as Mae Ella," Miss Foxworthy quoted the old land baron as having claimed in the braggadocio of his drunken stupor. His nauseating bravado jumped out at Lizzie from the face of the old legal document as if Willis himself were present and uttering the words, disgusting her as she read them.

"How could he?" she asked in disbelief. "First he ravished Mae Ella. Then, I suppose, to avenge the disintegration of his family he had wrought by that heinous crime— miscegenation, you law men call it; to me it's rape, plain and simple—he deflowered Mae Ella's daughter and let his own son take the rap! What a bastard he must've been."

"Things like this happen all the time, Lizzie," the old detective said with a hint of remorse in his gravelly voice. "Take my word for it. I've seen lots worse."

"I don't believe it." She nearly spat the words at him, contempt and loathing in her reply. "What could be worse than what this man did?"

Mikey took the statement back from Lizzie and set it on the middle shelf of the safe. Then he slammed shut the ponderous door, firmly engaged the handle, and rotated the dial of the combination lock full circle.

"I checked the old case files today. The ones we store in the warehouse. The statement Venus gave was there, all right. Tucked away with all the other evidence we used to convict the wrong man in the case of State versus Purdy."

"Did you take it?" Lizzie asked him.

"Yes." Mikey strolled back to his Naugahyde La-Z-Boy and sat down. "I took it back to the office and copied it. Then I returned the original with care to its file in the warehouse," he said with a certain smugness.

"That's the trap, Lizzie. You see? Prescott will think about that statement as soon as all this comes to light. He'll try to find it, destroy it, before the court and the commission can get their hands on it."

He paused momentarily, distracted by the subliminal urge to fetch his next Guinness.

"As far as Prescott knows, I destroyed Janelle Foxworthy's statement decades ago. That being the case, the only piece of evidence to concern him is Venus' statement."

"But what will you do, Mikey? What if he gets to it and destroys it before it can be preserved? Then all you have is the copy. The solicitor will swear it's a fake."

"Ah, Lizzie. You have such little faith in your husband. Leave that part to me, will you?" He got up and went to the refrigerator.

"And what about Merriman? What makes you so sure he'll play ball?"

Lizzie sensed a bit less confidence in her husband's pat reply. "You worry too much. Leave it to me, Lizzie. It'll all work out."

Lizzie sighed as she heard the pop of the cap on Mikey's last bottle of Guinness for the evening. Italy and the Caribbean seemed more remote than ever.

PART THREE

CHAPTER TWENTY-NINE

Leland was resting peacefully under the butcher's block when the doorbell rang. May was upstairs, tending to the laundry. Merriman was poring over the morning newspaper, hoping to stumble upon an account of some tragic automobile accident or other catastrophe, whose hapless and vulnerable victim he might prey upon with the allure of a fast cash settlement—for a reasonable fee, of course. Money was tight, thanks to his medical condition and those outrageous doctor bills, about which he complained to May with regularity and frequency.

Irritated by the interruption, Merriman tapped over to the front door, gold-headed cane in hand, and took a look through the peep hole. It was that gumshoe Barrow. What in the world could he want of me? Merriman wondered. At first he considered ignoring him. Then he decided to play along with whatever surprise the detective lieutenant had in store.

"Come in, Mr. Barrow," Merriman feigned politely. "Welcome to my humble abode."

Hat in hand, Barrow wore a trench coat, even though the day was bright and pleasant. His trademark plug was snugly in place between his left cheek and gum.

"Sorry to interrupt, Mr. Merriman. I'm not here on business—uh, official business, I mean. Can we talk?"

The law man's humble request, out of character for this rough and ready, street-seasoned brawler, immediately aroused suspicion in Merriman's devious mind. The two had never been other than adversaries before, trading barbs and insults in the courtroom not unlike a couple of kids swapping baseball cards and marbles on the playground.

"Yes. Of course," Merriman offered with transparently fraudulent grace. "You'll excuse my appearance, Lieutenant, I'm sure." Merriman was still in his pajamas and robe. "I've not been quite up to snuff lately."

Merriman led Barrow into the parlor, which May's lovely cousins Euphonia and Euphoria had so pleasantly decorated with their presence just weeks earlier.

"So I've heard, Mr. Merriman. Certainly hope it's nothing serious," Barrow replied with his own brand of equally transparent false courtesy. The detective lieutenant knew full well that Merriman knew full well that Barrow could care less about the health of the old fox.

"No, no. Nothing serious. Just a good excuse to take a little vacation, Detective." Merriman offered Barrow a seat, near the cold hearth. "What can I do for you?"

Just then May called from the top of the stairs. "What is it, John?" Ever since Dr. Fairchild had broken the news to her, May was anxious whenever there was even the slightest interruption in their routine.

"Nothing, May. Just a visitor for me," Merriman reassured her. "You remember Detective Lieutenant Barrow."

"Oh," she replied from above, with an admixture of relief and curiosity. "Of course. Welcome, Mr. Barrow."

"Thank you, ma'am," came his return.

There was an awkward moment of silence. The mantel clock ticked away. Then Barrow said, "I'll come to the point, Mr. Merriman."

"Yes. Why don't you, Detective." Merriman was anxious to return to his newspaper.

"Can we agree to talk confidentially?" Barrow asked, even though he knew he could repose little trust in the veracity of Merriman's reply.

"Of course, Barrow. Of course. Let's just treat this as we would a conversation between lawyer and client. Totally confidential. Privileged, as we are fond of saying." A slight, wicked smile flickered across Merriman's unshaven face.

"All right." Barrow knew he had no choice. "It's about Mr. Prescott. You know how closely I've worked with him over the years. How much I respect him and his abilities."

"Yes, yes. Of course I do, Barrow," Merriman said in his most comforting baritone, as if speaking down to a child. "I've witnessed it firsthand, you know."

Barrow paused for a moment, choosing his next words carefully. He decided a direct approach was best.

"There comes a time in the career of each one of us," he began, "when it's best to step down. Retire with dignity. I believe that time has arrived for Solicitor Prescott."

Merriman's interest was suddenly piqued. The newspaper could wait. He decided to hold his tongue and let Barrow get to his point.

"Frankly, Mr. Merriman, your client Dabney Peters should never have been acquitted. Don't misunderstand, sir," Barrow hastily added, "I'm not being critical of the fine job you did in representing the scoundrel. It's just that Solicitor Prescott has lost his edge.

"Now. I happen to know that he will not step aside voluntarily. He's an old soldier, Mr. Merriman. And it will require a wee bit of pressure, I'm afraid, to convince him."

Merriman was fascinated, but more curious as to what motivated Barrow. Thanks to years of practice he was able to conceal that fascination and curiosity behind a stoic demeanor—a legal poker face, one might say—which over the years had proven invaluably conducive to putting the witness—in this case Mr. Barrow—at ease with confiding in the old fox.

"Years ago you defended a man named Jake Purdy. A rape case."

"I remember it quite well," Merriman interrupted him. "What of it, Mr. Barrow?"

For the next half-hour Barrow unfolded the plot. Merriman was transfixed. Of course, the opportunity to free an innocent man—even a former client—never crossed his mind. But the chance to witness the pompous, self-righteous Prescott receive his comeuppance was something Merriman had never dreamed would happen—particularly now, in the eventide of his miserable lifetime.

When Barrow finished his presentation, Merriman kicked into lawyer mode.

"Have you attempted to locate this woman, Janelle Foxworthy?"

"Yes, of course. She died four years ago. Apparent victim of a snakebite. The coroner's report said a couple of fishermen found her badly decomposed body on the west bank of the Cumberland River in a clump of bushes. She was naked as the day she was born. No evidence of sexual assault. But there was a mark on her right calf. Two pinholes, it looked like. And there was a trace of moccasin venom in her coagulated blood.

"Best he could tell, the coroner figured she was either swimming or bathing in the river when luck would have it, and she inadvertently came too close to the nest of a cottonmouth."

"Hm-m-m. A shame. What about Willis Purdy?"

"He hasn't been seen or heard from in years. The computer turned up nothing on him since the charges involving Mae Ella Brown. He might well be dead himself, for all we know. He's got to be pushing ninety if he still has a pulse."

"Well," Merriman parried, "that leaves one other person, Detective. Venus Brown."

"Yep," Barrow replied, a little more confidently, now that his cards were on the table. "I'm afraid she won't help us either, Mr. Merriman."

"Why's that, Mr. Barrow?"

Barrow sauntered over to a casement window, cranked it open, spat a glob of brown fluid out into the courtyard, then reversed the crank handle and shut the window.

"She's in the insane asylum, Mr. Merriman. Crazy as a loon. Her psychiatrist says she can't even remember her own birthday, much less what might have happened on the night Willis Purdy paid her a little visit."

"Well, then," Merriman concluded, "all you've got to go on is an out-of-court statement given by a lunatic—which was withheld improperly, I'll grant you—and an affidavit of a dead woman, who is obviously in no condition to be cross-examined on its contents. Prescott will fight to his death to keep both of those statements out of evidence in any grievance proceeding against him—or on a motion for a new trial for Jake Purdy. And he'll probably succeed. That's my opinion, Detective. What's yours?"

Barrow had predicted the resistance Merriman expressed on legal grounds, and was ready with an answer. He knew that the legal problems wouldn't matter in the end. They wouldn't stop Merriman. Like a shark trailing an injured swimmer he would pick his moment and attack. Barrow only needed to provide Merriman the opportunity to smell the blood in the water.

"I've got two things to add, Mr. Merriman. I'm no lawyer, but I'll venture to say this. Admissible or not, those witness statements will make their way into the newspaper. And the public outcry alone will be sufficient to bring Prescott down. He's smart enough to know that.

"And secondly, Jake Purdy might just agree to give a fresh blood sample. The boys in the lab tell me the semen stain on the panties of Venus Brown is still available for testing, and they'll swear that it's a reliable sample. If the DNA in that semen doesn't match the DNA in that fresh vial of blood from our friend Jake, Malcolm T. Prescott's guilty verdict goes up in smoke. And so does his career. That's my opinion, Mr. Merriman."

The mantel clock chimed eleven times.

"Let me see that copy of Janelle Foxworthy's statement, Mr. Barrow."

Merriman examined it with care. He focused on the admission by Willis Purdy of tasting the girl's succulent young fruit, of plucking the juicy plum. "As sweet as Mae Ella herself when she was a girl," it quoted the drunken Willis as declaring. The sheer depravity of the act pricked even Merriman's dismal conscience. He abhorred sex crimes.

"The perverted braggart!" Merriman muttered to Barrow.

Suddenly Merriman had a beatific vision. There was Prescott, dressed in his white linen suit, his silver mane perfectly combed, standing in the chambers of the Commission on Character and Fitness. Except this time the good solicitor was not occupying his usual place behind the burnished mahogany bench, resting comfortably in one of the soft leather-bound chairs reserved for the honorable commissioners. He was instead ensconced in the dock reserved for the wretched lawyer under scrutiny.

And there was Merriman himself, on the witness stand, his unkempt mop of dark locks flowing down to his shoulders, clinching in his right hand the exculpatory affidavit of Janelle Foxworthy, and in his left, the statement of Venus Brown, fraudulently concealed by Solicitor Prescott during the rape trial of Jake Purdy. Vindicated! Vanquished at last!

"Vengeance is mine, and the year of redemption has come!" he could hear himself cry out to the Commission, prophesying like some modern-day Isaiah as the train of righteousness and justice steamed down the track, bound for everlasting glory, on a collision course with Solicitor Malcolm T. Prescott. The image was more than Merriman's weakening heart could bear to absorb.

The taste of blood was in the water, and the shark was poised for the attack.

CHAPTER THIRTY

Malcolm T. Prescott occasionally smoked a cigarette. In secret. He was ashamed of his lack of self-control, particularly in light of his full knowledge of the health risks. He had meticulously researched the medical literature, concluding that one or two cigarettes a month posed less than a four-percent probability of contracting lung cancer. The experts called that statistically insignificant. It was a chance he was willing to take.

Prescott did not view the habit as evidence of unrighteousness. After all, Jesus Himself imbibed alcoholic beverages, and surely a cigarette or two was no worse in the eyes of God than a few glasses of wine. He concluded that he was safe from eternal damnation. Thus, on the evening following Judge Bailey's shocking denial of his motion for a new trial in the Dabney Peters case, Prescott stood in the dark, in seclusion behind his two-car garage attached to his ultra-modern, comfortably furnished four-bedroom townhouse, puffing away.

The wife and children were in their beds. When he had sucked the last mentholated draft of tar-and-nicotine-laden smoke from the filtered Kool and exhaled the noxious second-hand fumes into the atmosphere, he slipped inside, took a long, hot shower, and brushed his teeth assiduously. The evidence of his personal failing swirled neatly down the drain.

The weeks that followed were difficult for Prescott. There was the encounter with Barrow over the appeal. And the constant pressure of appearing before Judge Bailey in other criminal cases, singing to one jury after another the same, tiresome old song of justice and righteousness. The once-pithy refrain rang hollow to him now. The relentless questions about his surprising defeat in the Peters case and the smirks on the faces of his fellow parishioners at First Scots on Sunday mornings added insult to injury.

Then came the crescendo.

He was sorting through a stack of unattended-to correspondence on his desk one morning when Myrt buzzed him on the telephone's intercom.

"What is it?" he groused, snatching the receiver.

"It's Detective Lieutenant Barrow, sir. He'd like to meet with you." Myrt was sweet, even when having every reason not to be.

"About what?" he asked, irritably.

The unflappable Myrt replied calmly, "I don't know, sir. But it seems important to him."

Prescott groaned. "All right. All right, then. Send him in." He grimaced as he thought of Barrow's sickening oral habit. Then he slammed the receiver back into its cradle.

The detective lieutenant entered the solicitor's private office a moment later. He stood uncomfortably until Prescott acknowledged his presence with a nod in the direction of one of his desk chairs.

"What is it today, Mr. Barrow? More drivel about appealing the Peters case?"

Prescott's tone was unusually harsh toward his erstwhile comrade-in-arms. Barrow decided to let it go. After all, Prescott was still technically his superior according to the organizational chart.

"No, sir," Barrow fawned. "I've given that matter a great deal of thought, actually. I suppose you're right about the appeal after all. I just came by for, well, for a little chat."

Prescott looked up from his papers, bemused. "A chat, eh? About what, might I ask?"

Barrow glanced at the open doorway leading into Myrt's outer office. "Uh, something personal, I suppose you might say." He seemed a bit nervous.

"Oh. I see. Well, in that case, why don't you shut the door and take a seat, Mikey." Prescott's foul humor was beginning to evaporate.

"Sit down, sit down, old friend," Prescott offered with grace and suspicion. "Tell me, old man, what's vexing your mind." The solicitor pointed to another, more comfortable

140

armchair next to the window.

Barrow took his designated seat.

"I'll come right to the point, Mr. Prescott."

The Silver Seal eyed him cautiously. "Please do."

"All right," the detective lieutenant started, a little fidgety. "This isn't easy for me." It was true.

"No, I'm quite sure of that," the solicitor responded with seeming understanding. "But never fear. You can confide in me. Are you in some kind of trouble, Barrow?" The suddenly avuncular Prescott was totally clueless. He had misread his colleague's intentions entirely.

Prescott's blunder threw Barrow off track for a moment. He recovered quickly, then remembered his quarry. "Oh, no. It's nothing like that. You see, it's you I came to talk about, Mr. Prescott. Not me."

Realizing his haphazard, mistaken impression, Prescott stiffened.

"Me? What on earth do you mean, Detective? I'm a busy man. No time for chit-chat. Come out with it." Then, before Barrow could speak, Prescott blurted, "I know! You're angry, aren't you? Bitter about the outcome of the Peters case. Is that it?"

Prescott's manic behavior startled Barrow. "No, sir. I'm not angry about the Peters case. I told you, I think you're right about the appeal."

"Well, then," Prescott thundered, "what is it, man? Speak!"

A period sufficient for thought of consequence followed.

"It's time you retire. That's it." Prescott disgorged the words with relief, as if from an illness. "You've had a long and distinguished career, Mr. Prescott, but . . ."

In that fleeting yet eternally significant moment Malcolm T. Prescott snapped.

"You have the temerity, the nerve, the unmitigated gall, Mr. Detective Lieutenant Barrow," Prescott hissed, spitting out the man's title with as much sarcasm as possible, "to come here—to my office, no less—and make the ludicrous, insupportable suggestion that it's time to turn me out to pasture? Why, you insolent dog, you unappreciative cur. Do you take me for an utter fool? I'll have your head for this!"

Prescott rose from his desk chair and placed his hands, palms down, on the leather-covered desk top, leaning forward in a threatening stance. His throat and cheeks were veined and florid from his little tantrum, his blood pulsating palpably in the swollen arteries of his neck.

"Get out!" he screamed.

An unexplainable tranquility came over Barrow. He crossed his legs and leaned back in the armchair. He reached in his briefcase and retrieved a manila file folder. He removed from it a single sheet of paper and slid it across Prescott's desk.

"Not just yet, Mr. Prescott," declared Barrow in a calm, steady voice. "You'll hear me out first." He gazed deep into Prescott's flashing blue eyes, then said with a measure of complete control, "I suggest you simmer down, Mr. Solicitor. Your blood pressure seems precariously high."

Angrily, Prescott snatched the piece of paper Barrow had placed before him and read through it.

"So this is it. The old Purdy case. You made your mark, Detective, as I recall, by assisting me in the prosecution of this affair. Now you try to use this false, incredible statement given by a whore, no less, to intimidate me—no, worse than that, to blackmail me—into resigning. Well, I won't do it! And I'll turn you in for it, you little scum-bagger. Don't you know, Detective, that it's a crime to attempt to blackmail a public official?"

Prescott glanced back over the statement of Janelle Foxworthy. "I suppose you have the original, notarized copy of this rubbish somewhere?"

"Yes."

"I seem to remember directing you to destroy this worthless document, Mr. Barrow."

"You did."

"So I can add insubordination to the list of charges against you."

"If you like."

142

"Damn you, Barrow," he cursed him bitterly. "I'll have you behind bars before the sun sets."

Just then Myrt interrupted with a knock on the door.

"Come in, Myrt! You're just in time to escort Mr. Barrow out."

"Sir," Myrt whispered, "Mr. Merriman just stopped by. He wouldn't stay. But he insisted that I deliver this to you immediately. I told him you and Mr. Barrow were in conference, but . . ."

"It doesn't matter. Give it to me. And see Mr. Barrow out."

She handed her longtime boss an envelope. The detective lieutenant stood. "It's all right, Myrt," he offered politely. "I'll see myself out. I believe I know what Merriman's delivery might be."

"Oh, ho! You do, do you?" Prescott glared at Barrow as he spoke.

"Well, then, that'll be all for now, Myrt," Prescott said to her. "Shut the door behind you."

The solicitor tore open the envelope and read the cover letter. It was a copy of a letter addressed to the clerk of court, in reference to the case of State versus Jake Purdy, and signed by Merriman.

"Dear Madam Clerk," it began. "Please find enclosed my Motion For a New Trial in the above-referenced matter. The fee is enclosed. Attached to the motion is the original Affidavit of Janelle Foxworthy, after-discovered evidence which has just recently come into my possession. By copy of this letter I am serving the motion and affidavit on Solicitor Prescott, who prosecuted the case."

Prescott slammed the letter down on his desk. "So! You and that vermin Merriman are in cahoots, are you? Never in my wildest dreams, or in my most horrific visions, did I think I'd live to see this day." His hands trembled as he spoke.

Barrow picked up his briefcase. He sauntered over to the window, opened it, and spat a big brown slug of tobacco juice through the orifice. "I'll take my leave now, sir," he said.

CHAPTER THIRTY-ONE

Judge Bailey waited impatiently in his chambers for the hastily arranged meeting with Detective Lieutenant Barrow and Merriman. His wall clock read ten-thirty-five. They were five minutes late.

Just then his secretary stuck her head in and said, "Judge, Mr. Barrow and Mr. Merriman are here."

"About time," the old jurist grumbled. "Send them in."

His visitors were familiar to their host. Barrow had testified before him in numerous trials, sought dozens of warrants, and attended every barbeque and Christmas party put on by the court personnel over the last thirty years. Merriman, strange duck that he was, had made frequent appearances before Judge Bailey, usually representing shady characters like the obese Harritt and the inane Dabney Peters.

"Come in, gentlemen."

Merriman detected a slight edge to the judge's tone of voice. He and Barrow took their seats.

"Now," Judge Bailey began, glancing at the clock, "what can I do for you two?"

Barrow took the lead.

"This is a rather unusual situation, Judge. Let me try to explain."

The judge glanced at Merriman, who was staring at the floor, then turned his attention back to Barrow. "Go ahead."

"You see," Barrow started, "I have reason to believe a crime is about to be committed by an elected official."

"Hm-mph!" Judge Bailey snorted. "That's nothing unusual, is it, Mr. Merriman?"

"No, Your Honor," Merriman agreed with a slight smile. He had a grudging respect for the old judge. He was tough, but fair.

"Go ahead, Barrow. Sorry to interrupt your train of thought," the judge said.

"Not at all, Judge. You see, Mr. Merriman here has filed a

motion for a new trial in the case of State versus Jake Purdy."

"What?" the judge remarked. "In that old case?"

"Yes, sir," Barrow continued. "Certain evidence in the case—critical evidence, I might add—was withheld from defense counsel, Mr. Merriman, and another piece of exculpatory evidence was ordered to be destroyed."

Judge Bailey peered over his reading glasses and squinted at Barrow. "How do you know this, Detective?"

"From my own personal knowledge, Judge. At the time I was a young deputy assigned to the Purdy case. Solicitor Prescott, who wasn't much older than me, was calling the shots in the investigation and the prosecution. I'm sure you remember, Judge, this was a rather sensational trial with lots of publicity."

"I remember, Mr. Barrow. But get to the point. Tell me what the evidence consisted of, and who ordered its concealment and destruction?" The matter now commanded Judge Bailey's undivided attention.

"Yes, sir." Barrow cleared his throat. "The first piece of evidence was a sworn statement given by the victim, Venus Brown. Here's a copy, Your Honor," Barrow said, handing the document to the judge. "The solicitor never gave a copy to Mr. Merriman here, who represented Jake Purdy. I didn't know it at the time."

Barrow paused, giving the judge a few moments to read through the affidavit.

"By the way," the judge inquired, "is this man Jake Purdy still alive?"

Merriman interposed the answer. "Alive and well, Your Honor. And occupying a cell at the Killough Correctional Facility as we speak."

"Well, now, Mr. Merriman. Since you've chimed in, let me ask you this. How does the concealment of the sworn statement of the victim prejudice your client's case?"

"Simple, Your Honor. Notice about halfway through, Venus offers what little description of her assailant she can. She characterizes him as an older man with wrinkles on his face. Jake Purdy was smooth-complexioned and in his early thirties when this crime was committed."

"And you want me to grant Purdy a new trial on the basis of that?"

"In part," Merriman replied. "Yes, sir."

Judge Bailey returned his attention to Barrow. "What else, Detective Lieutenant Barrow? You said a crime was about to be committed—by an elected official, if I recall correctly."

"You do," Barrow said. "And here's the rest." He handed the second document to the judge.

"This, Your Honor, is a sworn statement given by a woman named Janelle Foxworthy. She came forward during the trial. Solicitor Prescott and I read the statement but never interviewed the lady. She's dead now. But here's the rub: Solicitor Prescott instructed me to destroy that statement. I knew it was wrong, but he was my boss. So I hid it. I put the statement in my safe at home. It's been there ever since."

"You should've brought it to the attention of the court, Detective."

"Yes, sir. I know that now. I reckon Prescott figured he had himself a guilty verdict on the way against Jake Purdy, Judge, and he wasn't about to let anything mess that up. Not with all those reporters hanging around.

"You'll notice that Ms. Foxworthy clearly incriminates Jake Purdy's father—Willis Purdy—who just happened to be keeping house with her at the time." Barrow gave the judge plenty of time to study the statement carefully.

"Well, well," Judge Bailey said after perusing the document. "Looks to me like Mr. Merriman here might just have himself some grounds for a new trial after all." He turned to Merriman.

"This is after-discovered evidence, isn't it, Counselor?"

"Absolutely, Judge," Merriman declaimed. "I had no knowledge of this lady's statement—or of the fact that she was even alive, much less shacking up with Willis Purdy down by the river—when the trial took place."

Then the judge looked back at Barrow. "And if what you say is true, Detective, it further appears that our esteemed Solicitor Prescott might just have himself a little ethical problem, too. It's one thing to disregard evidence; but it's quite another altogether to order it destroyed. Are you prepared to testify to this, Mr. Barrow?"

"You bet I am, Judge," Barrow admitted, a little too hastily, Merriman thought.

Judge Bailey removed his reading glasses and scratched his balding head. "But you said a crime was about to be committed, Mr. Detective Lieutenant."

"Yes, sir. I hate this part. Judge, you know I have the greatest respect for Solicitor Prescott. I don't want to do anything to harm him." The law man paused for a moment.

"But, you see, Mr. Prescott doesn't know yet that I located that affidavit of Venus Brown in the storage warehouse where his office keeps old files like this one. I think he's going to go there, try to find that affidavit, and destroy it before it comes to light, too.

"Mr. Merriman only attached Ms. Foxworthy's affidavit to his motion, Your Honor. The solicitor doesn't know we also have a copy of the sworn statement Venus Brown gave."

"Hm-m-m," the judge grumbled. "The problem with your theory, Mr. Barrow, is that it would be perfectly normal for the solicitor to fetch the old file from the warehouse, if he is called upon to defend a motion for a new trial."

"Yes, sir," Barrow replied, "but if all he takes is the original statement of Venus Brown, the motive and opportunity are pretty clear, at least to me."

"So, what do you want me to do, Mr. Barrow?"

"Issue a search warrant, Judge. Let us go on the property of that warehouse and install a hidden video surveillance camera. If we don't move quickly, it might be too late. If Mr. Prescott is caught on video monitor removing from the file that affidavit Venus Brown gave, I believe we have grounds to arrest the solicitor for obstruction of justice."

"For what it's worth, Your Honor," Merriman added, "I agree. I would argue that exigent circumstances exist in the case so as to justify a warrantless arrest, if Mr. Prescott is found to be absconding with the Venus Brown affidavit."

"Our own version of the case of the purloined letter, eh,

Mr. Merriman?"

"Quite a good analogy, Your Honor," Merriman said.

"Anything else?" the judge inquired, peering over his spectacles first at Barrow and then at Merriman.

"No, sir," they replied in unison.

"I have something else, gentlemen," Judge Bailey added with gravity. "As you both know, this court normally requires an affidavit in support of the grounds asserted for issuing a warrant." Merriman and Barrow exchanged glances. "I'll dispense with that usual prerequisite under the circumstances, but I will insist on this: Raise your right hand, Mr. Barrow."

The detective lieutenant stood, sucked his plug firmly against his cheek, and complied.

"Do you solemnly swear that the averments of fact you have presented to this court are the truth, the whole truth, and nothing but the truth, so help you God?"

"On my honor I do," he firmly replied.

"Very well. I find that probable cause exists to issue the search warrant and install the surveillance device. Draw it up and bring it to me, Detective. I'll sign it."

Barrow couldn't stifle a grin as he handed a third document to the old jurist. "I took the liberty of drawing one up this morning, Judge, before we came. That's why we were late."

Merriman thought he noticed the judge's lips curl up on the ends, in a smile, as he issued the warrant.

CHAPTER THIRTY-TWO

Jake received the envelope from Nellie on the same day Detective Lieutenant Michael O'Shea Barrow had his little chat with Prescott. When he finished reading its contents, Jake slipped the surprise epistle back into the envelope and set it down on the shelf over his toilet, next to a yellowing Kodachrome photograph of Nellie and the kids. The shelf was the one spot in his cell at Killough where he was permitted to display his personal effects.

Then he broke down and sobbed.

It had been fourteen years, two months and twenty-one days since he last heard from Nellie. He figured she had taken his advice and relocated, remarried, and relegated him to the status of a bad dream.

Of course he wanted to get out. And to see Nellie. And to try to make contact with the children. But he was afraid. Afraid of the outside. What would he do out there? And what would the children think, after all these years? It had been a mighty long time.

Jake peered at his reflection in the mirror the next morning when it came his turn to shave. He was an old man now. What would an old duffer do on the outside, in a young man's world? He wasn't trained to find work at any of the high-tech companies that had sprouted and blossomed and covered the earth like kudzu since his conviction. And he was neither strong enough to go back to the Westinghouse plant nor tough enough to re-enlist with the Marines. He wasn't even sure either one would take him back, what with his record.

And then there was his daddy. What if that Foxworthy woman was lying? After all, she was a shameless whore, wasn't she? Not exactly the most credible witness. What if his daddy was innocent, just like Jake? And what if that newfangled DNA test turned out to be rubbish? It might well be as unreliable a proof of the identity of the perpetrator as the blood test had beennthe one that matched his blood to the stain on that colored girl's panties. Where would they be then?

Jake refused to get his hopes up. They'd been dashed before. He began to rationalize. Life in prison wasn't all that bad, not after all these years of learning to manipulate the system. He was a trusty now. A model prisoner. They let him watch TV and smoke whenever he wanted, even mill about the exercise yard twice a day. And the chow wasn't as god-awful bad as everybody let on. Shoot, it was better than hospital food, and a far cry from military rations. And there were still more books in the prison library he hadn't read than ones he had.

He was, well, believe it or not, comfortable—content, you might even say—in his circumstances. A Pauline prisoner. Why rock the boat now?

That afternoon the guard came to Jake's cell, announcing his arrival by rapping the bars with his billy stick.

"You got yourself a visitor, Jake. Fellow named Merriman. Claims to be a lawyer. Here's his card," the guard said, passing it through the bars. "He says you'll remember him."

The guard turned to walk away, then stopped and threw a casual remark over his shoulder toward Jake. "Doesn't look like a lawyer to me."

"Hey! Lefty," Jake called to him. Lefty was an amputee. "You be nice to that man. You might need his services one day." Jake laughed. So did Lefty. Jake liked Lefty. There wasn't a mean streak to be found in that old guard's mutilated body.

"Hey!" Lefty hollered at Jake. "I'll be back to fetch you. Lemme just get this lawyer patted down and parked in the visitors room. You know the drill."

A few minutes later, when Lefty escorted Jake into his half of the conference area, he recognized Merriman through the clear plastic window, standing on the other side of the dividing wall and leaning against a gold-headed cane. He didn't look too much different than Jake remembered. His hair was longer, but it was still thick and dark, with just a streak or two of gray. His face was thinner, as if gravity and time had sculpted a respectable drawn look, but without too many wrinkles, except the crow's feet around his eyes and a deep crease or two across his forehead.

Jake didn't remember the cane. When Merriman represented Jake he was bold and brash with a don't-give-a-damn attitude, like some courtroom swashbuckler. He didn't need a cane then. What Jake remembered most about Merriman was his rich, strong baritone. That syrupy, mellifluous voice was mesmerizing. When Merriman took his seat after delivering an hour-long closing argument to the jury, there was hardly a dry eye in the courtroom, except for those damn Yankee reporters. Jake felt sure the jury was going to cut him loose.

Merriman said it was politics, pure and simple. National politics. And the timing was all wrong, Merriman told him. The colored people in Cumberland County had been oppressed long enough. A violent, rushing wind was blowing a gale of freedom through the South like the Spirit of the Lord on Pentecost. What happened long ago between Jake's daddy and Mae Ella was one thing, Merriman told him. The white folks called it miscegenation back then, a consensual crime. Why else would a white man with a pretty wife have sex with a Negro? But the colored people didn't use fancy words. They called a spade a spade. And Jake's daddy raped Mae Ella, plain and simple, pretty white wife or not.

Now, what Willis Purdy's son Jake supposedly did to Mae Ella's daughter was something else altogether, Merriman explained to his client. At least that's what the big fat foreman of the jury told the hot-shot reporter from *The Atlanta Journal*. He got his picture on the front page of that newspaper, too, for saying what he did about Jake.

A man who breaks and enters the inner sanctum of a young colored girl's bedroom in the middle of the night, presses a knife to her throat, jerks down her panties, penetrates and violates her—well, he's done something worse than rape, the big fat foreman declared. Something even white folks don't call miscegenation any more. That's what the big fat foreman told that liberal big-city journalist. All for a snatch of fleeting fame and the unanticipated obloquy of having his porcine image, pouring sweat and beaming like a Cheshire cat, plastered on the *Journal's* front page and circulated nationwide.

And Jake committed that unspeakable act, according to the detailed and colorful description provided by the big fat foreman as if he'd been standing right there in that colored girl's bedroom observing it all happen, under cover of darkness. Now, he snickered knowingly to that liberal big-city journalist, doesn't that tell you something?

But like the penetrating eyes of God Almighty, the spotlight shining down from the lofty heights occupied by the national news media illuminated that darkness. It uncovered, it exposed, the despicable crime that Jake Purdy attempted to cloak in the darkness of sin and evil, the big fat foreman told him. The brilliance of that light simply would not allow for any shadow, he declared.

Before the first mortal witness ever took the oath, before Lawyer Merriman ever opened his unclean lips to defend Jake Purdy, before Solicitor Prescott ever lifted his crooked, righteous finger to prosecute him, the jury had already found Willis Purdy's son guilty of raping that colored girl. A colored girl who just happened to be Willis Purdy's daughter.

"Dee-spicable." The big fat foreman spat it out. "Jake Purdy is guilty beyond a reasonable doubt," he told that reporter. "Beyond any shadow of a doubt," he emphasized, just to be clear. "Hell," he told him, "Jake Purdy's as guilty as sin."

But it was more than that. Much more. Jake Purdy was found guilty in the court of public opinion long before the big fat foreman ever announced the verdict in the Criminal Court of Cumberland County. Long before his perspiring porcine image ever graced the front page of *The Atlanta Journal*. And that's what sealed Jake Purdy's fate. The verdict in the court of public opinion.

And Merriman told him, "Jake, my boy, there ain't no appeal from the court of public opinion."

Jake remembered these things as he took his seat in a metal folding chair and strapped on the headphone-and-microphone set that enabled him to confer with his counsel. The conversation was recorded and monitored, of course, by the officials of the Killough Correctional Facility. There was no reasonable expectation of privacy here.

Merriman took his seat directly across the Plexiglas window from Jake and tuned in.

"Remember me, Jake?"

"Yep. I do, Mr. Merriman. And I remember that twenty-eight hundred dollars me and Nellie paid you to defend me, too."

"Any hard feelings, Jake?"

"Nope. You done what you could. I don't fault you. I just wish Nellie had that money now, that's all."

Merriman paused. "I'm glad of that, Jake. I worked hard for that paltry twenty-eight-hundred-dollar fee. I'm just sorry the result wasn't different. Okay?"

"Okay," Jake said, not grudgingly or submissively, either. It was just matter-of-fact. Enough for a reconciliation—no more, no less. And it was all Merriman could expect.

"Have you heard from Nellie, Jake?"

Jake paused. "If you mean about the new trial, yes, I have." His affect was flat, like a mental patient on Thorazine.

Merriman squinted at his former client, trying to assess Jake's reaction to the news Nellie's letter delivered. Jake's eyes were dull, glazed, like those of a man who has given up hope.

"Look, Jake. You got a bum deal," Merriman started. "We have a chance to fix that now."

Jake interrupted his old lawyer. "Fix it? Is that what you think?" Jake's eyes were beginning to flash signs of life. "How are you going to fix thirty years, Mr. Merriman? By turning me loose now? By giving you another chance to be a hero, and win my case?

"It's too late for that, Mr. Merriman. You see, I'm a

prisoner of my own devices now. These bars don't hold me in any more. I wouldn't try to escape from this prison if they left my cell door wide open one night. Where would I go? What would I do?

"I'm locked in, Mr. Merriman. Up here, I mean," Jake said, pointing to his head. "And long ago—long ago, Mr. Merriman—I threw away the key."

Merriman readily perceived that he had his work cut out for him. He had never considered the possibility that Jake might refuse to go along. On the one hand it seemed odd that an innocent man, imprisoned for years for a crime he didn't commit, would balk at a chance of being set free. On the other, Merriman knew from a lifetime of experience in the justice system that imprisonment was about as conducive to transforming a criminal into a productive member of society as the dog pound was of converting a vicious canine into a docile household pet.

The task at hand—convincing Jake Purdy not only to consent to, but to actively participate in, the motion for a new trial—required Merriman to summon his most prepossessing powers of persuasion, if he was to have any reasonable chance for success. The sly old fox considered his cardiomyopathy and the stress the impending courtroom battle with Malcolm T. Prescott would have on his life expectancy. Was he willing to risk his life for this cause of Barrow's, a man he had spent his career opposing?

No one, certainly not the old Merriman whose shingle hung on rusty nails against the side of a dilapidated building on the corner of Champagne and Northampton streets, would have predicted his answer. But things were different now. And the new Merriman suddenly viewed the situation as an opportunity to prove his worth, a chance to do the right thing—not just for his old client Jake Purdy, but for the system of justice itself. It was a cause far greater than Barrow's. By succumbing to his overarching ambition, Solicitor Malcolm T. Prescott perverted the very system of justice he had sworn to uphold.

An intentional miscarriage of justice had occurred.

Jake Purdy spent thirty years in the penitentiary because Malcolm Prescott refused to accept the truth. This was not the time for Merriman to seek personal vengeance for petty offenses Prescott had committed against him over the years. This was the moment to stand up and do the right thing.

For the first time in his otherwise miserable life, John Merriman experienced an epiphany: he realized that the oath he had taken thirty-seven years ago was more than mere words. The practice of law was a profession of service to others, not just a means of making a decent living. It was as though the scales had fallen from his eyes: For the first time he comprehended the privilege that had been entrusted to him when he was granted a license to engage in this noble profession.

Through the lenses of a new pair of eyes, John Merriman saw before him a final, golden opportunity. He had been given a second chance. A chance to demonstrate that justice, righteousness and mercy—the ancient and eternal pillars of the law—still meant something today, something real and vital and effective. To Jake Purdy, to Mike Barrow, to Malcolm Prescott, and to John Merriman.

And by God, he wasn't about to let this opportunity slip through his fingers, cardiomyopathy or not.

CHAPTER THIRTY-THREE

The surveillance camera was mounted in place, well hidden, within an hour of the issuance of the warrant. The monitor was set up in Detective Lieutenant Barrow's office, out of sight of the rest of law enforcement staff.

Barrow figured that Prescott would make his move today. The detective resolved to stay at his desk, staring at the monitor, for as long as it took. He stationed two officers in a cruiser a block down the street from the warehouse. They had no idea why they were there, except that Detective Lieutenant Barrow, who was a big dog at the office, had ordered it. All he told them was that a high-profile arrest might be in the offing.

It was nearly one o'clock in the afternoon when the surveillance got underway. Merriman knew the stake-out was in place, and waited impatiently at his office for a call from Barrow.

At three o'clock Barrow took a quick trip to the men's room and ordered his secretary to watch the monitor in his absence. When he returned two minutes later she reported no activity. Barrow resumed surveillance.

At a quarter to four an anxious Merriman phoned.

"Anything yet, Detective?"

"No," Mikey replied. "The place is as dead as a graveyard. I'll call you if anything happens. Take it easy, Merriman. Police work requires patience."

Merriman clicked off without a goodbye. "Impertinent bastard," he muttered.

At ten after four the officers in the cruiser contacted Barrow.

"A white Crown Victoria just pulled into the driveway leading to the warehouse," one of the officers reported.

Barrow's feet were propped on his desk, his eyes bleary from viewing the monitor. He jumped up and approached the screen. Barrow knew that Prescott drove a white Crown

Vic, standard issue for upper-echelon law enforcement personnel.

Three minutes later a man entered the storage area under surveillance. At first Barrow couldn't be sure, but then the man turned in the direction of the surveillance camera. It was Prescott. He was almost certain.

The camera had been positioned such that it would record a perfect image of anyone opening the container in which the Purdy file resided. As the man walked directly toward the container, and thus the camera, Barrow positively identified Prescott.

Barrow grabbed his phone and contacted the officers in the cruiser.

"Get ready. And stay on the line. The target just entered the surveillance area."

Barrow was now operating on full adrenaline. He stared at the monitor and held his breath while Prescott rummaged through the container. He located the file he was searching for and set it on a small table next to the container. Barrow had set up the convenient table arrangement, well within the watchful eye of the camera, the afternoon before.

"Boys," he whispered through the phone to the officers, "exit your cruiser and walk down to the entrance to the warehouse. Be prepared to make an arrest of Solicitor Prescott on my order only. Don't forget to take your cell phone—and keep the line open to me."

"Excuse me, sir," the officer replied, clearing his throat. "Did you say Solicitor Prescott?"

"That's a big ten-four, Officer," came Barrow's response. "Be gentle with him. I don't anticipate any resistance."

Prescott opened the file and flipped through the contents. Barrow had reinserted the affidavit in its proper order after copying the document, placing it about midway through the papers in the file. It shouldn't take long for Prescott to locate it.

Within a minute Prescott stopped flipping through the contents. He removed a document with a blue backing. It has to be Venus' affidavit, Barrow said to himself. Prescott read through it, folded it so that it would fit into his inside coat pocket, and returned the remains of the file to its rightful place in the container.

"Okay," Barrow barked at the officer with the cell phone. "Get ready. This is your order to detain and arrest Solicitor Prescott when he exits the building. And for the love of Pete, don't forget to read him his rights. I don't want any slip-ups. Cuff him before you put him in the cruiser. He could benefit from eating a slice of humble pie." Barrow had an ulterior motive for the handcuffing. He knew this would prevent Prescott from removing the affidavit from his coat pocket.

"Yes, sir."

Barrow listened through the phone as the officers made the arrest. Prescott exuded shrieks of surprise and howls of outrage. Barrow paid close attention as one of the officers read the standard Miranda warnings to their stouthearted solicitor.

"Where's the warrant?" he heard the still-sharp legal mind and tongue of Prescott demand of the officers.

This is where things got sticky from a legal perspective. Barrow prayed Merriman's judgment was correct—that the exigency of the circumstances, coupled with the search warrant Judge Bailey had already issued, would obviate the need for an arrest warrant prior to taking Prescott into custody.

"He wants to know where the warrant is," the officer with the cell phone said to Barrow.

"Tell him the arrest is on order of Detective Lieutenant Barrow. Then bring him straight to my office. I'll handle the warrant here."

Barrow listened through the phone a moment longer. When he was sure they had Prescott cuffed and in the cruiser, he clicked off. As planned, he had Suzie, his longtime secretary, run the videotape over to Judge Bailey, who was waiting to view it, and hopefully return with an already prepared arrest warrant signed by the judge.

Then he telephoned Merriman. "We got him."

The sly old fox curled his lips in a smile. "Good work, Mr. Barrow," he conceded.

CHAPTER THIRTY-FOUR

Malcolm T. Prescott was a fool, but he knew better than to represent himself. And although he despised criminal defense lawyers as a lot, he had the good sense to hire the very best. Solicitor Prescott was going to need the very best.

Devon Jennings, Esquire, was fifty-one years old and in the prime of his career. Burly and ruddy with a shock of pale red hair, he exhibited a commanding presence in the courtroom. Unlike Merriman, Jennings maintained a large office staff including two young, ambitious lawyers and a seasoned trial paralegal. Prescott had tried many a case against Jennings, winning some and losing more. But no matter the outcome, Prescott always came away with a grudging respect for the awesome litigation skills of Devon Jennings.

If only the solicitor had taken Mikey Barrow's advice and announced his resignation, there would have been no need to humiliate himself by retaining Jennings. But he did not. Solicitor Prescott flatly rejected the offer and put in motion the destiny that lay before him.

"Ah, Mr. Prescott," Barrow offered with muted respect when his men delivered the good solicitor to his office. "Take off the cuffs," he instructed the officers, "and leave us alone."

Barrow waited patiently while the officers fumbled with removing the handcuffs from their once high-and-mighty solicitor turned high-profile detainee. When they were done and gone the detective lieutenant turned to Prescott.

"I'd like to play a videotape for you, Mr. Solicitor."

Prescott stood in stony silence, burning holes in his former subordinate with his fiery blue eyes.

Seemingly unaffected by the palpable tension in the air, Barrow sauntered over to his credenza and punched the play button on the video cassette player. He took his seat at his desk.

"Have a seat, Mr. Solicitor," the detective lieutenant offered, nodding in the direction of one of the two metal-and-vinyl chairs in front of his desk.

Prescott tacitly elected to stand, but he diverted his attention to the screen. As the tape rolled forward he saw himself enter the warehouse area, approach the container, and locate the file. The sudden turn of events was eerie. There he was, on screen, committing a felony. He looked on in horror as he took Venus' affidavit out of the file, folded it and slipped it into his coat, returned the file to its container and walked out of range of the camera.

Then it was over. The screen turned to snow. Barrow pressed the stop button and buzzed his secretary.

"Do we have the warrant, Suzie?"

"Yes, sir."

"Bring it in."

In just a moment Suzie was at the door, warrant in hand. She passed it to Barrow.

"Ask Officer Christopher to join us, please," the detective lieutenant instructed Suzie. Unlike Prescott, he always treated his subordinates, particularly the women such as Suzie who were under his command, with respect. He was once a lowly subordinate himself.

Prescott continued to stand, dumb as a post, like a lamb before the slaughter.

Officer Christopher entered Barrow's office.

Barrow took the warrant and handed it to Prescott. "You're under arrest for obstruction of justice. I believe you've already been informed of your rights, Mr. Prescott."

"I know my rights, Detective Lieutenant," he snapped back.

"Very well. Officer Christopher, kindly search Mr. Prescott's inside coat pockets and place the contents on my desk."

They consisted of a handkerchief, slightly soiled; a black plastic pocket comb, sticky from the mousse Prescott used; and a folded legal document with a blue backing. Barrow picked up the document and glanced at the title: "Sworn

Statement of Venus Brown Purdy." He took a moment to read through it, assuring himself that the exculpatory paragraph in which she described her attacker as a wrinkle-faced, aging man, had not disappeared. Then he set it back on the desk with the handkerchief and pocket comb.

"Now," Barrow directed Christopher. "Let's follow proper procedure, shall we? Place each item in a separate bag, label each one with name of the accused, date, time, and description of the item it contains, then sign each bag, seal them and place them in a case basket in the evidence vault."

Barrow had done this hundreds of times over the years, adhering to a procedure which Solicitor Prescott himself had designed and approved long ago. Chain of custody, it was called. He glanced at Prescott, who stared at Barrow in utter disbelief at the irony of the upside-down circumstances.

"That will be all, Officer," the detective lieutenant said to Christopher.

When Christopher made his exit Barrow turned to the solicitor. "Sit down, please, Mr. Prescott. Let's have a little chat."

A little chat. The suggestion blew Prescott's mind. He replayed the little chat he and Barrow had engaged in just days before in his office. He was a free and powerful man then, shackled only by his own ambition.

"No, Mr. Barrow," the still-prideful Prescott declared. "I shall exercise my constitutional right to remain silent."

"Very well, sir," Barrow said. He loathed constitutional rights. "Then I'll talk, and you listen."

Barrow produced a ball point pen and a sheet of paper and set them before Prescott.

"Submit your irrevocable intention to retire, effective immediately, sign and date it. You can attribute any reason you like to the decision. If you do, the charges will be dropped, and the record expunged. You will be free to go. If you don't, Officer Christopher will take you down the hall and book you. And I would imagine the *Tribune* will have the information on their front page in the morning. You can read the news in your jail cell while you're waiting on your lawyer and a bond hearing."

"Damn you, Barrow," Prescott cursed him. "I won't do it. I'll fight these trumped-up charges to the end. And then I'll have your neck, Barrow. You'll see."

"Why not take the easy way out, Prescott?" It was the first time Barrow had called him by his surname. "Be kind to yourself—and your family. Think of Mrs. Prescott, sir."

"I've already thought of her, thank you," Prescott replied bitterly. "But the answer is no, because the charges are not true."

"True?" Barrow asked in disbelief. "You want to talk about the truth, Mr. Solicitor? After how you mangled and choked the life out of the truth in Jake Purdy's case? Well, I suppose you'll get your chance, then, when you testify at your trial. That is, of course, unless you exercise your constitutional right not to." His voice was tinged with sarcasm.

"I'd like to make a phone call, Mr. Barrow. I believe I am entitled to that."

"Of course," Barrow said calmly. "As soon as Officer Christopher books you."

Barrow reached over to his phone and depressed the intercom button.

"Suzie. Ask Officer Christopher to come in, please."

After he was photographed, fingerprinted, inventoried, and booked into the records of the Cumberland County Sheriff's Department, Malcolm T. Prescott was provided access to a telephone.

An hour later Devon Jennings, Esquire, arrived at the county jail. Before leaving his home to drive there, Jennings telephoned a friendly magistrate and arranged for a bond hearing to be held at nine o'clock that evening.

Barrow appeared and didn't object to the release of the defendant, Malcolm T. Prescott, on a personal recognizance bond. "No, sir, Your Honor," he declaimed to the magistrate when it came his turn to respond to the request for release. "We have no reason to believe there is any risk of flight before trial by Mr. Prescott, or that his release would pose a danger to the community."

Prescott gritted his teeth as he listened to Barrow speak these insufferable words. He, the righteous one, the longstanding solicitor of Cumberland County and defender of the law, a flight risk? A danger to the community? The very suggestion was preposterous.

"Very well, then," the magistrate ruled. "Mr. Prescott, you are released on your personal recognizance. This court will require no bail to be posted. You will be informed of your trial date. Anything further, gentlemen?"

"Not from the defense, Your Honor," Jennings replied meekly.

"Nothing further from the State, Your Honor," Barrow echoed.

After a brief and embarrassing meeting with Devon Jennings, Prescott went home. It was late. His wife and children were asleep. They were used to his long hours. He smoked a Kool filter behind the garage, showered away the odor, brushed the tar and menthol off his teeth, and went to bed. He slept like the proverbial full-bellied baby, confident that righteousness and justice would prevail.

The next morning he awoke to find a photograph of his smiling face plastered onto the front page of the *Tribune*, next to a bold headline that read, "Solicitor Charged With Obstruction of Justice."

"Angela!" he called to his wife. She was in their bedroom, dressing for the day. Something tan or light gray, no doubt.

"Yes, dear?" she replied.

"We need to talk."

CHAPTER THIRTY-FIVE

Judge Bailey had his secretary schedule a conference in his chambers with Barrow and Merriman for eleven o'clock the morning the story broke. Both men appeared a few minutes early.

"Send them in," the judge barked at his secretary over the intercom.

When they entered the old jurist's chambers, Barrow and Merriman could see stacks of law books covering his desk. One was open before him, alongside a yellow legal pad. He had obviously been studying. Merriman assumed the subject of inquiry was the law on search and seizure.

"Come in. Sit down," the judge ordered, peering over his reading spectacles. The two took the same seats they had occupied in the meeting the day before.

"Well, boys, we're in it now, aren't we?" The judge remarked with a twinkle in his eye, looking straight at Barrow as he spoke.

Barrow tried to reply. "Your Honor, I can assure the court that all police procedures were properly . . ."

Judge Bailey cut him off. "I didn't call you here to question that. It's water over the dam now, Mr. Barrow. Either you did it right or you didn't. I'll have to rule on that, I'm sure, at the appropriate time. It wouldn't be proper to take up the matter without Mr. Jennings taking part in the discussion. I am assuming Devon Jennings is on board for the solicitor. I read the article in this morning's *Tribune*."

"Yes, sir." Barrow lowered his head and waited. Merriman stared at the floor.

The judge leaned back in his chair and removed his spectacles.

"The reason I called you here is quite simple. We're prosecuting the solicitor of Cumberland County. And therefore we don't have a prosecuting attorney to handle the case. Prescott has an assistant solicitor for administrative matters, of course, but that poor lad couldn't find his way to the courthouse, much less try a case once he arrived. And there's an obvious conflict of interest in his doing so. I have therefore decided to exercise my authority to appoint a special prosecutor to take over for the State.

"Last night I had, shall I say, an informal discussion with the attorney general. He concurs with my plan. I have decided to appoint you, Mr. Merriman, to serve as Special Solicitor for the case against Prescott. You will be the prosecuting attorney. I have drafted an order to that effect to be filed this afternoon. Any questions, gentlemen?"

Merriman was dumbfounded. Barrow wasn't sure what to make of this turn of events.

After a moment Merriman replied. "Your Honor may know that I have recently been diagnosed with health problems."

"I heard that, Mr. Merriman. I'm sorry. But you look fit enough to me. Would your physician rule this out?"

"I don't know, Your Honor."

"Well, then, find out today. And call me. I intend to appoint you this afternoon."

Merriman took a deep breath. He had never prosecuted a case.

"There's another problem I foresee, Your Honor," Merriman continued. "I would envision being a key witness for the prosecution. How could I serve as both prosecutor and witness?"

"I've thought about that, Mr. Merriman. I don't believe it's a problem. Barrow here can testify that the Foxworthy affidavit was ordered to be destroyed, and that defense counsel was never given the victim's statement. I won't let anyone tell the jury you were defense counsel. And even if we do need some type of record of your testimony, I'll handle all that outside the jury's presence. Then I'll instruct them what to do based on my findings and conclusions of law, once I hear your testimony. If necessary, they can have your testimony read anonymously to them by the court reporter if any real questions of fact remain. Any other concerns?"

Merriman thought a moment, then said, "One more thing, Judge. Would I not have a conflict as well?"

"Not if you can truthfully take the same oath Prescott took when he was sworn in as solicitor: to seek neither reward nor gain, but above all justice. Can you take that oath, Mr. Merriman?"

Merriman thought of Jake Purdy and his wife Nellie, and the twenty-eight-hundred-dollar fee he had earned so many years ago. The sense of purpose this whole affair had finally aroused in him came rushing back. He looked Judge Bailey straight in the eye.

"Yes, Your Honor. I am prepared to take such an oath."

Before Merriman could think of anything further, the old jurist wrapped up the meeting.

"Very well, then. It's all settled. Mr. Merriman, I expect to hear from you by two o'clock on the medical question. And tell your physician if he has any real question about your service, I want to see him here, in my chambers, at three o'clock.

"Seems to me, Mr. Merriman, that if you're healthy enough to argue the motion for a new trial and to serve as a witness in Prescott's criminal case, you're fit to carry the prosecution ball as well. Let me hear from you. I want this order filed—today."

Barrow and Merriman exchanged glances.

"Yes, sir, Your Honor," the duet responded in harmony.

CHAPTER THIRTY-SIX

For his birthday May presented Merriman with a cell phone. To him it was a newfangled gadget for which he envisioned little use. But he was glad to have it now. He called May from the hallway outside Judge Bailey's office.

"I have to see Dr. Fairchild at once, May. Can you pick me up at the courthouse and drive me there?"

May nearly swooned. "You idiot!" she popped off at him. "Call an ambulance at once! I'll meet you there."

Merriman realized his mistake. "No, sorry, May. I'm not ill. Judge Bailey wants me to prosecute the Prescott case, and I need Steve Fairchild's clearance by two o'clock."

"What?" May cried again, louder than before. "Are you crazy?"

Merriman quickly interjected. "Just pick me up now, May. I'll explain on the way to the doctor's office."

Thank God the doctor was in. Merriman and May waited in the lobby until Dr. Fairchild's normal lunch break, between one and one-thirty. The nurse came out at five after one o'clock and ushered Merriman back. "Dr. Fairchild can see you now," she explained, Abut just for a moment. I told him it was not an emergency."

"That will do nicely," Merriman replied. "It shouldn't take long."

Merriman was wrong, at least about the length of the meeting.Steve Fairchild had grave concerns about his patient taking on such a strenuous role. They sparred over the matter for nearly half an hour.

"Do you remember anything I told you, Merriman?" the doctor finally asked, in desperation.

"Of course I do. I don't have Alzheimer's yet, do I, Doc?"

"I was beginning to wonder," Fairchild retorted.

"Look, Doc. I've been a good boy. No smoking, drinking or carousing since I last saw you. And you just told me my blood pressure's nearly normal. I promise to stay off the sauce and behave during the trial.

"I really want to do this, Doc. Believe it or not, I've had a little epiphany lately—about lawyers and justice and mercy and greed. You know, little things like that. And the Prescott prosecution—along with Jake Purdy's new trial—would once and for all enable me to fulfill the oath I took years ago, when I was admitted to the bar. Maybe when I look in the mirror I'll see a different man. I don't know. What do you say, Doc?"

Steve Fairchild leaned back in his soft, blue leather desk chair and scratched his head. Just behind him, in a frame on the credenza, stood his wife in her rose garden, their ivy-covered Tudor mansion in the background. A moment or so passed before he spoke.

"Damn you, Merriman. You're a persuasive old goat. It's your life. You know the risks. I won't hold you back. Go for it."

Merriman stood and extended his hand. "Thanks, Doc," he said.

"You're welcome," the sometimes brash physician replied, grasping Merriman's hand. "And just for the record, I hope you nail that prick Prescott. I know that's not what my pastor at First Scots would like to hear me say."

"I won't tell him," Merriman said with a chuckle.

"Go get him, Tiger! I'm late for a cath. Gotta go," Fairchild said.

The two walked out to the lobby together. May was the only one there.

"Hello, May," Dr. Fairchild said.

"Hello, Dr. Fairchild. Will he live through this?"

Fairchild glanced at Merriman. "He'll probably extend his life a year or two, May. I'm not worried. We were just talking sports back there, mainly."

May knew it was a lie. Merriman had no interest in sports.

"All right," she said. "He's a new man, Doctor, in many ways. I suppose he deserves a second chance at this lawyering stuff."

As they turned to leave, Merriman glanced over his

shoulder at Dr. Fairchild, who was rushing back to his office for the keys to his car. He was a half-hour late to the hospital for a heart cath procedure on another patient.

"Slow down, Doc!" Merriman called to him.

Fairchild turned for a moment and gave him a knowing wink.

"I like that guy, May," Merriman said as he opened the driver's door of the Packard for his wife.

May sighed. "So do I, John. I just hope this gamble pays off."

Merriman jumped out of the Packard when they reached the courthouse. "I'll walk home, as usual. Hope to see you around six." And then he did something very unusual. He walked around to the driver's side and leaned into the open window.

"John!" May declared. "What on earth do you want?"

"A kiss, May." He didn't bother to glance around to see who might observe his aberrant behavior.

They kissed, and then he was gone, tapping up the steps of the courthouse to seek out Judge Bailey.

CHAPTER THIRTY-SEVEN

The various pending legal matters were enough to throw an average lawyer into a maelstrom. But Merriman was not your average lawyer. The day after his appointment as Special Prosecutor he went to his Champagne Street office, locked the door, and let the answering machine pick up the messages. No visitors. No interruptions. No phone calls. He had work to do.

Merriman took out a legal pad and listed the three upcoming proceedings. First, there was Jake Purdy's motion for a new trial. Next came the criminal prosecution against Prescott for obstruction of justice. Last but not least, someone was sure to file the inevitable grievance proceeding against Prescott before the Commission on Character and Fitness.

Merriman decided this was the order in which the cases should proceed. If Merriman was successful in winning a new trial for Jake Purdy, then certainly Devon Jennings, Esquire, would advise his client to fold, and seek the best plea bargain money could buy. Once Prescott entered a plea of guilty, the grievance proceeding should be a slam dunk. Any lawyer found guilty of a crime was headed for a sanction, most likely either a suspension or disbarment.

So it came down to the motion for a new trial. Everything else rested on the success of that motion. Merriman turned to a fresh page in the legal pad and made some notes. What would he need in order to prove that Jake Purdy was entitled to a new trial?

First and foremost, he would need Jake Purdy's cooperation. The best he had been able to do with the recalcitrant Purdy was to convince him to give a fresh blood sample. This would be extracted under the auspices of Detective Lieutenant Barrow and his boys in the crime lab. It was up to Barrow to ensure that procedures were carefully adhered to, and that no slip-ups occurred with respect to chain of custody. Assuming success on that end,

Judge Bailey would surely order that DNA testing using the fresh sample be conducted.

The second piece of that puzzle was the DNA testing on the semen sample, which the crime lab had preserved in its temperature-controlled storage vault. The question was the reliability of the evidence. After so many years, would the sample hold up under the scrutiny of the experts Devon Jennings was sure to hire? All of them would opine that the semen was stale, had disintegrated over time, and simply could not be relied upon as probative of anything.

To combat this attack Merriman needed his own outside, independent expert to corroborate the opinions of the boys from the crime lab. The boys were good, but they were no match for DNA experts from Johns Hopkins or Harvard or Duke, the likely institutions from which Jennings' experts would hail. These guys with bow ties, horn-rimmed glasses, and Ph.D.'s in biology and chemistry and genetics were sure to overwhelm the court with their erudition. Merriman drew a giant star in the margin next to this note and plowed on.

The most important evidence would come from Barrow and his team. The ordered destruction of the Foxworthy affidavit, the intentional failure to turn over to defense counsel Venus Brown Purdy's statement, and, finally, Solicitor Prescott's attempt to secrete or destroy Venus' affidavit—all of this would come in through the detective lieutenant and his officers. Barrow simply had to come through on this part of the case.

It was enough to think about for now. Merriman would go to the library and search for an expert witness—someone who had published papers in the peer review literature on the subject of DNA analysis, and whose point of view correlated with Merriman's on the reliability of the semen sample for purposes of extracting and determining the DNA it contained. "Who knows?" he chuckled to himself. "Maybe I'll get one of those young librarians to show me how to surf the net."

Merriman left his inner office and prepared to leave. He

opened the front door and exited the building, his briefcase in one hand and the key to the office in the other. It was raining, and a wet, chilly wind blew against his back. As he turned to lock the door a hand grasped his shoulder. Startled, he glanced behind him and observed a quite elderly man whose face resembled a wrinkled egg, peering at him.

"Are you Merriman?" the man asked.

"Who wants to know?" Merriman replied gruffly.

The man released his grip on Merriman's shoulder and looked him in the eye.

"Willis Purdy," he said. "That's who."

CHAPTER THIRTY-EIGHT

The meeting of the Commission on Character and Fitness was a solemn occasion. The commission itself had the power to bring grievance charges against a lawyer, upon receiving evidence that disciplinary proceedings were warranted. When the front-page story detailing Prescott's arrest broke, the chairman called a special meeting.

"Ladies and gentlemen," he began the conference, "I convened this special meeting because one of our own members is in trouble." He passed around packets containing copies of the newspaper article, the search and arrest warrants issued by Judge Bailey, and the booking information sheet from the Cumberland County Sheriff's Department.

"Most of you I am sure have already heard the sad news about our colleague, Solicitor Malcolm Prescott. Let me give you a moment to read over the documents our staff attorney has collected at my request, so that we'll all be singing from the same page of the hymn book."

The chairman, Edmund Stuart, had served in that capacity for seven years. Quite a long tour of duty for such a thankless job. But each year, when the Chief Justice met with Stuart and made her annual request that he continue his work, there was really only one response: "I'll do it." Edmund Stuart was sixty-five years old, well-respected, and semi-retired from one of the largest corporate law firms in Cumberland County. He had the time, the experience, the guts, and the wisdom to take on the task of chairman.

After five minutes Edmund Stuart asked the committee, "Everyone had time to catch up?"

There was a unanimous affirmative groan. No one relished the unavoidable job of tackling the problem brought about by Prescott's arrest on charges of obstruction of justice. There were a few questions.

"The allegations of misconduct date back thirty years or

so. Isn't there a statute of limitations that comes into play?"

The chairman had already thought about this. "Possibly, Betsy. At least as to the old stuff. But what about the allegation that only a week ago Prescott attempted to destroy evidence critical to the motion for a new trial, his criminal case, and any subsequent grievance proceeding? In my opinion, for what it's worth, all of the old stuff gets bootstrapped into the more recent charge. I'm afraid we're not going to be able to shuck this case on a technicality."

Another member spoke up. "It seems to me the grievance proceeding is not yet ripe. Presumption of innocence, and all that. Once we have the results of the new trial motion in the Purdy case and the Prescott criminal prosecution, we'll know the universe of charges—if any—we are faced with. I think we should bide our time. See what happens. Then take action appropriate to the circumstances."

"I agree, Charles, at least for the most part. The thorny question is, what do we do about the arrest? Can we simply ignore it?" Edmund was groping for help on this final point.

The only African American member of the committee weighed in. "The rule governing this Commission says 'upon conviction,' Edmund, not 'upon arrest.' We don't have jurisdiction to do anything yet. Let the solicitor have his day in court. He has excellent defense counsel assisting him. Then let the chips fall where they may."

Edmund Stuart glanced around the conference table. "You're dead right, Desmond. I agree. Anyone dissent?"

There was unanimous silence.

"All right. The matter is tabled for now. I'll call this Commission back together when the matter is ripe for our consideration. In the interim, if anyone has any additional thoughts, you've got my telephone number. We can convene a meeting via conference call if necessary."

As the members gathered their belongings, Desmond turned to the group. "The newspaper yesterday ran a story about the criminal prosecution against Solicitor Prescott. It was reported that our old friend John Merriman has been appointed Special Prosecutor. Excuse me if I sound disrespectful, but has Judge Bailey taken leave of his senses? I wouldn't have thought Mr. Merriman was up to the task."

Edmund Stuart responded. "You might be surprised, Desmond. I've heard good things through the grapevine about Merriman lately. He might be just the right man for the task—oh, excuse me Betsy. My age is showing. The right person for the task."

"Hm-m-m," Desmond mused. "Well, Edmund, you're closer to the situation in Cumberland County than I am. I just hope you're right. For the sake of our system of justice. As imperfect as it may be, it's the best in the world. I for one would like to keep it that way."

PART FOUR

CHAPTER THIRTY-NINE

Ensconced in a recently renovated building on Seville Row, just off Main Street, the Law Offices of Devon Jennings were less than a block from the courthouse. The building's exterior was clapboard, like so many of the old houses downtown that had been converted into office space, but it gleamed with two sparkling coats of white satin stain. The trim was painted a traditional Charleston green. The Seville Row office stood in stark contrast to the dilapidated old structure on the corner of Northampton and Champagne streets, which Lawyer Merriman inhabited.

The building's refurbished interior was light and bright thanks to the installation of large bay windows on all sides and the tan and mauve hues of wall coverings throughout. The mostly youthful staff were energetic, cheerful, and upbeat folks. The office itself perpetually bustled with lawyers and paralegals running to and fro, frequently treading a path in and out of Jennings' private office. His long-time secretary, Mrs. Otis, also served in the capacities of office manager and gatekeeper for her boss's inner sanctum. Nothing escaped her watchful eye.

Devon Jennings was obsessive when it came to trial preparation. A credo he adopted long ago was that talent and skill would get you nowhere in the courtroom unless you were fully prepared. He worked long hours as a result, and expected the same from the younger lawyers that served him and his clientele. This singular characteristic of the Law Offices of Devon Jennings earned him the respect of both bench and bar.

Judges have a nasty little habit of gossiping privately about the lawyers who appear before them. Whenever Jennings and his firm were the topic, the judiciary's comments were nearly always complimentary. He was intelligent, prepared, hard-working, respectful to the court, and one hell of an advocate for the cause of his client. All of which justified his charging hefty fees. Devon Jennings made a good living.

The criminal defense business was not always pretty. Many a shady character passed through the heavy mahogany door on Seville Row, received top-flight representation, and went on to serve ten, twenty years, even life in prison. Nearly always the clients who were found guilty and sentenced to lengthy terms eventually filed post-conviction relief petitions against Jennings on the ground of ineffective assistance of counsel. What did they have to lose? Typically the court appointed a lawyer free of charge to represent them. It didn't ruffle Jennings. The jailbird tactic came with the territory, and over the years he developed a thick skin. His fee took into consideration the possibility of having to defend a petition in every case he undertook.

In all his career no judge had ever overturned a conviction on the ground that Jennings and his firm were ineffective in their defense of a client. This post-conviction relief hassle was one of several that motivated him to obtain his fee in full, up front. Such an arrangement was perfectly ethical, and well within the bounds of the rules governing the practice of law. Devon Jennings wasn't a hard-boiled cynic, just a realist.

Prescott walked into the Seville Row office for his first appointment a bit apprehensive. He was certain the entire staff must be whispering about his case, delighting in the fact that their boss had been tapped to defend the good solicitor. It would be another high-profile case for the firm. And that meant lots of free publicity. This wasn't the kind of notoriety Prescott craved. Seeing his photograph on the front page of the newspaper in a complete reversal of his established role was sobering. Now he was reduced to seeking counsel—defense counsel, no less—as if he were some common criminal.

The obsequious Mrs. Prescott had done all she could to reassure him, but Prescott knew in his heart of hearts that he had a problem. A big problem. It accounted for his coming out of the closet. He now smoked openly at home. His faith in the God he had created was wavering. His self-righteous confidence was shaken. He was, in short, a broken man.

Judge Bailey held a pretrial conference on Merriman's motion for a new trial in Jake Purdy's case. The court ruled that Mr. Prescott was still the Solicitor for Cumberland County, and therefore would represent the State in that proceeding, over the objection of Merriman.

"Mr. Merriman," the judge declared, "I see no reason at this point why Mr. Prescott should be disqualified. This is not a jury matter. I shall rule on this motion from the bench. If Mr. Prescott is called as a witness, I am perfectly capable of distinguishing his role as advocate from that as witness. And the same applies to you, sir, in the event you are called upon to take the stand."

Merriman glanced down at his legal pad. "Yes, Your Honor."

The judge did grant Prescott's request to permit Devon Jennings to participate pro hac vice as special associate counsel to assist Prescott in opposing the motion for a new trial. Prescott and Jennings both realized that a successful outcome for Merriman on Purdy's motion for a new trial most likely dictated the result in the criminal prosecution against the solicitor. The stage was set for a battle royal.

And so when Prescott appeared, hat in hand, at the desk of Mrs. Otis, there was a trace of new-found humility in his voice. "Good morning, ma'am. The receptionist sent me in your direction. I'm Solicitor Prescott, here to see Mr. Jennings."

"Of course, Mr. Prescott," Mrs. Otis replied in a tone that was at once affable and subservient. "Please have a seat here in the foyer. I'll let Mr. Jennings know you're here." She immediately rose from her desk and entered the inner sanctum. A moment later she returned.

"Mr. Jennings will see you now."

Mrs. Otis opened the maple paneled double doors to Jennings' private office and ushered the solicitor inside. Jennings rose from his desk and warmly greeted his new client, offering him a seat in one of two overstuffed chairs placed at the ends of a beveled glass-topped coffee table.

Jennings liked to put his clients at ease, at least in their first meeting, by avoiding the typical seating arrangement that called for the lawyer to be seated behind an imposing desk separating him from the client. The coffee table arrangement made lawyer and client more like friends—or comrades at least—yoked together in the struggle to solve the problem.

"It's good to see you looking well, Solicitor," Jennings said. "Would you like some coffee?"

"No, thank you, Devon," Prescott replied a bit stiffly. "Your secretary already asked."

"Good. I know this is a difficult time for you," Jennings began. "Let me say in all candor that I have nothing but the utmost respect for you, Malcolm, and it's a privilege to be asked to help you through this." The compliment was only half a lie. Jennings prevaricated on the respect part, but was genuinely flattered to have picked up the case. It represented another feather in his headdress.

The kind words served their purpose of relaxing Solicitor Prescott.

"On second thought, I believe I will take a cup of coffee if you don't mind, Devon." The two were beginning to act like old school chums, addressing each other by their Christian names as if they'd been friends, rather than adversaries, for years.

"Of course, Malcolm." Devon Jennings rose and went to the double doors. He cracked one open and asked Mrs. Otis to fetch some coffee for them both.

The truth was that Jennings personally despised Prescott. Like other criminal defense lawyers, Jennings had always encountered an aloof, uncooperative, and downright arrogant adversary in his dealings with the pompous solicitor. In Jennings' view, there was a place for taking hard, uncompromising positions. And that place was the courtroom. But in the day-in-day-out practice of law, courtesy and cooperation were the lubricants that kept the system running smoothly. And such attributes were wholly lacking in Solicitor Prescott. From that perspective Jennings and Merriman were of the same mind. They had both been on the receiving end of Malcolm T. Prescott's blind pride.

As for Prescott's abilities as an advocate, Jennings rated him capable, but not stellar. He could remember many a case in which he had simply out-lawyered Prescott. There may have been more than a client or two who, although probably guilty as sin, walked free as a result of Jennings' superior litigation talent. Jennings wasn't proud of those cases. But the system of justice presumed that each party's advocate was roughly equivalent in proficiency. If not, there were built-in safeguards to balance any substantial inequalities, such as an impartial judge and the rules of law, procedure, and evidence. But because the system was designed and employed by human beings, by definition it was imperfect. Perfect justice was never guaranteed by the founding fathers. Fairness—or the right to due process and equal protection, as the judges and lawyers described it— was the only protection assured by Lady Liberty's grand instrument we call our Constitution.

Mrs. Otis brought in on a tray a stainless steel coffee pot, a sugar dish, a small pitcher of cream, two spoons, and two ceramic cups. She set the tray in the middle of the coffee table.

"How do you take yours, Solicitor?" she asked Prescott.

"Two sugars and a splash of cream," he replied.

Mrs. Otis fixed Prescott's coffee first, then poured a cup of black coffee for her boss. She quietly left the men to themselves and shut the double doors.

"I've read Merriman's motion for a new trial," Jennings began, taking a sip of his fresh ground coffee. "Seems to me that the Foxworthy affidavit and the request for DNA testing are his big guns.

"Let's take the Foxworthy affidavit first. Correct me if I'm wrong, Malcolm," Jennings invited him, "but my understanding is that, in a criminal case, the prosecutor has the unbridled discretion to accept or reject any evidence tendered to him. In the Purdy case, you exercised your discretion to reject the Foxworthy affidavit."

Prescott made no response.

"I would guess you based your decision on her lack of credibility," Jennings continued. "She was, after all, a kept woman. And the fact that Willis Purdy left her high and dry certainly gave her ample motive to do whatever she could, including lie, to get revenge. I'm sure you never instructed Barrow to destroy the affidavit. He must've misunderstood. He was young and inexperienced. I would imagine you simply told him to lay it aside, to forget it."

Jennings was trying his best to lead Prescott to verbalize these rational conclusions himself. But again the solicitor made no reply.

Undeterred, Jennings carried on.

"As far as the DNA testing is concerned, we don't yet know what the crime lab boys will come up with. But assuming they don't find a match between Jake Purdy's fresh blood sample and the old semen stain, I have no doubt that several experts in the field would be willing to opine that the semen stain on Venus Brown's panties is far too stale to be reliable. This expertise will cost a pretty penny, but it's money well spent, Malcolm. You know that. Juries and judges these days place great reliance on DNA testing. It's as if they consider the results infallible, almost scriptural. We have to discredit the underpinning—the semen sample—in order to convince the court to reject the crime lab's conclusions."

Jennings hoped that between the coffee and his gentle prodding the solicitor would rise to the occasion. After all, there was much at stake here for Malcolm T. Prescott. But he continued to sit mute.

When Jennings was a young pup of a lawyer, he learned the hard way never to ask his client the sixty-four-thousand-dollar question: did you do it? He discovered early on that the wrong answer to that question just made his job all the more difficult. And the right answer was many times almost impossible to swallow. So he developed a style of constructing the most logical and reasonable explanation for his client's innocence. Then he would trot it out and see if it fit. If the client agreed that the spin Jennings put on the evidence was apropos, the defense was settled. Jennings and his team would set about uncovering evidence to support the constructed defense. And the sixty-four-thousand-dollar question never needed to be asked—or answered.

Only rarely did the constructed defense require that Jennings' client testify. Too risky. The judge would instruct the jury that the defendant had the absolute constitutional right not to testify, and the choice not to do so should not—could not—be held against him. That would have to suffice. No doubt the jury in such a case wondered why the defendant didn't voluntarily take the stand and tell them what happened, explain why he was innocent. But they would just have to wonder—and hopefully accept the judge's instruction on that point.

One thing Jennings had already decided. He wasn't about to let the arrogant, high-minded Prescott take the stand in his own defense. The jury would despise him.

Suddenly the solicitor came out of his coma.

"What is your fee going to be?" he asked abruptly.

Jennings drew a deep breath, then expelled it, as if the question bored or irritated him.

"For a case such as yours, where only the criminal charge is involved, my standard fee is thirty-five thousand dollars. That doesn't include the expenses of the expert witnesses. Here, we have not only your criminal case to deal with, but Merriman's motion for a new trial as well. And, of course, we both anticipate a disciplinary proceeding will ensue before the Commission. If I am to assist you in those ancillary proceedings as well, my fee would have to be a minimum of fifty thousand dollars. I estimate the expert witnesses will cost another twenty-five.

"Malcolm, this case is already charged with publicity. It will be tried in the newspaper as well as in the courtroom. That always means more complexity, and more work for me. I believe fifty thousand is a fair and reasonable fee under the circumstances."

Prescott swallowed hard. He had the money tucked away, in a place even his wife didn't know about. He had dreamed of spending it traveling the globe upon his retirement, not paying some defense lawyer to fight these scurrilous charges. He gave no reply.

Jennings was growing tired and frustrated with Prescott's stonewalling. He changed course.

"There is one major element to the case we haven't yet touched upon. My friends at the sheriff's office tell me that Barrow has a videotape that is quite damaging. Something about your removal of a key affidavit from the file. Can you elaborate on this?"

Prescott set down his coffee cup. "Yes. Of course. I've viewed the tape. It's nothing to be concerned about.

"When I received the motion for a new trial, I did what any lawyer would do. I located the old file of the trial of the case and searched through it to refresh my memory. I saw a statement given by the victim I had forgotten about. Rather than take the time to study it in the storage facility, I put it in my pocket and intended to take it home and read it over carefully that evening. If nothing else, it should refresh my memory of the events that occurred so long ago.

"For reasons I cannot fathom, Detective Lieutenant Barrow set up a surveillance camera and videotaped my actions. I should tell you that Mr. Barrow, just days earlier, approached me with the suggestion that I retire from office. I don't know why, but my guess is that he was bitter about the unfortunate result we obtained in the Dabney Peters' case. Surely you read about that fiasco in the newspaper. I rebuffed his impudent suggestion. I can only conclude that he resolved to build a case against me—to force me to retire. The night I was arrested, he offered me the choice of resigning, with a complete expungement of the arrest and charges against me, or face trial. I flatly rejected the former and steadfastly chose the latter."

Jennings leaned back in his chair and tried to process this new information. It certainly aroused suspicion in his mind as to the motivation for Prescott's arrest. But one thing bothered him.

"Why did you take only the victim's statement, and not the whole file? Surely you would want to have the entire file in order to prepare you to oppose the motion for a new trial."

Prescott had anticipated the question. "Purely a matter of procedure. Before my office removes a file from the storage facility we are required to submit a request for it. Then the officer in charge of the evidence room reviews the request, and approves it unless there is some extraordinary circumstance warranting denial of the request. He procures the file for you, and requires you to sign a receipt. This process takes several days. I didn't have the luxury of time to wait on the procedure. It would've taken too long. I was, I guess you'd say, a bit impatient. I readily concede it was a mistake in judgment. But it certainly wasn't a crime."

Jennings wouldn't let it go. "But Malcolm, you still haven't given me a satisfactory answer as to why you took only the statement of Venus Brown Purdy. Was a copy of that document furnished to defense counsel before the trial? Surely Merriman had the right to obtain it in his defense of Jake Purdy."

Prescott cleared his throat. "I don't believe it was ever furnished to the defense, Devon." His face reddened.

"I see," Jennings replied. "Did the statement contain any exculpatory evidence?"

There was a lengthy silence. Jennings sipped the last of his black coffee as he waited for the response.

"I'm afraid one could interpret a portion of it that way."

"Hm-m-m. That's a bit of a dilemma, isn't it, Malcolm?"

"Yes, Devon." Prescott squirmed a bit in his overstuffed chair. "I suppose it is."

"Well," Jennings said as he rose from his chair, "I believe we've covered as much as I can absorb and process for one day. Let's meet again next Monday. Mrs. Otis can schedule the appointment when you leave. The hearing on the motion for a new trial is two weeks away. It's time to plot strategy."

Prescott stood, a bit shaky. He craved a cigarette. "Devon, I want you to take the lead in opposing the motion. Of course I'll participate. But I would rather you take first chair." He paused, steadying himself. "You'll have my check for fifty thousand in the morning."

CHAPTER FORTY

Elizabeth Flenniken Barrow was a good soul. She attended mass from time to time, prayed regularly for Mikey, and tried to do good deeds. Most elections she pulled the lever voting the straight Democratic Party ticket. She knew this meant a vote for such abominable things as a woman's right to choose—abortion, the Church called it—but on most social issues this good soul aligned herself with the party platform. For the occasional sin she was penitent.

Mikey did not vote. At least, not since John F. Kennedy ran for president. "It's a waste of time, Lizzie," he told her. "The wheels of government grind on just the same whether George W. or Al Gore wins." Lizzie didn't believe him, but it wasn't worth arguing about. She simply went to her precinct on election day and pulled the lever.

She was worried about her man. The pressure on him had been intense lately. Dealing with Merriman was bad enough. But fighting Prescott and Jennings seemed at times insurmountable. Lizzie was proud of him, though. He had gambled on Prescott attempting to purloin Venus' statement, and his instincts proved correct. He was all over the news. Mostly, his pat response to the reporters' questions was, "No comment," but that made the whole affair all the more mysterious. And the reporters all the more curious.

On the day Prescott met with Jennings on Seville Row, Barrow spent most of the afternoon in Merriman's dismal Champagne Street quarters strategizing. It was a profitable session. Merriman's head was clear for a change, and the sly old fox had mapped out a pretty good flow chart of how to proceed with the motion for a new trial.

"If we could just persuade Jake to come to the courtroom," Merriman remarked, "even if all he did was sit at counsel table. His presence would evoke some sympathy. And he could at least give the appearance of a righteously indignant innocent man." Merriman stubbed out his cigarette and turned to Barrow. "Any suggestions?"

"Maybe," Barrow replied. "Let's send Lizzie back to talk to Nellie. Perhaps she can persuade the old girl to pay Jake a visit. Convince him to come."

Merriman leaned back in his chair and thought it over. "All right. It's worth a try. I'll wait to hear from you."

That night Mikey Barrow came home exhausted. After depositing his wad of tobacco slush in the trash can, he went straight to the fridge and grabbed his first bottle of Guinness.

"Lizzie!" he hollered as he popped off the cap. "Where in the world are you?"

"Where do you think, Mikey?" she hollered back. "Where I always am this time of night. In the wash room scrubbing your grimy collars and doing the laundry."

Mikey made straight for his Naugahyde La-Z-Boy and crashed in it. He sipped the cold, dark brew and waited patiently for Lizzie to join him. By the time Lizzie came downstairs he was beginning to relax a little.

"What's for supper, dearie?" he asked.

"Pot roast," she replied. Lizzie could read the exhaustion in her husband's face. "How was your day?"

"Long. But interesting. Merriman's not the slouch I always pegged him to be. He has a sharp legal mind, particularly when he's sober. I suppose that accounts for his brilliant defense in the Dabney Peters' case." He took a long pull on the Guinness. They sat in silence for a moment.

"We have a mission for you, Liz. That is, of course, if you're willing."

Her eyes lit up. She suddenly had a vision of Venice, of them winding their way through the canals of the old city in a gondola. Then she envisioned them aboard a cruise ship, sipping fruit-laden alcoholic beverages in chaise lounges on the ship's deck, somewhere far away in the clear blue and green waters of the Caribbean.

"What is it you want me to do, Mikey?"

"Let me fetch my other Guinness, Liz. Then I'll explain."

At first Lizzie was hesitant. She had invaded Nellie's

space once before, and she felt uncomfortable doing it again.

"Do you think Nellie really wants Jake to come home, Liz?"

"I have no doubt about that, Mikey."

Barrow sipped his second Guinness and pondered Merriman's strategy. There was something the old fox had up his sleeve that he wasn't telling anyone, including the detective lieutenant, about. Ah, well, he thought, that's the lawyer's business. Not mine. His thoughts returned to Nellie.

"I can tell you this, Liz. Jake Purdy is afraid. Afraid to come home. Afraid of what he'll find awaiting him after so many years in the Big House. Merriman tells me he's comfortable there now. He's a trusty. His life is a monotonous but safe routine. He's not afraid there anymore."

Lizzie spoke quickly. "It's absurd, Mikey. Nellie still loves him. I can tell. Even after all the years, and all the pain. Jake would find safe haven there with Nellie. God knows, it has to be better than prison. Can't he see that?"

Mikey seized his opportunity. "Not without Nellie opening his eyes to it, Liz."

Liz gazed deep into her husband's eyes. "Are you convinced that Jake Purdy is an innocent man, Mikey?"

"I am, Liz."

"Do you swear it, Mikey? On your mother's grave?"

Barrow took a final draft of the stout and set the bottle down on the table beside him. He thought of Miss Foxworthy, and of the description Venus had given him and Prescott of her assailant. He pictured the solicitor, videotaped as he slipped Venus' statement out of the file and into his coat pocket. Then he remembered the look on Prescott's face as he viewed the video in Barrow's office.

"I swear it, Lizzie. On my mother's grave."

"Then I'll go," she answered. "First thing in the morning."

CHAPTER FORTY-ONE

Leland lay quietly in her spot under the butcher's block. Keenly observant, the Jack Russell sensed that today was an important milestone in their lives. Perhaps she might take another ride in the Clipper.

Merriman stirred nervously about the kitchen, waiting for the coffee to brew.

"Damn Steve Fairchild," he cursed aloud. "I've been a good boy long enough." He hadn't taken a drink in weeks. And he smoked only at the office. He knew May would have his head if he lit up in front of her.

He continued his schoolboy soliloquy. "When this trial is over, May and I shall surely celebrate. She deserves it as much as I do. We might even invite Barrow and his wife."

The motion for a new trial was scheduled to begin at nine-thirty. It was seven-fifteen.

"May!" he yelled up the stairs of their Station Avenue townhouse. "We have to get moving. All of my papers are at the office." It was pouring rain outside.

"Hush, John," came her calm reply. "You have plenty of time. I'll drive you there and then on to the courthouse." He would have tapped along the sidewalks with the assistance of his gold-headed cane, as usual, but the rain and the heft of his briefcase prevented it.

Merriman grumbled under his breath and continued to fidget. Finally the coffee was ready. He poured a generous amount into a mug and sat at the breakfast table. The raindrops blew against the kitchen window and then ran down the panes like little rivulets searching for the mother stream.

Late last evening, after Barrow had checked with him by telephone on the final arrangements, Merriman prepared a list of the main points to be presented. He removed it from his shirt pocket and set it on the table. The after-discovered Foxworthy affidavit, the concealed statement of Venus

Brown Purdy, the DNA test results, and the dénouement—the videotape of Prescott purloining the undisclosed, exculpatory statement of the victim. Lastly, Merriman had written an item at the bottom of the list: "Surprise." He was not at all sure his surprise would materialize. If not, he was confident that he had enough evidence to warrant a new trial. But if his surprise came to pass, it would surely drive the final nail into the coffin of Solicitor Malcolm T. Prescott.

Arrangements were made with prison officials to transport Jake Purdy to the courtroom. Merriman envisioned him dressed in his prison fatigues, handcuffed and shackled, seated next to him at counsel table. Nellie reported the result of her meeting with Jake through Lizzie. It had gone reasonably well, she thought, but the meeting had been difficult for them both. Nellie could give no firm assurance that he would come to the hearing.

Leland got her wish. May threw the pup into the front seat of the Packard, where she assumed her *Winged Flight* position with front paws on the dash. Merriman sat in the back seat, just as Brocadia had done so many times during her Sunday visits before the crash.

They sped across town to the corner of Champagne and Northampton. Wife and dog waited patiently in the car, parked illegally at the curb, while Merriman fumbled with the key and finally entered the office. May stared at the pathetic sign affixed to the brick wall to the right of the office door. "John Merriman," it read. "Attorney at the Law." The wooden shingle was cracked and the paint was faded and worn, but the lettering was still legible. May considered having a new sign made for a surprise, but upon reflection she changed her mind.

"It suits him, I suppose," she said to Leland, who nodded in apparent agreement.

When they reached the courthouse, Merriman leaned forward toward the front seat.

"May," he said. "I don't want you to come inside. You'll only make me nervous. Take this damnable dog and go home. Engage in your normal routine. I'll use this contraption of a cell phone you gave me to call you after it's over. Whatever happens, we have a date for tonight. Eight o'clock. The Gloucester. I know it's not grand, but it's our spot, May. We may even rent a room for the night in the Bonnie Prince Charlie."

He alighted from the car, grasped his old briefcase, and tapped over to the driver's window. Rain was still falling. He didn't care. May rolled down the window, wondering. He leaned inside the car and kissed her on the lips. It was a tender kiss, brimming with emotion. Stunned, all May could do was smile.

"Good luck, John," she said, her eyes beginning to moisten. And then she and Leland drove away.

CHAPTER FORTY-TWO

The courtroom was packed. While Jennings and his minions scurried about the solicitor's table, Prescott sat stoically, like some grand emperor. He was attired in his white linen suit. Plug in place, Barrow selected a perch behind the defense table. The detective lieutenant was a bit uncomfortable on that side of the aisle. Normally he would be seated behind Solicitor Prescott. He flipped through the pages of the morning *Tribune*, pretending to be unaffected by the intensity of the moment.

The gallery was abuzz with curiosity-seekers of every stripe—members of the local bar, interested citizens, law enforcement officers, courthouse personnel, and a bevy of journalists and reporters. There was even a sketch artist. Judge Bailey disallowed cameras or recorders in the courtroom. Several academic types were scattered among the crowd, no doubt the expert witnesses Jennings and Merriman had employed to testify on the reliability of the DNA testing.

The scene reminded Merriman of the original trial of State versus Jake Purdy. The sly old fox surveyed the noisy crowd, then tapped his way down the aisle and took his seat at the defense table. His long dark locks were damp and disheveled. He set his gold-headed walking stick on the floor beside him and opened his briefcase. He laid out his papers in his own orderly fashion. Then he reached in his shirt pocket and retrieved the summary list he had gone over at the breakfast table earlier that morning. He perused it again.

A few minutes before nine-thirty, two officers from Killough Correctional Facility entered the courtroom through a rear door with Jake Purdy in tow. He was dressed in ordinary street clothes. Nellie had purchased them at Wal-Mart the day before. The officers didn't bother with handcuffs or shackles. Jake was, after all, a trusty. And they knew he was a harmless old duffer. Escape from the courtroom was unthinkable. The officers escorted him to an empty chair at the defense table beside Merriman and took their seats behind Jake, next to Barrow.

Merriman turned and gazed at Jake Purdy. His client's eyes flickered a little. Merriman wasn't sure whether they signaled hope or fear.

"Good morning, Jake," Merriman said in greeting. "I'm glad you decided to attend. Nellie's here." He threw a glance in her direction. "She took a seat in the back."

Jake nodded, but made no verbal reply. The shock of his return to the courtroom—and the world—was overwhelming.

At nine-thirty sharp Judge Bailey entered the courtroom through the door to his chambers. A hush came over the gallery. The bailiff cried, "All rise. Hear ye, hear ye! Persons having matters of business with the Court of General Sessions for Cumberland County, draw near. Judge Oliver Thornwell Bailey presiding. God bless this great state, and this honorable court."

Merriman hadn't heard the traditional cry of the bailiff officially opening a session of court in many years. The bailiff's cry was an anachronism now, a relic of the past. Judge Bailey must have instructed the bailiff to resurrect the solemn announcement. It was a portent to Merriman, a sign that the old jurist considered this matter to be of great significance.

"Be seated," the judge allowed after taking the bench. His desk was littered with motions, briefs and law books. He fumbled through the papers for a moment, located a document setting forth the caption of the case, and slipped his gold-rimmed spectacles onto the bridge of his nose. The metal arms of the antique eyeglasses curved at the ends, securing the spectacles nearly completely around the backs of his ears. A black nylon strand was attached to each end of the arms, allowing the judge to remove the reading glasses when he didn't need them and let them dangle around his neck, coming to rest below his Adam's apple.

"The matter before the court is the case of State versus Jake Purdy, Criminal Action number 76-481. Mr. Merriman, the court will hear your motion for a new trial now."

Before Merriman could grasp his cane and stand to address the court, Devon Jennings was on his feet.

"Your Honor, as you know, the court has appointed me Special Counsel to assist Mr. Prescott in this hearing. Before we begin I have several motions *in limine* to take up. These motions were filed this morning. I have just handed Mr. Merriman and Mr. Purdy copies. We'd like to have those preliminary motions heard first. They may well be dispositive of Mr. Merriman's motion for a new trial."

Judge Bailey removed his spectacles and slammed the palm of his right hand down on the bench.

"Mr. Jennings," he replied sternly, "I have nothing but the highest respect for you. But to file these motions the morning of trial, when neither defense counsel nor the court has had the opportunity to study them, is unfair, untimely, and prejudicial. You've had two weeks to get your ducks in a row, so to speak, and file these motions in an orderly manner. The court will not delay these proceedings. Your motions are denied, without prejudice to their substance, at this time. I'm quite sure you'll find an opportunity to make your arguments as we proceed with the motion for a new trial."

Merriman, who had been poised to object, curled his lips in a faint smile.

A slow burn made its way up Prescott's throat and onto his florid cheeks. He yearned to be in control.

"All right," Judge Oliver Thornwell Bailey continued. "Let me hear from you, Mr. Merriman."

Merriman gathered his gold-headed cane and his summary list of items and approached the podium. He feigned a slight, painful-appearing limp as he tapped his way there. A stillness pervaded the crowded courtroom.

"May it please the court," he began respectfully. "Today we celebrate the triumph of our system of justice and the rule of law. This morning we come before you as ordinary folk seeking something extraordinary—the reversal of a jury's verdict delivered decades ago, here in this very courtroom, and the entry of an order by this court righting a wrong. A wrong that convicted an innocent man—Jake Purdy—and catapulted him headlong into the penal system of this state."

Merriman was on top of his game—in the zone, so to speak. His rich and mellifluous baritone, delivered in his stentorian best, captured the attention of all who were present. The weeks he had abstained from pummeling his throat and vocal cords with scotch whiskey had paid off. Not only was his mind sharp and clear, but his voice was strong and deliberate. Dr. Fairchild would be proud.

"We have filed with this court—timely, I might add—an extensive memorandum with supporting affidavits setting forth the reasons why we ask Your Honor to grant the extraordinary relief we seek." Merriman was proud of the papers he had filed. Each one had been written by the sly old fox himself.

"Allow me to summarize those points."

"Proceed, Mr. Merriman," the old jurist growled.

"Thank you, Your Honor." For the occasion Merriman adopted a tone of humility, which came neither easily nor naturally for him. He was accustomed to playing the street fighter.

"First, we have the affidavit of Janelle Foxworthy. As the court knows, this affidavit is after-discovered evidence. Detective Lieutenant Barrow has submitted an affidavit to that effect, and is here to testify if the court deems it necessary."

Devon Jennings, Esquire, rose to address the point. He was wearing his most expensive dark blue suit, a hand-tailored white dress shirt with gold cufflinks, and a subdued burgundy silk tie. He exuded confidence and success.

"Your Honor please," he began, "the State will insist that Mr. Barrow testify. We can't cross-examine his affidavit, but we certainly look forward to the opportunity to confront this man on a number of issues raised by this so-called after-discovered evidence."

"Noted, Mr. Jennings." The judge paused briefly, reflecting on Devon's demeanor, then added, "The State may insist, as you put it, on any number of things, counselor. But have no doubt that this court shall be at the helm of these proceedings, Mr. Jennings. Not the State—nor the defense either. Bear that in mind as we go forward." He turned to the defense. "You may continue, Mr. Merriman."

Judge Bailey's firm, gentlemanly reminder that he was in charge of the courtroom was not lost on Lawyer Jennings. He had tried many cases before His Honor, and understood full well that Judge Bailey would not be pushed around. Devon had witnessed more than one cocky out-of-state lawyer have his head handed to him by the crusty old jurist when the lawyer attempted to wrest control over Judge Bailey's fiefdom.

Jennings took his seat, sufficiently chastened. Prescott's respiration rate increased by seven.

Merriman carried on, unflustered by the interruption. "The Foxworthy affidavit unequivocally establishes that Willis Purdy committed the crime for which his son, Jake Purdy, stands convicted. I shall not defile this court's record by reading the depraved, perverted statements made by Willis Purdy to Miss Foxworthy—statements by which he openly and shamelessly confesses his culpability for the abhorrent crime committed against Miss Brown—reputedly his own daughter! The court has the affidavit."

Jennings jumped to his feet.

"Object, Your Honor!" he boomed with an attitude of righteous indignation. "Mr. Merriman is testifying now. His characterizations of these drunken ravings of a delirious man are, number one, pure hearsay, and number two, inappropriate argument on a motion to the court. This isn't the time for passionate closing arguments to a jury. This is the place for rational and deliberate discussion of the factual and legal issues in play."

Prescott's pulse rate increased by ten. Merriman remained calm.

Judge Bailey exhaled a long sigh and leaned back in his chair. "Noted, Mr. Jennings. And overruled. You may proceed, Mr. Merriman."

Merriman cleared his throat and picked up the thread of his argument.

"My point, Your Honor, if I may go there, is simply this. The Foxworthy affidavit was a vital piece of evidence. Solicitor Prescott not only failed to take it into consideration in his pursuit of the truth, which we all agree should have been the cornerstone of the prosecution of my client—or any other person charged with a crime, for that matter—but he deliberately and intentionally ordered Mr. Barrow to destroy this exculpatory statement.

"Of course it should have been turned over to the defense. I never knew it even existed. It's a blatant violation of Rule 6, Your Honor. And a clear obstruction of justice. Had we known that Janelle Foxworthy summoned the courage to come forward and give this sworn statement, her testimony at the trial could have substantially affected the outcome."

Prescott crossed his legs and turned his silvery profile to the court. A slight wrinkle, an imperfection, in his trousers was exposed. His ordinarily stone-cold heart burned with malice toward Barrow and Merriman.

"That's number one, Your Honor." Merriman glanced at his summary list of points.

"Number two. The sworn statement of Venus Brown Purdy, the victim herself. Here, Your Honor, continues the skillful weaving by the prosecution of a tangled web of deceit—a web in which the spider, and not the fly, ultimately found itself trapped. The silky strands of that deceitful web are criss-crossed ever tighter by the recent actions of Solicitor Prescott, culminating in his arrest. We shall get to that point in due course."

"Object," Jennings interrupted, starting to stand.

Before Devon could rise, the judge snarled, "Overruled. Sit down, Mr. Jennings, and be patient. Your time will come. And you may rest assured that, when it does, this court will operate on a level playing field. I predict you will inject your own brand of melodrama into your argument as well. I am accustomed to lawyers doing that. It doesn't sway me from the truth. Let me remind you both: I have no friends to reward, no enemies to punish. The court has but one goal—that justice be served."

Prescott flinched slightly, almost unnoticeably to the untrained eye, but Merriman's eye was trained—and he took note. Otherwise the solicitor sat still and dumb as a statue, at the very table from which he had delivered his own fiery sermonettes so many times throughout his career. His lustrous, silver mane was perfectly coiffured. His posture was stiff and straight as an arrow. His attire, with the exception of the slight wrinkle in his trousers, was spotless and impeccable. At his feet lay an oversized black umbrella he had remembered to carry earlier that morning. It served its purpose in keeping his hair dry and his linen suit protected from the onslaught of inclement weather.

Merriman proceeded. "The import of that statement, Your Honor, is that Venus Brown Purdy gave a description of her assailant to the solicitor—and to Mr. Barrow, who was in charge of law enforcement's investigation of this crime.

"She described her attacker in details that any reasonable juror could see did not match the appearance of the defendant, Jake Purdy. Jake was a young man, Your Honor, when this crime was committed. His wife, Nellie, is prepared to testify this morning on that very point. We have submitted her affidavit already. Jake was, in her words, a smooth-complexioned, handsome young man."

"Object!" again came Jennings.

"Overruled," rejoined the judge, with perfect equanimity. "I am perfectly capable, Mr. Jennings, of distinguishing argument from evidence. And I have read with some care the affidavits submitted by both sides. Proceed, Mr. Merriman."

"And Your Honor, the point to be made here," continued Merriman, plodding steadfastly along, "is that Mr. Prescott secreted that sworn statement, knowing that the description it contained of the assailant was exculpatory. Once again, his failure to turn that statement over to the defense was a gross violation of Rule 6 of our Rules of Criminal Procedure, not to mention the due process clause of the Constitution of the United States."

"All right," Judge Bailey interjected. "What else, Mr. Merriman? It's after ten-thirty and the court reporter will need a break shortly."

"I can finish my next point very quickly, Your Honor."

"Take your time, Mr. Merriman. I'm not rushing you, and I shall give Mr. Jennings all the time I feel he needs as well. Let's hear your next point, then, and we'll recess afterwards."

"Thank you, Your Honor," Merriman replied.

"Point number three. As the court knows, the Law Enforcement Division lab has conducted certain DNA analysis. There was a semen stain on the panties of the victim, which has been meticulously preserved by LED. At the original trial the forensic evidence only matched the blood type found in the semen to Mr. Purdy's blood sample. There was no DNA testing available in our lab at that time. As the court knows, millions of people share Mr. Purdy's O positive blood type.

"My client has submitted not one, but two blood samples in the course of this matter. The first sample was taken by court order when Mr. Purdy was arrested—before the original trial. The second sample is fresh, having been voluntarily given by Mr. Purdy less than three weeks ago. The supervision of the procedure, including chain of custody of the second sample, was overseen by Detective Lieutenant Barrow. He, his officers, and the lady and gentlemen from LED's laboratory are present and prepared to testify today. Of course, the sum and substance of their testimony has already been presented to the court by affidavit.

"The lab boys—uh, excuse me, Your Honor. My age is beginning to show. The persons from the LED lab have concluded to a reasonable degree of scientific certainty that the DNA contained in the semen does not—repeat, does not—match the DNA of Jake Purdy found in both of his blood samples. This evidence alone, Your Honor, is sufficient grounds for this court to grant a new trial—or set the man free."

"I have your point noted, Mr. Merriman. Anything further on that one at this time?"

"No, sir," Merriman replied.

"Very good. Gentlemen," the judge said, addressing the lawyers, "let's take a ten minute break. When we return I will expect Mr. Merriman to wrap up. Then we'll hear from you, Mr. Jennings. I anticipate you have a few arguments you would like to advance in opposition to this motion."

A titter wafted through the gallery. It served to melt away, if only for the moment, the palpable tension that was present in the courtroom.

Jennings stood. "I do, Your Honor."

"I look forward to hearing you," Judge Bailey said, rapping his gavel. "This court stands in recess."

"All rise," the bailiff intoned, as the judge made his way back to his chambers.

The representatives from the news media rushed into the hallway and punched the speed dials set up on their cell phones, racing to see whose advance to their respective editors would be the first to make the midday news reports.

CHAPTER FORTY-THREE

During the break Detective Lieutenant Michael O'Shea Barrow positioned a large screen television with built-in videotape player so that the judge and the lawyers, and the audience for that matter, would have an unobstructed view. He loaded the tape, rewound it, and showed Merriman how to operate the remote control. He had never operated a VCR in his life.

"When you're ready to show it," Barrow instructed, "simply press 'play' and it should start. When the video is finished, just hit 'stop' and that should turn off the machine. I'll come to your aid if any technical problems crop up." He returned to his seat and his newspaper and sucked quietly on his plug. Just then he heard Prescott signal to him, "Ps-s-s-t! Barrow!"

The detective lieutenant hesitated, then walked over to where Prescott was seated. Jennings and his staff were outside the courtroom, huddled in a conference in the hallway. Merriman was fiddling with the remote control. Barrow crouched down to Prescott's eye level.

Prescott leaned toward him. "You bastard," the solicitor hissed into his ear. A light spray of spittle flecked across Barrow's cheek. "I'll get you for this. Mark my words." The solicitor's normally florid cheeks burned bright red with anger. The blood vessels in his neck stood erect, pulsating with pressure.

It had been quite a while since Barrow had experienced the emotion, but as he gazed into Prescott's bloodshot eyes, his heart filled with compassion. He withdrew his handkerchief from the inside pocket of his jacket and wiped the spittle off his cheek. Then he leaned forward, nearly touching Prescott's face. Barrow could smell the pungent odor of the solicitor's bitter breath in his nostrils.

"I pity you, Prescott. Your pride has swallowed your capacity to reason. Think now, man. My offer still stands.

Resign and be done with this. For the sake of your children, if nothing else."

Just then Devon Jennings and his troops returned to the courtroom. Barrow stood. His eyes met Prescott's for a second, and then he turned away and saw Merriman, standing ready at the podium. In that little window of time as their eyes met, Barrow caught a glimpse deep into Prescott's very soul. Like a boy peering down a dark, forbidden well Barrow shuddered, for all inside seemed empty and dead.

"All rise!" ordered the bailiff as Judge Bailey strode toward the steps leading to the elevated bench.

"Are you ready to proceed, Mr. Merriman?" the judge inquired, taking his seat.

"I am, Your Honor."

Merriman's argument set the stage nicely for the videotape. Over the vigorous objection of Devon Jennings, he explained the rationale for obtaining the warrant to install the surveillance camera, and the suspected motivation of the solicitor to remove, and possibly destroy, the statement of Venus Brown Purdy. Of course Judge Bailey was intimately familiar with all this, having issued the warrant himself, but the record had to be made. If the judge's ruling were appealed by either side, the appellate court would require a complete record.

"At this time, Your Honor, I would like to play the videotape, which was filed with the court along with the affidavit of Detective Lieutenant Barrow."

"Any objection, Mr. Jennings?"

Jennings conferred for a moment with one of his associates. "Your Honor, nothing more than we have already stated as to this entire issue. We believe the actions of the solicitor in retrieving a document from the file of the original trial are absolutely irrelevant and highly prejudicial. That would include the introduction of this videotape. We further believe it is perfectly natural to expect the solicitor to collect documents from the file, when faced with a motion for a new trial—especially in a case as old as this one is. Memories do fade.

"We don't question the authenticity of the tape, but just how or why it could have any relevance to the motion for a new trial is beyond me. I can find no support for it in the rules of evidence."

It was, indeed, a close evidentiary call for the judge. No small amount of his research in preparation for the hearing had been spent on the admissibility of the solicitor's secretive procurement of the victim's statement. In the final analysis, the judge decided the night before the hearing that it was probative on the issue of the solicitor's alleged obstruction of justice, one of several grounds advanced by Merriman in support of the motion.

In his memorandum to the court Jennings put forth his constructed, but unconfirmed, explanation that the solicitor had simply forgotten about the statement in the heat of a very high profile case. Venus intended to testify at the trial, Jennings argued, and in fact she did so. Solicitor Prescott merely placed the statement in the file, concentrated on preparing Venus to testify at trial, and allowed the statement to slip his mind. Or so went the theory advanced by Devon Jennings and company. When Jennings ran the theory by Prescott before filing the brief, he sat mute, as usual, neither adopting nor rejecting his lawyer's seemingly plausible explanation.

The judge turned to Merriman. "Anything further you wish to add, Mr. Merriman?"

Throughout the night before the hearing, as Merriman paced the floor and rehearsed his arguments, he worried over this part of his case. Certainly it was the essential evidence in the upcoming criminal prosecution of Prescott. There would be no problem with its admissibility then. It was proof of his continuing effort to obstruct justice, the very charge for which Prescott stood accused. And a conviction for obstruction of justice was the cornerstone of a grievance proceeding before the Commission on Character and Fitness. The question now was whether it tended to prove or disprove any issue pertinent to the motion for a new trial—in other words, was it relevant?

But another thought had sprung to Merriman's mind as he paced the floor overnight.

"Yes, Your Honor. Two final points on relevance."

Prescott twitched. Jennings and his associates paid close attention, wondering what the sly old fox had up his sleeve.

"First, Your Honor, we contend that the solicitor obstructed justice during the original proceedings against Mr. Purdy by ordering the destruction of the Foxworthy affidavit and by failing to turn over the exculpatory statement of the victim. His recent conduct in attempting to remove and, by inference, destroy the victim's statement is further evidence of his continuing effort to obstruct justice. That makes it relevant."

Prescott, who was seated next to Jennings, started to rise in his own defense. Jennings, a former college linebacker, extended his arm across Prescott's chest to restrain him. "Sit down, Malcolm," he whispered to his client. "Let me handle this." The solicitor bristled, but obeyed.

"Yes, yes, Mr. Merriman. I know that's your position," the judge replied impatiently. "I've read your brief."

So far Jennings had heard nothing particularly new or nettlesome. More succinctly stated, maybe, but not a new argument. The introduction of the video was the very issue he was banking on to save him on appeal, in case the judge granted the motion for a new trial. He glanced at Prescott, and thought he noticed a bead of perspiration forming on his upper lip.

Then Merriman dropped his little bombshell.

"Second, Your Honor, and this is critical," Merriman emphasized as he tapped his way from behind the podium and approached the bench. He was speaking extemporaneously now.

"The actions of Solicitor Prescott in secretly—or so he thought—removing the victim's statement from the file, completely discredit the argument of his counsel that he simply long ago forgot about the existence of the statement. Excusable neglect, they contend, perfectly understandable in the heat of such a battle. Unfortunate, even careless, they concede. But not an adequate legal ground for the granting of a new trial.

"Hogwash. If their contention were true, and the solicitor truly forgot about the statement three decades ago, why did he suddenly remember, go straightaway to the storage facility three weeks ago, immediately after being served with the motion for a new trial, and purloin the very statement he purportedly forgot all about? Was he struck by a bolt from the blue?

"Nothing in my papers tipped him off that the victim's statement was to be an issue in the motion for a new trial. If Solicitor Prescott experienced a great awakening as to the existence, and significance, of the old statement, why did he bypass routine procedures and proceed in secret, all alone and without any notice to anyone, to retrieve only that one document from the file in the storage warehouse?

"I'll venture to say why. It was because Solicitor Prescott knew from the very beginning that the statement Venus Brown Purdy gave the prosecution undermined his case against Jake Purdy. A case that brought him fame and, more than that, security in his re-election for years to come. And so he stashed it away. Detective Lieutenant Barrow was wet behind the ears. He wouldn't be any the wiser. After all, it's the solicitor, not the investigator, who is duty-bound to turn over any exculpatory evidence to the defense.

"I submit that Solicitor Prescott succumbed to the siren calls of the evil twins—unrestrained ambition and blind pride. Sin was already crouching at his door, ready to pounce during a moment of weakness."

Jennings rose to object.

"Tone down the histrionics, Mr. Merriman," Judge Bailey cautioned him before Jennings could speak. "There is no jury here."

"Yes, Your Honor." Merriman turned to observe Prescott, his mottled scarlet face covered with beads of perspiration, rigid and stoic but struggling inwardly to retain control of his fury. Merriman's fiery darts had found their marks.

Merriman continued. "When he received my motion,

Malcolm T. Prescott knew that if Venus' statement suddenly turned up in the dusty old file of State versus Jake Purdy, it would spread like a cancer throughout his otherwise unblemished career. And so he resolved to venture out to the storage warehouse alone, and secretly remove the one piece of evidence he thought still existed that might torpedo his renowned conviction of Jake Purdy by an all-white jury for the brutal rape of a Negro girl—a conviction that made Solicitor Prescott a hero in the eyes of the liberal press and a poster child for the so-called New South.

"I believe the videotape speaks, as they say, volumes on the question of the good solicitor's motive and intent—intent to obstruct justice and motive to destroy the evidence of his original malfeasance. In so doing he committed a crime. And that's why this whole issue, including the videotape, is relevant to these proceedings."

There was a tense moment of silence. Jennings placed a firm, restraining hand on Prescott's knee. In so doing he detected a slight tremor. Merriman quietly tapped back to the podium and waited. Then the judge ruled.

"I agree, Mr. Merriman. The evidence is relevant to these proceedings. Play the videotape."

The images of Prescott on the tape were shocking. Seeing him warily flip through the file, locate the blue-backed statement and remove it, was like opening a window into his devious mind. Merriman hadn't noticed when he first reviewed the tape in Barrow's office, but this go-round he observed Prescott cock his head from one side to the other, obviously surveying the premises to assure himself that no one was watching. Then he folded the statement, placed it inside his jacket pocket, and returned the remainder of the file to its storage container. The videotape was as damning a piece of evidence as Merriman had ever encountered. He pushed the "stop" button on the remote and tapped over to his seat.

The only sound to be heard in the ornate old courtroom was the furious scribbling of notes by the reporters and journalists.

"Anything further, Mr. Merriman?" Judge Bailey asked.

Merriman turned to the gallery and searched the crowd carefully, as if he were trying to locate a key witness. Barrow and all of his law enforcement people were present and ready, as were the crime lab technicians. Merriman's DNA expert sat unobtrusively in the rear corner.

Merriman cleared his throat and addressed the court. "Your Honor, I believe the defense has presented overwhelming evidence to support the granting of a new trial." Merriman paused, glancing at Prescott. "However, Mr. Jennings has indicated that he intends to put witnesses on the stand. I would like to reserve the right to offer testimony in reply. With that stipulation, the defense rests."

Judge Bailey removed his spectacles, allowing them to hang loose on the black nylon cord about his neck. "Very well. Mr. Jennings, the ball is in your court." Judge Bailey was a sports enthusiast.

CHAPTER FORTY-FOUR

May sped to the Station Avenue townhouse and parked the Packard Clipper at the curb. She snapped the leash onto Leland's collar and took her straight inside.

"In your spot!" she ordered. "And stay there. I'll be back."

The little yapper comprehended the tone of voice of her mistress and chose to obey. Her outpost under the butcher's block consisted of a foam rubber, oval-shaped pillow on whose patriotic red-, white-, and blue-striped cotton cover was stitched the inscription, "The Queen Sleeps Here." Quite true.

May checked Leland's supply of food and water, which was ample, and left the beast to her own diversions. She returned to the courthouse. After her encounter with the obese Harritt and his sidekick Dunleavy early in her marriage, May made it a rule never to come to court to observe Merriman in action. She preferred to imagine. But today was different. Her intuition told her that her husband needed her presence today.

This case was not some routine fender-bender or petty criminal matter. It was John Merriman's opportunity to redeem himself, to show Malcolm Prescott and Judge Bailey and Devon Jennings what it meant to be a lawyer, to discard his image as a shyster, and to assume a position of respect among the members of the Cumberland County Bar. May would be there.

Even though the sky was ominous and dark as slate, with not even a hint of sun, May wore her sunglasses as a cover. When she entered the courtroom Merriman had just begun his argument. She spied an empty seat in the back, next to Nellie. May recognized her immediately. They had met during the course of the original trial. On the other side of Nellie was a woman May didn't recognize. She was holding Nellie's hand. When May took her seat Nellie glanced over at her.

"Hello, Nellie," May whispered. "How are you holding up?"

Nellie squinted at her. "Who are you?"

May realized her sunglasses were the problem. She removed them and smiled. "I'm May Merriman, Nellie."

Nellie's creased, wizened face brightened. "Of course you are! I remember you. I'm glad you're here."

Just then Liz, who overheard the women's exchange, turned to May and said, "I'm Lizzie Barrow. Mike's wife."

May reached over Nellie's lap and squeezed Lizzie's hand. "I suppose we're in this together, the three of us. I'm proud to be counted among you ladies."

Lizzie smiled. "The Three Musketeers, we are. Feminine version."

The musketeers unsuccessfully stifled a giggle.

A serious-minded man in the row in front of them turned and shushed them. "Quiet, please. I'm trying to take accurate notes."

May could see Prescott seated at the prosecution table, dressed in white linen, stiff and proud and ridiculous, like some cigar store Indian. She didn't know Jennings, but by reputation she recognized him from his expensive habiliment and impressive demeanor. "He doesn't come cheap," she said to herself. But Merriman had always told her that the courtroom was the great equalizer. It didn't matter how much money the client had, or the prestige he might enjoy in the community, or how the lawyer was attired or even how eloquently he spoke. The thing that counted, Merriman always said, was the ability to persuade. To convince, whether by force of reason or pure nonsense or by any other means available, that your cause was right and just and fair, and that your client, however mean or poor or unattractive, deserved to win. That, Merriman told her, was the *sine qua non*.

May replaced her sunglasses just in case Merriman turned and looked her way. Then she settled in and listened. She cringed whenever Jennings boomed out his objections. But Merriman kept his cool and withstood every onslaught. She was rightly proud of him.

May couldn't make out the images on the videotape too well, but from the looks on the faces of Jennings and his team, she could tell the little movie must be devastating to Prescott's cause. When it finished playing, and Merriman turned and searched the gallery, she lowered her head, hoping the sunglasses disguised her well enough. She didn't know that Merriman was oblivious to her presence. He was looking for someone else.

Judge Bailey turned the hearing over to Jennings. He came out swinging. Devon Jennings and company took no prisoners. First he picked away at the points Merriman had laid out for the court.

"Let's be candid, Your Honor. Janelle Foxworthy was a whore and a convicted felon. On top of that she was a woman scorned. And hell, someone smarter than me has written, hath no fury like a woman scorned. Particularly one who is a whore and a convicted felon. She yearned for revenge against Willis Purdy, who left her penniless, high and dry down by the river. And that so-called affidavit she gave the prosecution provided her the means of achieving that revenge.

"Janelle Foxworthy's proffered testimony has a credibility gap as deep and wide as the Grand Canyon. It reminds me of one of those lurid, sensational stories found every day on the front pages of the tabloids. Entertaining, yes. But absolute rubbish.

"How can this court in good conscience second-guess the discretionary call Mr. Prescott made in the heat of a fierce battle to ignore that admittedly colorful but totally fictitious statement? I, for one, applaud his judgment in rejecting it. The poor woman's tale simply didn't rise to the level of reliability required by the law, and therefore Solicitor Prescott was well within his rights to disregard it. Having done so, I submit he had no obligation under Rule 6 or otherwise to turn it over to the defense."

Jennings was everything Merriman had described him to be, and more. Forceful, eloquent, with a commanding presence and, yes—persuasive. May was worried. Prescott seemed to relax for the first time since the hearing began. A slight glimmer of satisfaction appeared on his face.

Jennings moved on.

"Now. Let me make short shrift of this whole business about Venus Brown Purdy's statement.

"First, and contrary to the speculation—and that's all it amounts to—of my friend Mr. Merriman, the failure of the prosecution to provide the defense with a copy of that statement was an oversight, pure and simple. We admit that. We are guilty of that omission. But to say that such an oversight—when viewed in the context of the most sensational, complex trial this county had ever seen—was so prejudicial as to warrant the granting of a new trial, is to turn an ant into an elephant.

"That statement was available. It was in the solicitor's file. If Mr. Merriman had simply taken the time to walk down the street to the solicitor's office and request to review the evidence file, he would have found it there. But he made no such request. He relied solely upon the generally recognized obligation of the prosecution to make available to the defense any exculpatory evidence in its possession.

"Well, Judge, I contend that it was made available— for the asking. Is Solicitor Prescott required to do Mr. Merriman's homework for him? Of course not. As the court knows, I normally practice in the area of criminal defense. In every case I handle, the first thing I do is serve a written request upon the solicitor pursuant to the authority of Rule 6 of our Rules of Criminal Procedure. In that request I always—always—specifically request the production of all statements given by the alleged victim. It's standard procedure. Any criminal defense lawyer worth his salt will confirm that.

"Well, my friend Mr. Merriman made no such request. I'm sorry. But it's too late to come crying to this court now, decades later, and say, 'Oops. I screwed up. I failed to request the production of the victim's statement. I omitted to take the opportunity to look through the prosecutor's evidence file. I utterly failed to do the minimum required of me in the defense of an accused. So grant me a new trial. Give me a second chance.'"

Jennings paused to let his own stinging arrows find their targets. He buttoned his dark blue jacket and walked around the podium with copies of a few documents in his hand. Prescott fairly gloated as he turned his gaze toward Merriman.

"Let me add this," Jennings continued his harangue. "Your Honor has the statement. The portion of it in question is one little sentence. You'll find it midway down the page. Venus says, 'He was older, maybe in his sixties—I could tell from his voice, and he had wrinkles.'

"That's it, judge. The sum and substance of the so-called exculpatory evidence. But let's take a closer examination of Venus' statement. At the beginning she states very clearly that the rape took place in the pitch black dark, so dark she couldn't recognize the assailant as either someone she knew or a complete stranger. Your Honor will recall that Venus testified at trial. Mr. Merriman, to his credit, thundered away at her on cross-examination. I would have done the same.

"But the point is this: when Mr. Merriman brought her to the climax, so to speak, of her testimony, he popped the question. And I'm quoting from the trial transcript now, Your Honor, page one hundred sixty-one, at line fourteen. 'Can you tell this jury—and I remind you, young lady, that you're under oath here—that Jake Purdy, the man sitting there at the defense table, was the same man who raped you?' Her answer was, 'No, sir. I can't say for certain. It was too dark.'

"Now. What further good would it have done the defense to have gotten a copy of her statement? None whatsoever. She testified that she couldn't identify Jake Purdy as the assailant. What more could Mr. Merriman want from her? So, what can we conclude from this inadvertent oversight by Mr. Prescott? No harm, no foul, as the old saying goes. That's what. And no prejudice to the defendant.

"One final point on the oversight of Mr. Prescott in failing to produce a copy of the statement. There was nothing stopping Mr. Merriman from asking Venus Brown Purdy at trial to describe her assailant as best she could. Had she been asked, presumably Miss Brown Purdy would have given the very same information she provided in that one little sentence that Mr. Merriman now relies upon—no, seizes upon—to ask this court to overturn the unanimous verdict of a jury following a three-week trial, and to reverse a conviction that was never appealed."

Jennings, having finished with his argument on the facts, cut to the chase. He turned his attention to the law.

"This court knows the two-step standard our Supreme Court has laid down for the granting of a new trial in a criminal case. I'm quoting now, Your Honor, from the recent case of *State v. Adams*. It's cited in our brief at page nine. 'First, was the omission of the prosecution to turn over the alleged exculpatory evidence so prejudicial, under the circumstances of the case, as to constitute a denial of the defendant's constitutional right to due process?'"

Jennings turned to face Merriman. May noticed a very slight change in the defense lawyer-turned prosecutor's expression, revealing a hint of a sneer on Devon Jennings' countenance. She boiled with anger over his criticisms of her husband's defense of Jake. She didn't understand that such argument was simply good advocacy. Merriman anticipated it, and harbored no ill will.

"This inadvertent oversight by Mr. Prescott, entirely understandable in light of the pressure of this landmark trial and the fact that the victim's statement was never even requested by defense counsel, cannot possibly rise to the level of a violation of a constitutional right. There's plenty of blame to go around here, Judge," the persuasive Mr. Jennings continued, lowering his voice a decibel or two, "and we've admitted our part in it. I would suggest defense counsel do the same.

"Now, just for the sake of the record, should the court find it necessary to even reach the second step of the inquiry laid down by the Supreme Court, that standard is this: Would the evidence withheld by the State most probably cause a reasonable juror to return a verdict in favor of the defendant?

"Well, Judge, when the victim cannot point to the defendant, who is sitting in the courtroom not more than ten feet away from her, and say 'That's the man,' or even more importantly, say 'That's not the man,' how can this court fairly conclude that a reasonable juror would most probably—not possibly or perhaps, but most probably—return a verdict for the defendant, had this one little sentence in the victim's statement been added to the mountain of evidence the jury received during this three-week trial?

"I respectfully submit, Your Honor, that if this court were to reach such a conclusion, it would be committing reversible error that could not possibly stand up under the scrutiny of an appeal to the Supreme Court."

May sank lower and lower in her seat. Nellie squeezed her hand while Lizzie clasped both of hers around Nellie's other hand. They were bound together by fear and hope. There was power there.

Merriman maintained a stiff upper lip throughout the powerful arguments Jennings made, but underneath his calm exterior his enlarged heart was pumping overtime.

Judge Bailey glanced at his watch. "It's nearly lunchtime. What do you have left to say, Mr. Jennings?"

"I want to address briefly the videotape and the DNA evidence. I can do that in ten minutes, and then, if the court please, after lunch I would like to present a few witnesses."

"All right. Let's proceed."

Jennings dismissed the videotape as nothing more than gamesmanship on the part of Detective Lieutenant Barrow, who he intimated had an ulterior motive in these proceedings.

"Well, Judge, I can only say that if Mr. Prescott had not fetched and reviewed the file from the original trial, he would have been judged incompetent by any standard of prosecutorial conduct. How can anyone be surprised that he did so?

"And as for the aspersions cast by Mr. Merriman that he did so secretly and without following procedure, all I can say is this: Mr. Prescott is the boss. He has ultimate authority over the maintenance, protection, and access to those old files. And he needs no permission from anyone to enter that storage facility in broad daylight and retrieve any file he chooses. The court has Mr. Prescott's affidavit. He intended to copy the statement of Venus Brown Purdy and return it to the storage container the next day. That's all there is to it. And, of course, I renew my objections previously made to this entire matter involving the videotape and Mr. Prescott's actions in retrieving the old file."

He turned to the DNA match.

"Let me just say this one thing, and we'll all be ready for a lunch recess. That semen stain, which Mr. Merriman's laboratory technicians rely so heavily upon, is thirty years old. It was tested and retested before the original trial. It has been handled by literally dozens of people. And Lord knows the condition of our LED laboratories has never been up to the standards the directors of the lab have wanted. Year after year they beg the legislature to provide the funding to enable them to upgrade the lab. It hasn't happened. Through no fault of the employees of the Law Enforcement Division. My hat is off to those men and women. I shall not throw stones at them. They've done their dead-level best with the pitiful assets they have at their disposal.

"But the point is this. As my expert witnesses will testify, that semen sample is totally unreliable from a scientific standpoint. Semen, like any other bodily fluid, decomposes—disintegrates—over time and particularly when it is not preserved in the most delicately controlled environment. The sample relied upon by Mr. Merriman's witnesses in this case cannot hold up under the rigorous scientific standards my experts will lay out for the court. And if the bedrock evidence is unreliable, then the opinions based upon that bedrock are likewise unreliable. They are, simply put, fruits of a poisonous tree, and they must be disregarded by this court.

"We'll let the witnesses explain further, and better than I can, after lunch. Thank you, Your Honor."

The judge announced the lunch recess and the bailiff cried, "All rise." As he did so, Prescott smoothed the trousers of his white linen suit and turned to Jennings with a gleam of self-satisfaction in his eyes.

"Well, done, Devon." The tone of the compliment struck Jennings as a bit patronizing. "I am confident," Prescott added, "that righteousness and justice will prevail."

Jennings set his papers on the table. "Be careful what you wish for, Malcolm."

CHAPTER FORTY-FIVE

The Three Musketeers ducked out the rear double doors of the courtroom and found a little deli around the corner from the courthouse, on Seville Row, just a block from the splendidly refurbished Law Offices of Devon Jennings.

"How are you feeling, Nellie?" May asked her as they munched pastrami and rye.

Nellie thought a moment. "Tired. And beat up. The system has not been kind to me and Jake. Do you think we have a chance?"

Lizzie fielded the question.

"There's no doubt about the courtroom prowess of Devon Jennings, girls. But May, your husband has done a splendid job. I, for one, think he is winning on points. Sort of like a boxing match. Neither lawyer has scored a knockout, at least not yet. Let's see what the afternoon brings."

May was scared to death, but for the sake of Nellie and her own ability to persevere, she didn't show it. Most of all, she worried about Merriman's health. The hard blows he was receiving from Jennings must be having an effect on him, not only mentally, but physically as well.

"Thanks, Liz. John, deep down, yearns to be a good and decent man. I'm not sure I would have said that a year ago. Circumstances in life change. That has certainly been the case with John lately. Liz, you probably know about his cardiomyopathy. One day he'll be gone." She glanced at Nellie. "You know what it's like to lose your husband, Nellie. I shouldn't complain."

Nellie smiled. "A word of experience, May? It might even contain a smidgeon of wisdom."

"Please, Nellie," May replied.

"Live for today. There's no such thing as tomorrow. When you wake up in the morning it will be today. The past? I can't change it. And I sure as hell can't forget it, either. But time has a way of removing bitterness and replacing it with an occasional reason to hope. Lizzie brought me a reason to hope, and I've clung to it.

"So live this life for today, May. You never know what the future may hold for you and Mr. Merriman. You've got no control over that."

They finished their sandwiches and returned to the courtroom. It was nearly empty. The wall clock said a quarter to two. The spectators and reporters were still at lunch. Jennings and his staff had retreated to a conference table in his office, plotting their next moves while they gulped down sandwiches and coffee. Merriman and Barrow were seated at the defense table, deep in conversation. They anticipated that Jennings would call Barrow as his first witness.

When he heard the doors closing in the rear of the courtroom Merriman turned to see who was there. When he saw May he smiled, then elbowed Barrow.

"Our cheerleaders are here, my good Detective Lieutenant."

A bit embarrassed, Barrow winked at Lizzie and turned back to Merriman.

"What do I say if Jennings brings up my offer of resignation to Prescott?"

Merriman nodded. He had anticipated that questions along this line were sure to come. "I'll object, of course. It isn't really relevant. But Judge Bailey won't be surprised by it. We all but told him what our ultimate goal was. And I don't think there is any love lost between the old judge and our worthy solicitor.

"Just tell the truth, Barrow. Of course you would prefer that he resign rather than be dragged through these proceedings. That's all there is to it, as far as your motives are concerned. You offered him the easy way out, but Prescott chose the hard road. He'll have to travel it now."

The courtroom filled as the clock's minute hand approached twelve. Just at the stroke of two the judge entered the courtroom to the bailiff's cry, "All rise."

"Are you ready to proceed, Mr. Jennings?"

"I am, Your Honor."

And he was. As Merriman expected, Jennings first called Barrow to the stand. The examination was grueling, but Barrow held his own. He admitted he had offered Prescott the opportunity to resign, over the objection of Merriman, but the point didn't seem to cause Judge Bailey any concern. Jennings tried mightily to attribute some ill motive to Barrow's offer, suggesting his anger and embarrassment over the result in the Dabney Peters' trial, but Barrow stuck to his story.

"Mr. Jennings," Barrow summed up firmly, "I have served this state alongside my colleague—and I'll say my friend—Mr. Prescott for many, many years. I daresay you were still a boy when Malcolm Prescott and I tried the case against Jake Purdy." Barrow glanced at the solicitor, who allowed no indication of his emotions to show. AI have the highest regard and respect for Mr. Prescott. The last thing I wanted to see was his good name and excellent reputation sullied by a lapse in judgment.

"It is my humble opinion that the time has come for Solicitor Prescott to retire. I might add that my time is coming, too. I made the offer to Mr. Prescott out of a sense of care, not for any ulterior motive you may wish to suggest."

Before Jennings could pounce further Judge Bailey interrupted.

"Mr. Jennings, I believe I understand your point. And I have heard enough testimony on it. Move on."

"Yes, Your Honor."

Jennings wrapped up with Barrow, and then paraded his DNA experts before the court. Merriman insisted that the experts be sequestered, so that none could hear the testimony of the others. Thus Jennings herded them all out into a conference room adjoining the courtroom, and called one at a time back into the courtroom and onto the stand.

After each expert finished his testimony, the judge instructed, "You are not to discuss your testimony with either of the other experts until this hearing is completed. Do you understand, Doctor?" Of course they did.

Jennings didn't like it one bit, but he knew that

sequestration was an absolute right, specifically provided for in the rules of evidence, and if Merriman insisted upon it, he was entitled to it. There was no use in wasting time objecting. What, Jennings wondered, did the sly old fox have up his sleeve?

Each one of Jennings' troop of experts was impeccably qualified and thoroughly experienced in the burgeoning field of DNA analysis as a forensic evidentiary tool. Merriman cross-examined each one only briefly. He knew he couldn't touch their credentials. He closed his cross-examination of each expert with a set of questions that were designed to bring the DNA issue back down to earth.

"So, Doctor, your conclusion is that, because of the condition of the semen sample, you can offer this court no opinion, one way or the other, with regard to whether the DNA of the semen stain matches the DNA contained in the blood samples drawn from the arm of Jake Purdy, is that correct?"

The standard response went something like this: "Not only myself, but no one else can credibly offer an opinion to a reasonable degree of biogenetic certainty as to whether there is a match, as you call it, or not."

"But let's be clear, Doctor. And fair," Merriman hammered away. "My question was addressed to you. And so I'll rephrase it. You yourself, Doctor, have no such opinion. Isn't that true, Doctor?"

When Merriman pinned his first expert down, Jennings rose with a strong objection. "Asked and answered, Your Honor. He's badgering the witness."

Judge Bailey looked over the rims of his spectacles at Jennings and smiled.

"Mr. Jennings, your witness is a big boy, and well educated, too. Harvard, I believe he said. I'm confident he can take care of himself. And I don't believe Mr. Merriman's question can fairly be characterized as badgering. The witness has expanded upon the narrow question asked. Mr. Merriman is entitled to a simple yes or no. In other words, a direct answer to his question.

"Objection overruled. Answer the question, Doctor."

The answer, uniformly and begrudgingly uttered by all three scientists, was to this effect: "Yes. Yes, then, if that's all you want. The answer is yes, that is true. I have no opinion to offer, one way or the other."

Thus having extracted his little nugget of gold, Merriman would tap over to the defense table, pick up a large scientific-looking tome, turn back to the witness, and close with one last question.

"Doctor," Merriman addressed each witness respectfully, flipping through the pages of the book until arriving at a particular chapter, "are you familiar with the work of Professor Siegfried Zellund in the field of DNA analysis?"

"Zellund, did you say? No," came the consistent response from each member of Jennings' little band of Ph.D.'s."Never heard of him."

"Thank you, Doctor. Thank you very much, indeed."

"Damn him," Jennings muttered under his breath after his first expert stepped down. "Now I know why Merriman insisted on sequestration."

CHAPTER FORTY-SIX

"Anything further from the State, Mr. Jennings?" Judge Bailey inquired.

"Not at this time, Your Honor," Jennings replied, equivocating.

"You don't have another time, Mr. Jennings," the judge growled. "It's now or never. If you intend to call Mr. Prescott to the stand—or any other witness, for that matter—you'd better do it now."

"A brief conference, with the court's indulgence?"

"Yes, yes. Of course, Mr. Jennings."

Jennings huddled with Prescott and his associates for a moment. He finally stared Prescott in the eye and said, "Malcolm, I see no reason to put you on the stand. Do you?"

Solicitor Prescott hesitated. His thoughts ran to his obsessive beatific vision. He pictured the grand heavenly courtroom where righteousness always triumphed over evil. There he was, the divinely ordained prosecutor, dressed in his white linen suit, hurling question after unanswerable question at the chief of all sinners, the loathsome Merriman himself.

The moment of truth and the verdict of condemnation against his nemesis was so close, yet so far away. Wistfully, Prescott returned to this world. There across the courtroom sat Merriman, calmly preparing to cross-examine Prescott on such frivolous but embarrassing matters as the affidavit of that whore, Janelle Foxworthy, and the statement given by that poor mulatto girl, Venus Brown Purdy. And, of course, there was the unflattering videotape. Prescott concluded that his divine retribution was not meant to come to pass this day.

"No, Devon. Not today. But at my trial, Devon," he insisted, "I shall tell my story. I shall sound the trumpet of truth. And the towers of injustice and unrighteousness shamelessly fabricated by Merriman and Barrow shall come tumbling down, like the walls of Jericho." His eyes were gleaming now, sky-blue, as he stared fixedly over the broad shoulders of Devon Jennings, Esquire, heavenward.

Jennings glanced at his associates, who seemed stunned. He rose and announced, "The State rests, Your Honor."

Judge Bailey turned to Merriman. "All right, counselor, it's four o'clock. What do you have in reply?"

Merriman again surveyed the courtroom. Then, turning to address the judge, he said, "One witness, maybe two. Then we'll be done, Your Honor."

"Very well. Proceed."

"The defense calls Professor Siegfried Zellund."

Jennings elbowed his associate, Frank, and whispered, "Where in the world did this guy come from?"

"I don't have a clue, Mr. Jennings," the associate squeaked.

"Hm-m-m." Jennings scribbled a note on a yellow legal pad and shoved it in front of his trembling young colleague. "Remind me to fire you later," it said. Poor Frank felt a sharp pain in his abdomen. He had just signed a lease on a powder blue BMW convertible.

Merriman took Professor Zellund through his curriculum vitae slowly and deliberately. Frank took copious notes. He intended to google the man as soon as he returned to the Law Offices of Devon Jennings. That is, if he still had a job there. How did I miss this guy? he tortured himself. Frank jotted down the highlights: "training in biogenetics, graduate of Johns Hopkins, well-published in forensic pathology, teaches at graduate level and conducts research funded by endowed chair at Duke." Zellund sported a red polka-dot bow tie and a brown tweed jacket with patches sewn on the elbows.

"We tender Professor Zellund as an expert in the field of biogenetics, with specialized training in DNA analysis, Your Honor," Merriman declared.

"Any objection, Mr. Jennings?" asked the judge.

Jennings rose. "Not to his qualifications as an expert, Your Honor."

"Very well," the judge continued. "The court accepts

Professor Zellund as an expert, qualified to opine in the field stated by counsel. You may proceed, Mr. Merriman."

"Professor Zellund," Merriman began his substantive examination, "have you had the opportunity in the past to extract DNA from semen stains found on the underclothing of victims of sexual assaults?"

"I have," he replied.

"And can you tell the court, Professor Zellund, the age range of the semen stains you have examined in the past?"

The Professor opened a manila file folder and leafed through it. "Yes," he replied. "The sample stains ranged in age from thirty-four years to three weeks."

Merriman tapped back to the defense table and picked up the tome lying on top of his papers. He returned to the witness box and handed the book to Professor Zellund.

"Are you familiar with this text, Dr. Zellund?"

"Quite," came the reply. "I am one of the editors of this collection of papers, and the author of the article beginning on page seven hundred sixty-nine."

Merriman continued. "What, sir, is the title and subject of this collection?"

"The name of the text is *Examination and Testing Protocol for DNA Samples*. The subject is, well, explained most succinctly by the title."

"Thank you, Doctor. And what is the title and subject of the paper contained in this collection that you authored?"

"Uh," the professor stalled a moment as he flipped to the table of contents. "Yes. Here it is. When I first published this paper in the journal *Nature* it was given a slightly different name by the editors of that publication. In this text we have before us it is entitled, 'The Standard Protocol for Preservation, Examination and Testing of Aged Semen Samples.' Yes, that's it. See it here?" he asked Merriman, as if to demonstrate the veracity of his statement.

"I do, indeed, Doctor. Thank you. Now, in your work in this area, have you found any problem with aging, disintegration or the like with older samples which would cause them to be rejected as unreliable?"

"Absolutely not," the professor thundered. "That, Mr. Merriman, is the whole thesis of my research endeavor. As long as the fundamental techniques of preservation of bodily fluid samples are rigorously observed, semen samples can be preserved for reliable analysis indefinitely, in my opinion."

Jennings put his head in his hands and released an audible sigh. Frank stiffened in a state of pure terror.

"Thank you, Doctor," Merriman replied. "Allow me to ask you this question. In the course of your work in this case, have you examined the semen stain retrieved from the panties of the victim, Venus Brown Purdy?"

"I have."

"Did you find it to be properly preserved in accordance with the protocol set forth in your paper?"

"I did."

"Did you find the sample removed from the semen stain to be reliable to a reasonable degree of scientific certainty, Doctor?"

Professor Zellund cleared his throat. "More than that, Mr. Merriman. I found it completely reliable. In fact, I examined and tested it myself."

"And," Merriman pushed on, "were you able to extract from the sample an identification of the DNA it contained?"

"Yes, I certainly was."

Merriman took the textbook back to the defense table and set it down. Then, with the able assistance of his gold-headed cane, he tapped back to the witness.

"Dr. Zellund, did you also examine and test two samples of blood supplied to you by technicians from the Law Enforcement Division laboratory and identified as blood drawn from the veins of my client, Mr. Jake Purdy?"

"That is correct."

"And were you able to extract from those samples an identification of the DNA they contained?"

"Yes," the professor replied. "The blood samples and their DNA were identical."

"I see," Merriman said. "And one last question, Professor.

225

Did you have occasion to compare the DNA from the semen sample with the DNA from Mr. Purdy's blood samples?"

"I most certainly did," he replied. "That was the objective of my assignment, as I understood it. The DNA contained in the semen sample did not match the DNA in either of the blood samples."

"And, once again, Doctor, so that the record will be absolutely clear on this point, do you hold that opinion to a reasonable degree of scientific certainty?"

"Absolutely," Professor Siegfried Zellund declared.

Merriman limped slowly back to his table. He picked up the tome and glanced at it a moment, then turned to the witness and said, "Professor, please answer any questions Mr. Jennings may have for you."

The cross-examination was a nightmare for Jennings. He had no idea Merriman could come up with the apparent premier expert on the very subject of scientific inquiry in the case. He stumbled around briefly, tried unsuccessfully to bully Professor Zellund, then followed his own advice he had given young lawyers for years. Never, ever ask a witness on cross-examination a question to which you don't already know the answer. He sat down.

"No more questions," he remarked as casually as he could, pretending that the witness wasn't entitled to waste another moment of his precious time.

"Very well," Judge Bailey declared. "Mr. Merriman, you said one or two. I've heard one witness. Do you have another, or is that it?"

Before Merriman could respond, Jennings stood and asked the court, "May we have a brief recess, Your Honor? I would like to discuss a very serious matter with Mr. Prescott, in private, before we proceed further."

CHAPTER FORTY-SEVEN

Unlike his client, Devon Jennings, Esquire, was no fool. He knew when to hold them, and knew when to fold them. He escorted Prescott out of the courtroom and into a little antechamber available to counsel and their clients during trials. He closed the door. They sat across a little table from each other.

"Malcolm, you have paid me a handsome sum to advise and represent you throughout this ordeal. My fees are high because my clients obtain superb representation in the courtroom and excellent advice outside it. We are outside the courtroom now.

"I don't say these things out of arrogance. I believe my track record speaks for itself, and my former clients would corroborate the truth of what I have said. The fact that you chose me to represent you reflects that you have placed your trust and confidence in my ability and my advice.

"It is time for you to listen to my advice. Are you ready to do that?"

Prescott nodded suspiciously. He had a strong urge to smoke a cigarette.

"All right. Malcolm, we're going to lose this motion. I can sense it. I can read it in the judge's face. When we do, the house of cards will come tumbling down around you. Judge Bailey is assigned to try your criminal case, and you can bet that, even though a jury will ultimately decide your guilt or innocence, His Honor will gently but firmly guide them to the outcome he feels is appropriate. We've given it our best shot, and frankly it just isn't good enough. You're facing felony charges and the distinct possibility of serving time in the penitentiary. You might just end up occupying the cell Jake Purdy vacates. That is no way for a man of your stature and reputation to end a career.

"It's time to take the deal. That is, if it's still available. Barrow offered to drop the criminal charges in exchange for your irrevocable agreement to retire, effective immediately. At this point, I don't believe Judge Bailey would stand in the way of that deal. Particularly if the State consents to Jake Purdy's motion for a new trial, and then drops the case against him. He walks out of prison a free man, after serving time for three decades, and you walk into retirement with a fully vested pension and plenty of benefits. It's a no-brainer, Malcolm. I strongly recommend you take the deal."

Prescott was stunned. How could this be possible? All these years he had resisted the temptation to turn coat and open a private practice defending criminals. He would have made big bucks, just like Jennings. But he was a man of lofty principles. Malcolm T. Prescott stood on the side of justice and righteousness and truth. Throughout his career he had soiled his hands by working amongst men like Merriman and Jennings. Birds of a feather, he said to himself. The one's no better than the other. They both seek after money and headlines, not justice and truth.

No, he decided. I'll not compromise my principles. I'll see this through, if it costs me my retirement, my reputation, my family. Someone has to stand up for righteousness.

He stood erect and placed the palms of his hands on the table. His cheeks and throat turned bright red as he spoke.

"No. I will not compromise when it comes to the truth. I have committed no crime. I am blameless before the law. If you can't represent me, I'll represent myself."

Jennings released a long, audible sigh. "Malcolm, don't be a fool. Of course I can represent you, and I will to the best of my ability. But I would be remiss in my duty to you if I did not recommend in the strongest terms possible that you settle this whole affair.

"You've heard me. It's your case, and you're ultimately the boss. But if you go further, you will lose. And you can be sure that I will write you a letter tonight, memorializing this conversation, so that when this motion for a new trial is granted, and the jury returns a verdict of guilty against you, and the Commission disbars you, there will be no basis for misunderstanding between us. Am I making myself clear, Malcolm?"

"You are, Devon. Quite clear." Malcolm T. Prescott turned and walked out of the antechamber and back into the courtroom. Jennings took a moment to collect himself, then followed his client back to the prosecution table. He noticed that Merriman had stepped away. Jake Purdy sat alone at the defense table, head bowed, fidgeting.

Just then the bailiff cried "All rise," and Judge Bailey took his seat on the bench. "Are you ready to proceed, Mr. Jennings?"

"We are, Your Honor."

"Where is Mr. Merriman?"

Before Jennings could respond Merriman came through the rear double doors followed by an elderly, wrinkle-faced man who took a seat in the far corner of the gallery. Merriman tapped down the aisle and took his place, standing, at the defense table.

"There you are. I thought we had lost you, Mr. Merriman," the old judge remarked.

"No such luck just yet, Your Honor," replied Merriman, a bit out of breath.

Judge Bailey chuckled. He was beginning to develop a grudging admiration for the sly old fox.

"All right. Any more witnesses, Mr. Merriman?"

Jennings leaned forward in his chair, hoping against hope that there was no one else to contend with this afternoon.

"Yes, Your Honor. The defense calls Willis Purdy to the stand."

The spectators and reporters erupted in a melee of surprise and excitement. The Three Musketeers, hands clasped tightly together, gasped in unison. Jennings and his minions couldn't believe their ears. Willis Purdy? Impossible!

The judge rapped his gavel against a leather pad on the bench. "Order in this court!" He rapped the gavel again, for good measure. "If order is not contained, I will remove any and all who are responsible. These proceedings are of vital importance to the parties and to this community. I will not permit them to be disrupted again."

A hush fell over the courtroom as the bailiff said, "Come

around, Mr. Purdy, and place your left hand on the Bible. Raise your right hand and repeat after me: I do solemnly swear to tell the truth, the whole truth, and nothing but the truth, so help me God."

Willis dutifully repeated the oath.

"Have a seat in the witness box, Mr. Purdy," said the bailiff. Willis glanced at Jake, whom he hadn't seen since his son was a teenager, and took the stand.

Merriman approached the witness. He leaned against the rail so that Willis wouldn't have any difficulty hearing his questions.

"Mr. Purdy, how old are you?"

"I'm ninety-one years young," he said with a toothless grin.

"Do you know what a subpoena is, Mr. Purdy?" Merriman asked him.

"Yep," he replied. "That's one of them papers that order you to come to court."

"That's right, Mr. Purdy. Did you get served with a subpoena ordering you to come here to this courtroom today?"

"No, sir, I did not," Willis snapped. "I came here as a volunteer. For one reason and one reason only."

"What's that reason, Mr. Purdy?"

Willis drew in a deep breath and expelled it slowly. He glanced over at the defense table where Jake sat, as surprised as anyone.

"A week or so back I read in the newspaper that my son, Jake—he's sitting right there at that table—was asking for a new trial in the rape case involving Venus Brown. When Jake was charged with that crime I was long gone from here. I was a drunk. It ain't no secret that I fathered that girl. I took advantage of her mother, Mae Ella Brown, and ended up with a busted marriage and a family that disowned me. I lost a fortune because of my folly. Not just money, I replaced most of that eventually. But the things that matter most—a wife that loved me, a son that looked up to me, and a home to call my own.

"Liquor swallowed me whole. I lost control. I took off running, running away, I guess. I couldn't face the truth of what I'd done, and so I numbed it up with alcohol. Some people can drink a little and take it or leave it. I ain't one of those people. I blazed a trail through more states than I can remember. After changing my name, I lied, cheated, stole, and did a bunch more I'm ashamed to tell about. Some of it I can't even remember.

"But after years of running I made my way back to Cumberland County. I don't know. I suppose something drew me back here. I took up residence down by the river with a girl named Janelle Foxworthy. She's had her share of troubles, too, but she was a real sweetheart, and she genuinely cared for me. She washed my clothes and fed me and kept me sober some of the time. And I provided for her.

"Then one night I lost my mind. I had heard talk about Venus Brown, how pretty and shapely she was, just like her momma, except her skin was lighter, a coffee-with-cream color. I decided I wanted me another taste of Mae Ella, just like she was when she was a young woman. And somehow my alcoholic mind convinced me that I had a right to take that girl. And so I went there to where she and her momma lived one night. I was liquored up. The bedroom window was open, and I crawled inside. Before I could get my pants unbuttoned Venus woke up, startled, and I was worried she was gonna wake up her momma.

"I jumped on her and put my jackknife blade to her throat. 'I'll kill you if you even breathe a word,' I told her. I struggled to get my pants down and keep the knife at her throat. She had a little nightie on, and a pair of panties. I ripped that nightie off and didn't worry too much about the panties. I was as hot as a firecracker, as crazy as a loon.

"I believe that girl was a virgin. I know this much: when I penetrated her it was rough on that young thing. How many times I've relived that nightmare I do not know. But nothing was gonna stop me from tasting that forbidden fruit. My mind was pickled. When I finished my business I threatened her again, told her that if she made as much as a peep, I would come back and kill her. I can still hear her muffled sobs as I crawled out that window and took off.

"Well, I got a hold of another pint and rode the highway until I finished it off. Then I went home to Janelle. I was as drunk as a goat by then, tired and exhausted, too. She said, AWhere in the hell have you been, Willis Purdy?" And I told it all, every last detail. The last thing I remember is waking up and she was gone. It was her place. She left me a note. It said that if I wasn't gone by morning, she would be back with the sheriff.

"That's when I took off running again. As far away as I could get. I didn't read a newspaper until I was so far away, and so well hidden, that nobody could find me. I lived in the wilderness for years, coming into a little community in Missouri only to stock up on supplies. One day, not too many weeks after I left, on a lark I picked up a copy of a newspaper. That night, in the light of a campfire, I read the AP story that told about Jake's arrest, and the letter Venus had written him just a few weeks—maybe days, they kind of run together now—before I raped that poor little girl. And now here was my son, grown up to be a decent man. A veteran of the Vietnam War. A family man, married to a girl I didn't know—Nellie was her name, I believe—with two young kids.

"I took off running again. There wasn't enough liquor east of the Mississippi to numb my pain, and so I crossed the river and headed west. For years I lived a quiet life. I got off the booze finally, with a lot of help from AA and some newfound friends. I never told them everything about my ugly past. But I made a new life for myself. Laugh if you want. I wouldn't blame you, but I found God—or maybe He found me. But whatever happened, it saved my wretched soul. But the past kept haunting me. I guess I had never tried to make amends for all the hurt and all the misery I caused so many people.

"And so, at the ripe old age of eighty-nine I made a decision. God offered me a second chance. I could take it, and do the right thing, or I could go on living a lie. I started going to a little church out near Fresno, California. They had a full-time counselor on staff. He and I got right down to it. It took a year of therapy, but I finally figured it out. There wasn't a damn thing—oops, Judge, pardon my French—I could do to change what I had done. But here was something I could do to try to right some wrongs, to make amends.

"And so I came back to Cumberland County. I bought me a little farm down near the river, close to the place where Janelle let me stay. And I searched out Mae Ella, but she was long dead. Then I searched out Venus, but she was locked up in the insane asylum, crazy as a loon. I was on the verge of heading to Killough prison when I read in the paper about Jake's motion for a new trial. That's when I paid my visit to your office, Mr. Merriman.

"I told you I wasn't sure I had the strength and the courage to come here today. I don't mind saying I'm scared of what might happen to me. But I came anyway. I owe it to Jake.

"I raped that girl. Jake had nothing to do with it. He didn't even know I was in town. So let him go, Judge. And put me behind them bars. I'm the one who should be there, not Jake."

Merriman allowed time for the impact of this testimony to sink in. He knew Jennings was thinking, how in the world do I cross-examine this man? And the judge had to consider Willis' testimony the icing on the cake, as far as the decision to grant a new trial was concerned.

"One last question, Mr. Purdy," Merriman said. "And then I'll turn you over to the solicitor. Would you consent to having a blood sample drawn and tested for purposes of identifying your DNA?"

"You bet I would," said the old codger. "I'm confessing anyway, ain't I?"

"Yes, sir," Merriman said. "Your witness, Mr. Jennings."

Jennings hesitated. He dared not ask too much. Then his curiosity got the best of him.

"Mr. Purdy, why did you wait three decades to come forward with this confession?"

Willis Purdy eyed Jennings for a moment, trying to size him up before answering.

"Young man," he said, "I've grieved over that same question many a night. And I've drained many a bottle of whiskey so I could forget the answer to that question.

"I haven't claimed today to be a good man, or a courageous man, or a religious man. I'm a sinner. I know what it's like to be in a far country. You know the parable of the prodigal son. That's me.

"Well, it took me a long, long time to come to my senses. I had to hit bottom, and as long as I had enough money for a drink and enough distance between me and Cumberland County, I could pretend—no, lie—to myself and say everything's all right, Willis.

"One morning I woke up to the sound of someone banging on my door. It was the sheriff. He had a writ of eviction in one hand, and an arrest warrant in the other. He said, 'Old man, your luck just ran out.' He tossed me out on the street, took everything I owned, and stole every dollar I had in my wallet.

"That wasn't so bad. I'd been evicted before. And I'd been broke more times than I could count. But the sheriff drove me downtown, read me my rights, and charged me with negligent homicide. I had no idea what he was talking about. Turns out I stole a car, crossed the center line doing eighty-five miles an hour in a forty-five zone, and ran that stolen truck head-on into a little Mazda being driven by a sixteen-year-old girl. The car flipped over and pinned her underneath. She lived long enough for her parents to get to the scene of the accident. Her daddy held her hand as the life blood drained out of her and onto the sidewalk.

"I must have fled the scene after the collision and somehow made my way back to the little one-room apartment I lived in. I don't recall. I was in a total blackout.

"After watching the video the state trooper shot at the scene, and the other video of me at the police station the next morning, still stumbling drunk from the night before, I experienced what old-time religious folks call a conversion. I prefer to call it an awakening. I finally came to my senses. I served seven years of a ten-year sentence and was released on probation in 1997. I lived in halfway houses and the Salvation Army for over two years. A man I met at the Salvation Army, a complete stranger, offered me a job. The only condition was that I meet him for breakfast every morning, Monday through Saturday, at the IHOP restaurant on DeVries boulevard in Santa Monica. That man had been sober for twenty-one years. During that time he built a business, married a lovely woman, and raised three children. He gave me something all the money in the world can't buy, young man. That's hope, and a future.

"So, you see, it took me a while to get here. But by the grace of God and the kindness of one former drunk, I made it. If I can help somebody else, particularly my own flesh and blood, I'm ready. I've been to prison before. It ain't so bad if you behave yourself, and keep your head down. You might try it sometime, Mr. Jennings. Just a short visit will cure you, if you find yourself taking life for granted."

Jennings sat down.

"No more questions of this witness, gentlemen?" asked the judge.

"None," said Merriman.

"None," replied Jennings.

"Mr. Purdy—that is, Willis Purdy—you are excused. You may step down."

"You mean I'm free to go?" Willis asked, incredulous.

"You are as far as I'm concerned. And I'm the judge." Then, turning to the lawyers, he said, "Gentlemen, I'll announce my ruling from the bench tomorrow morning at ten o'clock. A written order will follow shortly. This court stands adjourned *sine die*."

CHAPTER FORTY-EIGHT

On their way out of the courtroom Jennings buttonholed Barrow. "Can we talk?"

"Sure," Barrow replied. They stepped into the little antechamber Jennings and Prescott had occupied earlier in the afternoon.

"I'll get right to the point," Jennings said. "Is your offer to drop the criminal charges in exchange for Prescott's retirement still open?"

"Well, now, Mr. Jennings," Barrow allowed, "a lot of water has spilled over the dam since that offer was made, hasn't it? Not to mention that your client spat in my face after calling me a bastard this afternoon. My wife says I've got a bit of an Irish temper. But that's all right. I pity the man. And a little spray of spittle won't kill me, now, will it? Nor will it hinder me from doing the right thing, Mr. Jennings.

"I believe your main impediment is Merriman. He has now been appointed Special Solicitor in charge of Prescott's prosecution. He'd have to check off on any deal. And you know as well as I that Merriman loathes and despises your client. For some good reasons, I might add."

"I understand perfectly," Jennings replied with a wry smile. "I myself have found the worthy solicitor to be a bit of a pompous ass along the way. Ridiculous, really. And such a waste of time."

"All right. It's getting late and I've had a long day, Mr. Jennings. I'll still go along with the deal if Merriman will sign off."

"Fair enough." Jennings started for the door, then turned.

"A thought occurs to me. Merriman will want a package deal, Detective Lieutenant. He will likely insist that a new trial for Jake Purdy be a part of that package. For that reason, I think it's imperative we strike a deal and notify the court before Judge Bailey announces his ruling at ten tomorrow morning."

"I agree," Barrow replied. "So you'd better get on the phone with Merriman right away. I understand he carries a cell phone now. Can you imagine? Merriman on a cell phone! Here's his number." Jennings scribbled down the number and Barrow was out the door, his mouth watering as he anticipated the taste of that first cold Guinness.

Merriman heard the jingle-jangle of the cellular device's ring tone, but couldn't find the phone. After rooting around in the pockets of his trousers and jacket, he finally located it in his raincoat.

"Hallo?" he answered it. "This is Merriman."

"Merriman? Devon Jennings here. Congratulations. You tried one hell of a case today."

"You're kind. But I'll wager that's not why you called."

"You would be correct, Mr. Special Solicitor." Jennings took a deep breath before coming around to business. "Look, Merriman, I've talked to Barrow. He's still amenable to trading the criminal charges for Prescott's resignation. Will you go along?"

There was a pause on the line.

"Merriman?" Jennings called out after a moment. "Are you still connected?"

"Yes," came Merriman's reply. "I'm still not quite used to thinking through what would be the right thing to do, as opposed to the thing that serves my own selfish interests. I am much more facile in my ability to come up with the latter. Pardon the delay."

"Certainly," Jennings remarked, a little amused. "Would you like to think it over and call me back?"

"No," replied Merriman. "I'll go along under one condition."

Before Merriman could verbalize his thought Jennings interrupted.

"I know. I know what you want," the younger lawyer interjected, moving the negotiations ahead a step, or so he thought. "That we consent to the motion for a new trial, and then drop the charges against Jake. I've been appointed Special Assistant to the Solicitor in today's proceedings.

Prescott has turned the defense of that motion over to me entirely. I think that gives me the authority to consent to the motion. And I will."

Merriman said nothing in reply, sensing there was more to come from Jennings. He was right.

"And, of course, if you think I'd even consider seeking an indictment against old man Purdy, you must believe I'm not only stupid, but crazy too. You'll have to take my word on Willis."

Merriman laughed aloud. "You've misjudged me, counselor. I'm confident that the Honorable Oliver Thornwell Bailey will grant the motion for a new trial. I'm willing to take my chances on that. And as far as Willis Purdy goes, I have two comments.

"First, I don't believe you're stupid or crazy, and I will take your word that you won't seek an indictment against him. Second, you will recall that I have been appointed Special Solicitor. That general grant of prosecutorial power trumps your authority as an assistant to the solicitor for the limited purpose of the new trial motion the court heard today. Your job is done, and along with it your authority is dissolved.

"I suppose that, now, the authority would reside in me, especially in the absence of our full-time solicitor Mr. Prescott, to decide whether that office would seek an indictment against Willis Purdy. Mr. Jennings, you may rest assured that I will not seek such an indictment.

"But all that palaver is really much ado about nothing. Jake Purdy's motion for a new trial and his father's potential exposure to an indictment were not the subjects of my condition."

A bit baffled, Jennings asked, "What in the world is it, then, Merriman?"

"Simply this, Jennings. You meet me in chambers with Judge Bailey tomorrow morning and join in my request that the judge turn this matter over to the Commission on Character and Fitness. We should make the joint request at the same time we put the deal before him for his approval."

Jennings was flabbergasted. "I can't do that to my own client."

"Yes, you can," Merriman replied calmly. "First, you have an obligation under the disciplinary rules to report any unethical behavior by a fellow lawyer, client or not. Your failure to do so itself constitutes a violation of the rules of professional conduct."

Jennings swallowed hard. Merriman was right, and Jennings knew it.

Merriman carried on. "Second, our request to the judge on a disciplinary matter is strictly confidential. Whether His Honor agrees or not, he is strictly prohibited from disclosing the conversation. Prescott will never know that you participated in the matter."

"You're right," Jennings conceded. "And if the judge won't turn him in, then what?"

"Then you're off the hook, Mr. Jennings. My condition was that you join in the request, not that the judge grant it. I'll take my chances on that as well."

Jennings couldn't help smiling. This is why he's called the sly old fox, Jennings suddenly realized.

"Okay," Jennings concluded. "We have ourselves a deal. I'll inform Barrow. I'm sure he'll want to join us in chambers."

"Yes," Merriman said. "But there's still one problem."

"What's that, Merriman?"

"What if your client won't consent to resign?" Merriman asked. "I gathered from the expressions on your and Malcolm's faces this afternoon that you had already put that question to him and been rebuffed."

"Your insight is remarkable, Mr. Merriman. But don't worry. I have an ace up my sleeve on that part."

"Very well. I'll leave that to you, Mr. Jennings. I'm too old to worry. But if Prescott won't resign, the deal is off and the criminal charges go forward."

"I understand," Jennings said. "Have a pleasant evening. Let's meet in the judge's chambers at nine-thirty."

"Sleep well," Merriman replied. Then he fumbled with the cell phone to disconnect the call. "Damned gadgets," he mumbled.

Just as he slipped the phone into his pocket it rang again.

It was May.

"Hello, May."

"Hello, John. How are you?"

"Tired. But good."

"I'm glad. I've changed our reservations for tonight at the Gloucester to tomorrow night. Let's wait until we're sure we have something to celebrate."

"Bless you, May. Exactly my sentiments. I'll be home soon."

"Sooner than you think, John. Leland and I are parked outside the courthouse, ready to taxi you home. No extra charge."

PART FIVE

CHAPTER FORTY-NINE

Devon Jennings, Esquire, returned to his office and found his entire staff hard at work. The poor associate whom Jennings threatened to fire was staring at his computer monitor. When he saw Jennings he jumped up from his credenza and rushed out into the hallway. Jennings was going over the day's office matters with Mrs. Otis.

"Mr. Jennings," the associate nearly whispered.

Jennings turned and smiled. "Yes, Frank. What is it?"

"I found him, sir."

"Who in the world are you talking about, Frank?"

"Oh," Frank said, realizing he was getting ahead of himself, and Jennings, too. "Professor Siegfried Zellund, sir."

"Ah. Yes. That part of the case was your responsibility, wasn't it, Frank?"

"Yes, sir, Mr. Jennings."

"And, if I recall correctly, I instructed you to remind me to fire you later, did I not?"

"Yes, sir, Mr. Jennings. You did."

"Well," Jennings continued, having a bit of fun at Frank's expense, "I suppose you'll now tell me how the professor from Duke evaded your radar screen."

"Yes, sir. You won't believe it, Mr. Jennings."

"Try me."

Frank took a deep breath and began.

"You see, Mr. Jennings, there happens to be another university whose name, phonetically, is pronounced 'Duke.' Only it's spelled 'D-o-o-k-e.' In the courtroom this afternoon I suppose we all assumed it was the university in Durham. Turns out it's an on-line college, with a mailbox in Santa Fe. Professor Zellund is on the faculty there, sir, but the school is not—well, it's not accredited by the American Association of Colleges and Universities. It seems that Professor Zellund is considered a bit of a fraud by the mainstream of scientists in the area of DNA testing.

"And the text that Mr. Merriman was waving around—you know, the one that contained the article written by Zellund—is out of print. It sold one hundred and fifty-one copies, most of which were purchased by Siegfried Zellund himself. And it has never been approved for use by any accredited school in the country.

"That's how I missed him, sir. I'm sorry."

Jennings nearly fell to the floor in paroxysms of laughter.

"That son-of-a-bitch Merriman," he said, laughing until he cried. "How did he come up with that guy? Bow tie and tweed jacket—the works! He had us all fooled."

"Um," Frank stammered, "sir, I think I know the answer. He employed this guy I know who hangs out at the library downtown. He's a complete nut, but remarkably talented when it comes to massaging and retrieving information from the world wide web."

"Ah-hah!" Jennings declared. "Sounds a bit like someone I know. All right, Frank. You're not fired. Relax. The guys you came up with as our experts were superb. They just got out-foxed by Merriman. And so did we."

Jennings laughed all the way down the hall to the men's room. "Damn," Jennings said to himself as he stood at the latrine, relieving himself from a long day of coffee and water. "I've gotta give credit where credit is due. Merriman's good. Maybe I could talk him into coming over here in an Of Counsel role to the firm."

As he walked past Mrs. Otis' desk, Jennings murmured, "Get Malcolm Prescott on the phone for me."

After a minute Mrs. Otis' voice came through the intercom. "He's on line two, Mr. Jennings."

"Thank you, Mrs. Otis." Devon Jennings would fold his tent if anything happened to Mrs. Otis. She was irreplaceable. Twenty years' experience in a large defense firm, the last seven of which were as administrative assistant to the senior partner, and then a two-year stint in the governor's office as Girl Friday to the state's chief executive. Jennings lured her away with an offer combining a substantial salary increase with a generous benefits package that included four weeks paid vacation annually. No secretary in Cumberland County had ever dreamed such compensation was possible.

"Hello, Malcolm. We need to talk. How about breakfast at Clancy's tomorrow morning at eight?"

Prescott crushed out the smoldering stub of his fourth filtered Kool since arriving home. He sat in his study with his starched pajamas on.

"Okay," the solicitor replied, attempting to blow a smoke ring with the toxic mentholated inhalation. "What's the topic?"

"A deal, Malcolm. And this time I want you to approach it with both feet planted firmly on the ground. See you at Clancy's." Jennings hung up, leaving Prescott holding onto a dial tone.

When they met over sausage and eggs the next morning, Jennings could sense that Prescott was nervous. About the outcome, perhaps. Or was it about their meeting? He couldn't tell. Jennings ordered more coffee and got to the point.

"Malcolm, we're going to do a deal this morning. The State will drop the criminal charges and you'll tender your resignation. That's it." The waiter brought more coffee. Jennings took another cup, but Prescott waved the server away. He glanced around the small diner to ensure there were no familiar faces.

"We had this discussion yesterday, Devon," said Prescott. "I thought I made myself clear."

Jennings sipped his coffee and stared over the rim of the cup at his client. "You did, Malcolm," he said, calmly and deliberately. "Now I'm going to make myself clear. Listen carefully. I'm only going to say this once.

"There's no doubt in my mind that Judge Bailey is prepared to grant the motion for a new trial at ten this morning. I held out a shred of hope, even after Professor Zellund testified. But when Willis Purdy came down from the witness stand he took with him any possibility of a decision in your favor. Face it, Malcolm. You're going to lose.

"And when you do, a guilty verdict on the criminal charge against you will be a slam dunk for Merriman. You're looking at serving time, Malcolm. And you're facing disbarment on top of that.

"Don't be a fool. Take the deal. Retire with dignity. Enjoy yourself. Go on that vacation you and your wife always wanted to take. Maybe a cruise. Forget Merriman and Barrow. Live your life."

The two sat quietly for a few moments. Jennings could sense that the self-righteous bravado undergirding Prescott's demeanor of the day before was beginning to crumble.

"I, I thought about it all night, Devon. I knew this was the end game. But I can't do it. I've spent my career fighting for truth and justice. How can I compromise now, when my own life is in the balance? I'd feel like such a hypocrite."

"Let me tell you the cold, hard facts about truth and justice, Malcolm. The truth is that you were a young, ambitious solicitor who made a couple of mistakes. Now, under the microscope of the current proceedings, those careless little mistakes have been magnified into grievous errors of professional judgment. The truth? I'll tell you the truth. Judge Bailey is going to nail us. I predict he will find that you violated Rule 6 and the defendant's due process rights by failing to turn over the Foxworthy affidavit and by not disclosing the exculpatory statement of Venus Brown. He'll leave the videotape out of it. He doesn't need to go there to grant Jake Purdy a new trial. And Judge Bailey knows that the videotape will be powerfully damning evidence against you at your criminal trial. The DNA evidence and the confession of Willis Purdy will be footnotes in the order, serving to buttress his decision in the event of any appellate review.

"Now. You want to talk about justice? There's only one conclusion any reasonable judge or juror could draw about justice from yesterday's proceedings. Jake Purdy was denied justice. And he spent thirty-odd years in Killough Correctional Facility as a result.

"So, Malcolm, if truth and justice are your issues, you're

gonna lose them both if you go forward. And if you choose to go forward, you'll go without me representing you."

Prescott's face reddened. The jaws of the trap were finally tightening around him. There was no exit.

"If you drop me," he replied weakly, "I'll expect a substantial refund of the fee I paid you." It was all Malcolm T. Prescott could think to say.

Devon Jennings reached in his shirt pocket and pulled out a piece of paper. He set it before him and signed it. The document was a check drawn on his law firm's operating account, made payable to Malcolm T. Prescott in the amount of fifty thousand dollars. He pushed it across the table.

"It's yours, Malcolm. That is, if you take the deal. I don't owe you that refund. I worked hard to prepare to try the motion for a new trial, and my firm did an excellent job yesterday, in my humble opinion. And those expert witnesses we put on the stand didn't come cheap.

"But there's more to the practice of law than money. I want you to do the right thing. And the right thing is simple. Take the deal. If you do, the money is yours. If you don't, I'll decide what my representation of you through this date is worth, deduct it from the fifty thousand you've already paid me, and cut you a check for the balance. Then you can go your merry way. Maybe F. Lee Bailey will take your case. My bet is that you're looking at prison and disbarment."

Prescott glanced down at the check. He sat straight as an arrow. Last night his wife dutifully ironed the wrinkles out of his white linen suit. He wore it again today, but with a fresh pinstripe shirt and a new club tie. Jennings noticed a slight tremor in Prescott's hands.

"I didn't know that what I was doing was wrong, Devon," he whispered feebly. "You believe me, don't you?"

"Yeah," Jennings said. "I believe you."

Prescott slid his trembling hand over the check, folded it, and slipped it into his pocket.

"You're a good lawyer, Devon." Prescott looked away after he spoke those words.

"Yeah," Jennings said. "Let's go do the deal."

CHAPTER FIFTY

It was just before nine-thirty when Jennings and Prescott entered the courthouse. Barrow and Merriman were already in the courtroom. Jennings walked over to them and nodded. "I'm ready. Has anybody notified the judge we want to see him?"

Merriman smiled. "I did, Devon. He's waiting for us."

As the three men made their way to the door leading to the judge's chambers, Prescott took his seat at the prosecution table and reminisced about the many battles he had fought from the very seat he now occupied. He ran his fingers over the oaken tabletop, feeling the scars of a hundred victories, a hundred defeats. Now it was over. He would never try another case. He would never wear his white linen suit again.

Judge Bailey was in a good humor this morning. "Greetings, gentlemen," he offered as they entered his office. "Take a seat. I understand you have something to discuss with me."

Jennings and Barrow deferred to their elder statesman. Merriman spoke for the trio.

"Your Honor, Mr. Jennings and I had a little talk last night. We have reached an agreement in which Detective Lieutenant Barrow concurs. We seek the court's approval. These are the terms of the agreement.

"Mr. Prescott shall submit, in writing, his irrevocable resignation from the office of Solicitor for Cumberland County, effective immediately. In exchange, the criminal charges against Mr. Prescott will be dismissed."

Judge Bailey gazed at the three men, then said, "Is that it?"

"Yes, Your Honor," said Merriman. Jennings and Barrow nodded their concurrence.

"What about the motion for a new trial?"

Merriman spoke first.

"Judge, for the defendant, we have every confidence that the court's ruling will be just and fair. I have not conditioned my assent to the agreement upon any settlement of the motion for a new trial."

"Very interesting, Mr. Merriman. And very risky," warned the judge.

Jennings spoke next.

"For what it's worth, Your Honor, I think everyone in that courtroom yesterday would agree that Mr. Purdy deserves a new trial. I, for one, believe he deserves to be set free. Immediately."

Barrow joined in. "I concur with that, Your Honor."

The old jurist leaned back in his chair and chuckled. "And what if I disagree with you both?" He winked at Merriman.

Before Jennings or Barrow could respond, Merriman said, "Judge, it's no secret that most of my career I have skated close to the edge. Occasionally I have crossed the line, skated too far. I can't explain to myself, much less to you, why that has changed recently. Maybe the heart condition is the cause, or maybe I've just finally grown up. But I've decided that, from here on, I will do the next right thing, whatever that may be, one day at a time.

"As far as Jake Purdy is concerned, the next right thing meant doing everything legally possible to right a terrible wrong, to correct a blatant injustice, that was wrought three decades ago. I hope that I have succeeded in doing so. But I want that injustice to be corrected, that wrong to be righted, not by some agreement between the lawyers, but by the system itself. I will accept the ruling of this court, no matter how it comes out.

"As for Mr. Prescott, he is no longer my enemy. I wish him well. And I plan to join him in retirement. This is my last case, too, Your Honor. I plan to take my wife on a much-needed and well-deserved vacation when this is all over. Perhaps when I return I can be of some small assistance to the young lawyers coming along. Perhaps not. We'll see. But there's no turning back now.

"Prescott had it right when he extolled the virtues of truth and justice. Unfortunately, like me, he is only a man. And like me, he is capable of making mistakes in judgment. He made some in this case early in his career. That's obvious. But who am I to throw stones?"

There was a moment of silence as the two lawyers, the judge, and the detective lieutenant considered the verity of what Merriman had said.

Then Jennings spoke. "Let me say two things, if I may, Your Honor."

"Please," the judge replied. "Feel free."

"Number one, I hope that one day I will have the guts to achieve the integrity Mr. Merriman possesses. It takes courage to do what he has done, and more courage to say what he just said. I have a stable of young lawyers who could benefit greatly from your wisdom and experience, Mr. Merriman. You have a standing offer to serve as Of Counsel to my firm, starting as soon as you return from vacation. Pick your own hours.

"Number two. I speak for both Mr. Merriman and myself in making this request of the court. The conduct of Solicitor Prescott in the prosecution of Jake Purdy, and his subsequent apparent attempt to cover up a portion of that conduct, warrants investigation by the Commission on Character and Fitness. Mr. Merriman and I feel that the court, not the lawyers, should initiate that investigation by filing a formal charge with the Commission.

"That is all I have to say."

The judge turned to Merriman. "Anything further from the defense, counselor?"

"Just this, Your Honor. I thank Mr. Jennings for his kindness. And I join in his request regarding the charge to the Commission."

"Very well. Give me a moment to get my robe on, and to absorb and digest what I've just heard."

The courtroom was packed with the same crowd of spectators, courthouse personnel, and reporters who occupied the gallery the day before. Merriman, Jennings and Barrow took their seats and waited for the judge to convene the proceedings. Jake Purdy sat next to Merriman, his head bowed as if in prayer. Merriman placed his hand on Jake's shoulder.

"All rise!" came the cry from the bailiff as the judge made his way to the bench. He was somber, almost grave in his appearance.

"Be seated," he said. "Is counsel prepared for the court to rule?"

Merriman and Jennings stood, and spoke simultaneously. "We are, Your Honor."

"Very well," replied the judge.

"This court finds that the evidence withheld by the prosecution from the defendant, consisting of the Foxworthy affidavit and the statement of the victim, was substantial and exculpatory. The failure to disclose those key pieces of evidence to the defense constitutes a violation of Rule 6 of the Rules of Criminal Procedure, and of the constitutional right of this defendant to due process of law. This court further finds and concludes that such evidence would most probably have caused a reasonable juror to reach a verdict of not guilty. For these reasons, it is the ruling and decision of this court that the Defendant, Jake Purdy, be, and is hereby, granted a new trial. Your motion is granted, Mr. Merriman. A written order will follow shortly, gentlemen.

"In the meantime, I will entertain a motion for release pending the decision of the solicitor's office as to whether to proceed with a new trial."

Merriman stood. "Thank you, Your Honor. I move at this time that the defendant, Jake Purdy, be released on his personal recognizance until such time as he may be required to appear for further proceedings in this matter."

Jennings rose to reply. "The prosecution does not object to the motion."

"All right," the judge intoned. "Mr. Purdy, please come around to the clerk's table and sign the papers she will present to you. You are thereafter free to go, but you may not leave the state and you must appear at any future proceedings that may require your presence. You will be notified of such proceedings, if any, by the court.

"If the Office of the Solicitor determines that it is not in the best interest of the State to retry you, you will be so notified, and all conditions of your release and your bond will be vacated. It is the opinion of this court that such a determination would be entirely appropriate under the circumstances. Good luck to you, sir."

The Three Musketeers, who were seated in their same spot in the rear of the courtroom, hands entwined, began to cheer. Nellie ran down the center aisle of the gallery and threw her arms around Jake. Then, she and Jake and Merriman proceeded to the clerk's table to complete and sign the bond.

The judge rapped his gavel, then said, "The court will recess briefly. I want counsel to stay in place. The rest of you are dismissed." The reporters flew out of the courtroom and scrambled to contact their editors, hoping to land the scoop that would hit the news first. Then they would be ready to pounce on Jake and Merriman as soon as they exited the courtroom.

When he was advised by his secretary that the gallery was empty, Judge Bailey came back into the courtroom and said, "Gentlemen, I believe you have another matter you wish to take up with the court. You may proceed."

Merriman restated for the record the terms of the deal reached with Jennings, who confirmed the agreement, and Barrow acknowledged it as well. Jennings handed the court Prescott's letter of resignation, and provided copies to Merriman and Barrow.

"Mr. Solicitor," the judge addressed Prescott, "you have served the people of Cumberland County in a manner that should make you proud, and the people grateful. I have had the privilege of presiding over many, many cases you have handled, and I congratulate you on your integrity and ability. You will be sorely missed by all who have had the pleasure of working with you, but the court speaks for all in wishing you many happy and healthy years of retirement.

"I hereby direct the court reporter to prepare an official

transcript of my remarks, and further direct the clerk of this court to frame the original and hang it on the wall of this courtroom in an appropriate place where it can be read and admired by the people of this county. And it is so ordered.

"There being no further business, this court stands adjourned."

Merriman rose. "There is one last thing, Your Honor. And I would like this to be placed on the record. With Mr. Prescott's resignation, I believe I am authorized by virtue of my appointment as Special Solicitor to speak for that office. I shall do so now. The Office of the Solicitor for Cumberland County will not pursue a retrial of Mr. Jake Purdy. No bond will be necessary. He is a free man, as far as this office is concerned. And the criminal charges against Malcolm T. Prescott are dismissed and forever ended, with prejudice."

"Very well, Mr. Special Solicitor," the old jurist replied. "This court gives its approval to both decisions. These being your last official acts in that capacity, I hereby dissolve your appointment. An interim solicitor will be appointed by this court. Mr. Purdy, you are free to go. Madam clerk, you may dispense with the bond."

A handful of court personnel, gathered in a knot by the entrance to the judge's chambers, began to applaud, one by one. Then the Three Musketeers joined in with whoops and cheers. Jennings clapped his hands alongside the little band of men and women honoring Merriman, and Barrow followed suit. Prescott sat mute and straight-backed in his white linen suit, his hands clasped tightly together and resting on the prosecutor's table. He stared fixedly at absolutely no one.

Judge Bailey slipped out of the courtroom, unnoticed, as the curmudgeonly old bailiff came over to shake Merriman's hand. "Congratulations, Mr. Merriman. You're one hell of a lawyer," he said.

As he left the ornate old courtroom with May at his side, Merriman glanced at the inscription on the plaque at the front door of the entranceway. "Do Justice, Love Mercy, And Walk Humbly With Your God."

He turned to May. For the first time she saw real, honest-to-goodness tears forming in the corners of his eyes. "It's been there all this time," Merriman remarked. "This little kernel of wisdom from antiquity. It's a verse from the minor prophet Micah, if I'm not mistaken, and it's been waiting patiently here all these years for me. Now I know what it means."

Then he kissed May, gently.

"Come on, John," she said. "Let's go home."

CHAPTER FIFTY-ONE

"Hurry up, May! We'll be late," Merriman groused.

"Back to your old self, eh?" May rejoined from the bedroom. "Don't fret, John. It's bad for your heart. And the Barrows won't mind if we're a few minutes late."

The Bonnie Prince Charlie was just a short drive from the Station Avenue townhouse. When Merriman and May arrived, they went straight to the Gloucester, where they spied Mike and Lizzie Barrow seated at a table for four. After exchanging greetings and congratulations all around, the foursome took their seats.

"Merriman," Barrow said, "I have a small token of appreciation for you, and I won't take no for an answer. Tonight's dinner is on me. I've already made the arrangements for payment."

Before Merriman could object, the waiter appeared with a chilled bottle of Chardonnay and a pint of cold, dark Guinness. He opened the wine and poured Lizzie and May a glass, then turned to Merriman.

"And for you, sir?"

Merriman didn't know what to say. He suddenly realized it had been quite a while since he had taken a drink of alcohol. He thought of Dr. Fairchild. Just then May said, "John, I have a little surprise for you, too. A note from a friend." She reached into her pocketbook and handed him an envelope.

Merriman took it and noticed it was addressed to "John Merriman, Esquire." He opened the envelope and found inside a sheet torn from a prescription pad. On the top of it was printed AW. Stephen Fairchild, M.D., F.A.C.C." The handwriting of the prescription itself was a little hard to decipher, but Merriman made it out: "Take two drinks of expensive scotch whiskey before your evening meal, preferably consisting of a prime cut of aged beef. Enjoy yourself. Then take May on a vacation. When you return, find a nice little firm with an opening for a crusty old lawyer willing to serve part-time as Of Counsel. You've accumulated a lot of wisdom. It would be advisable to impart as much as you can to the young guys. And congratulations. I hear you really kicked some butt today." It was signed at the bottom, simply, "Doc."

"Well," Merriman declared, "I'm legal! Waiter, bring me a Johnnie Walker Black and soda, in a tall glass with plenty of ice."

"Right away, sir."

The waiter opened Barrow's Guinness and poured it into a chilled mug. When he returned with Merriman's drink, the sly old fox raised his glass.

"I propose a toast! To health and happiness. And to vacation. And to my colleague, Malcolm T. Prescott. God bless him. In the end he did the right thing, thanks to you, Mikey. And so I raise my glass to you, too, my good friend, Detective Lieutenant Michael O'Shea Barrow. But most importantly, I wish to offer a toast in honor of my treasure—my loving and encouraging wife May, who stuck by me through thick and thin, through periods of abject misery and occasional mirth, but most of all, through sickness and health."

Their glasses clinked as they consummated Merriman's toast. There wasn't a dry eye among them. Then the table fell silent for a while, as memories of recent days and distant years flooded their individual and corporate consciousness. A bittersweet air settled amongst them, as if someone was missing from their little soirée.

Then Lizzie raised her glass. "To Jake and Nellie. May they have a glorious and peace-filled twilight, and may their reunion bring them great joy for a long, long time to come." Their glasses clinked again, and the atmosphere suddenly lightened.

Merriman turned to his partner of many years. "I love you, May," he said.

"I love you, John," she replied.

"But I do, May! I really do. I never realized it until I got sick." He was like a wide-eyed boy passing into manhood, entering a season of his life he never imagined was possible.

Merriman glanced at the prescription Steve Fairchild had written for him earlier that afternoon. The old fox felt his heart flutter momentarily, then settle back to its normal rhythm.

"God does work in mysterious ways, doesn't He, May?"

"Yes, John," she said. "He certainly does."

ABOUT THE AUTHOR

Born in 1950, Wilmot B. Irvin received his undergraduate degree in English literature and law degree from the University of South Carolina. He served in judicial clerkships for a South Carolina Supreme Court Justice and a Senior United States District Judge, which provided invaluable training for a writer.

Until he reached his late forties, Irvin's writing was almost exclusively the product of his career as a practicing lawyer. He began writing fiction at that time, and has since published six books: four full-length novels, a novella, and a novelette. Irvin has also written numerous short stories. He was chosen as an author presenter at the 2010 South Carolina Book Festival and was invited to serve as an author panel moderator at the 2011 South Carolina Book Festival. He and his wife, Jeannie, live in Columbia, South Carolina with their fourth child. They have three adult children and a grandson.

Wilmot Irvin's works explore the depth and vitality—and often the fragility—of human relationships. Fear and love, loss and fulfillment, evil and redemption, and guilt and deliverance are themes that frequent his evocative and colorful stories, populated by interesting characters poignant in their struggles and triumphs.

Visit Irvin's website at www.wilmotbooks.com.